Praise for *New York Times*
bestselling author B.J. Daniels

"You won't be able to put it down."
—*New York Times* bestselling author Jodi Thomas
on *Heartbreaker*

"Daniels is a perennial favorite on the romantic suspense
front, and I might go as far as to label her the cowboy
whisperer."
—*BookPage* on *Luck of the Draw*

"Daniels keeps readers baffled with a taut plot and ample
red herrings, expertly weaving in the threads of the next
story in the series as she introduces a strong group of
primary and secondary characters."
—*Publishers Weekly* on *Stroke of Luck*

"Daniels again turns in a taut, well-plotted, and
suspenseful tale with plenty of red herrings. Readers
will be in from the start and engaged until the end."
—*Library Journal* on *Stroke of Luck*

"Readers who like their romance spiced with mystery
can't go wrong with *Stroke of Luck* by B.J. Daniels."
—*BookPage*

"Daniels is an expert at combining layered characters,
quirky small towns, steamy chemistry and added
suspense."
—*RT Book Reviews* on *Hero's Return*

"B.J. Daniels has made *Cowboy's Legacy* quite a
nail-biting, page-turner of a story. Guaranteed to
keep you on your toes."
—*Fresh Fiction*

**Also by *New York Times* bestselling author
B.J. Daniels**

Look for B.J. Daniels's next novel
available soon from HQN.

For additional books by B.J. Daniels,
visit her website, www.bjdaniels.com.

B.J.
NEW YORK TIMES BESTSELLING AUTHOR
DANIELS

FROM *the*
SHADOWS

HQN

ISBN-13: 978-1-335-94817-5

From the Shadows

Copyright © 2021 by Barbara Heinlein

Recycling programs for this product may not exist in your area.

This edition published by arrangement with Harlequin Books S.A.

For questions and comments about the quality of this book, please contact us at CustomerService@Harlequin.com.

HQN
22 Adelaide St. West, 40th Floor
Toronto, Ontario M5H 4E3, Canada
www.Harlequin.com

Printed in Spain

I dedicate this book to my niece, Jennifer Pearson Weaver.
As the characters in my books discover—
things don't always begin well. But as we know,
it's how the story ends that really counts.
So glad that you and Charley have each other now.
Here's to many more happy endings!

FROM *the* SHADOWS

CHAPTER ONE

Friday

FINN LAY ON the dusty floor of the massive, old and allegedly haunted Crenshaw Hotel and extended his arm as far as it would go into the dark cubbyhole he'd discovered under the back stairs. A spiderweb latched on to his hand, startling him. He chuckled at how jumpy he was today as he shook the clinging strands from his fingers. He had more to worry about than a few cobwebs. Shifting to reach deeper, his fingers brushed over what appeared to be a notebook stuck in the very back.

Megan Broadhurst's missing diary? Had he finally gotten lucky?

The air from the cubbyhole reeked of age and dust and added to the rancid smell of his own sweat. He should have been used to all of it by now. He'd spent the past few months searching this monstrous old relic by day. At night, he'd lain awake listening to its moans and groans, creaks and clanks, as if the place were mocking him. *What are you really looking for? Justice? Or absolution?*

What he hadn't expected, though, was becoming invested in the history of the place and the people who'd owned it, especially the new owner—who would be arriving any day now to see the hotel demolished. Casey Crenshaw had inherited the structure after her grandmother's recent death. Word was that she'd immediately put it up for sale to a buyer who planned to raze it.

Finn had been looking for a place to disappear when he'd heard about the hotel, which had been boarded up and empty for the past two years. He'd known it would be his last chance before the hotel was destroyed. It had felt like fate as he'd gotten off the bus in Buckhorn and pried his way into the Crenshaw. He'd been in awe of the infamous hotel because of its illustrious history even before he'd stepped inside and seen how beautiful and haunting it was.

He'd only become more fascinated when he'd stumbled across Anna Crenshaw's journals. That was why he felt as if he already knew her granddaughter, Casey. He was looking forward to finally meeting her.

His fingers brushed over the notebook pages. He feared he would only push it farther back into the dark space or, worse, that its pages would tear before he could get good purchase. Carefully he eased the notebook out.

This was the first thing he'd found that had been so well hidden. He hoped that meant it was the diary that not even the county marshal and all his deputies had been able to find.

He coughed from the thick dust that floated into the air as he sat up, bringing the notebook with him as he got to his feet. As he did, he caught his reflection in the mirror on the wall and was startled by the man he saw. His dark hair was way too long, his beard scruffy.

Shaking his head, he had to smile. Most everyone in Buckhorn, Montana, thought he was homeless, and that was why he'd been holed up in the hotel for the past few months. He definitely looked the part.

He ran a hand over his beard, hardly recognizing himself. For months he'd avoided mirrors, avoided looking himself in the eye. At one time, it had made sense coming here. He'd known the place was empty. It had been boarded up due to the elderly owner's declining health and subsequent death.

But now new owner Casey Crenshaw was on her way. From what he'd heard, she couldn't wait to not only get the hotel sold, but razed. That seemed odd—unless you'd spent some time here at night, he thought with a laugh. Did she think leveling it would get rid of the ghosts?

Last night, he'd stood at the window looking out at the small town of Buckhorn and wondering who was looking back at him. That feeling of being watched had never been stronger. But it was what had been watching him *inside* of the hotel that kept him up at night. After all, the Crenshaw was famous for its ghosts—especially Megan's.

So was it Megan's ghost Casey Crenshaw wanted to get rid of? Or was destroying the hotel about covering up Megan's murder?

He'd come here looking for answers, but now he wondered if he was really ready to know the truth about this place—let alone the new owner. Shaking his head to clear his thoughts, he bent down and shone his flashlight into the hole. There was nothing more in the space.

Rising, he considered the notebook. He felt like an archaeologist who'd dug for days to discover nothing. Just this morning, he'd been telling himself what a waste of time this had been. But time was something he had plenty of, wasn't it?

He flipped open the notebook, hopeful, but was quickly disappointed. All there appeared to be were blank pages. Finn let out a curse. He was covered with dust and grime and had gone to all that trouble for nothing. He started to fling it away when his gaze caught on a page with scrawled words. He squinted to read the cramped handwriting.

I'm not a psychopath. I'm just sick. It's not my fault that I kill them.

Finn felt his pulse jump. What the hell was this?

I shouldn't write this down. I'm not supposed to tell anyone or they will put me away. But when I'm dead, no one will understand. They'll blame me. It's this hotel. There's evil here, and sometimes it makes me do things I don't want to do. I shouldn't keep a list of their names, but I do anyway because they shouldn't be forgotten.

I know other people don't feel like this. But I can't control it.

There is something wrong with me, and I have to hide it. She tells me to bury it deep so no one can ever know what I've done. But I can feel it building again, and it scares me.

I don't want to do it again. Someone, please help me.

Please don't make me do it again.

He examined the notebook, looking for a date, a name, anything else.

There was nothing. Just the one page, the writing becoming smaller and less legible toward the end. He told himself it could be nothing more than someone's imagination on paper.

But he didn't believe that. He could almost feel the author's pain and his own because it confirmed what he'd come to suspect.

The Crenshaw Hotel had a killer—and Megan Broadhurst wasn't the only victim.

CHAPTER TWO

THE SPRING SUN beat down on the compact convertible, but Casey Crenshaw refused to put the top up. For miles she'd let her hair blow back in a flame-red wave as she'd enjoyed the freedom and pretended she didn't have a care in the world.

Once she'd hit the Montana border, though, the pretending got harder. She was going back to her grandmother's hotel without her after all these years. And she couldn't keep pretending that she wasn't about to do something terrible to the town of Buckhorn to save herself.

As the massive, historic Crenshaw Hotel materialized on the horizon ahead, she let up on the gas. The hotel was just as it had been in her nightmares, ghost stories and all. Constructed of wood and native stone, it dominated the skyline. With seven stories, two wings and a tower, it was still the largest and tallest building in Buckhorn. It rose up against a backdrop of mountains and pines and Montana spring sky.

Casey felt that familiar jolt of mixed emotions, trepidation being the strongest. There'd been a time when she couldn't wait to come here to spend the summer with her grandmother. She'd always been filled with excitement. Then, at sixteen, all that had changed. Megan Broadhurst had been murdered, and for the next ten years the Crenshaw Hotel was the last place on earth Casey wanted to be.

It had meant not spending summers with her grandmother, something she deeply regretted. Especially now her grandmother was gone.

If Anna Crenshaw hadn't died and left her the hotel and land, Casey wouldn't be here now, she thought. But she'd promised her grandmother that she would return one last time to collect a few family items before the place was sold and demolished.

Casey concentrated on the feel of the sun baking her fair, freckled skin from the perfect blue sky overhead. But even her sunburn did little to distract her from the growing knot of dread roiling in her stomach. She glanced at herself in the rearview mirror and saw that her shoulders were as red as her hair. She would pay for not putting the top up miles ago. Even as a girl she'd always burned worse in Montana because of the altitude. Today would be no different, she thought as she slowed at the edge of town, turned onto the dirt road and drove into the huge, empty parking lot behind the hotel.

She purposely parked back here at the edge of the pines with the mountain looming over her and the hotel. The townspeople would find out soon enough that she was here. By now, most would have heard what she planned to do with the property. She could well imagine the uproar. Not that it would change anything. With luck, the hotel would be demolished by the end of the month.

She tried not to think about that or the impact the developer's proposed truck stop, motel, gift shop and restaurant would have on the tiny Western town miles from anywhere. Or how it would change the character of Buckhorn, which sat on a two-lane highway that sliced across Montana and was tucked into picturesque, evergreen-covered mountains.

Heart pounding, she concentrated on just breathing in the pine-scented air. She'd forgotten how amazing it smelled. Or how blue the sapphire sky was. It was hard to forget how chilly the spring could be. Most of all, she desperately wanted to remember the good times here with her grandmother instead of the nightmarish days before she left here planning never to return.

She'd always loved this time of year before dozens of tourists filled the streets to buy cowboy boots and hats, curios and maps, photos and artwork of mountains and streams, everyone wanting to take home a little piece of Montana.

Bessie Walker's bakery would be selling freshly made cakes and pies, turnovers and giant cookies that melted in your mouth. Earl Ray Coffield would always be the first to try whatever Bessie brought out of the oven. Axel Mullen would be behind the counter at the general store, his wife, Vi, back in the small post office slipping mail into the wall of metal boxes.

Soon the town would be packed with motor homes, trucks and trailers, camper vans parked in front of Vi's antiques barn and Dave's bar at the other end of town. There would be tourists on benches along the main drag—which was the highway that passed through town. Families would be eating ice cream looking up at the mountains as their kids took selfies and texted friends how bored they were.

For a few short months, the town would be alive as the tourists lapped up that old Wild West feeling. Once the snow began to fall, though, Buckhorn would become a near ghost town. Most businesses would be boarded up for the winter, the owners hightailing it south to warmer climes, leaving only a few hearty souls behind in the frozen north.

Not that Casey would see the change of seasons. Once she completed the sale of the hotel and property and picked up the things from her grandmother's list, she would be gone before the summer tourist season even set in. She'd never see her grandmother's huge hotel and outbuildings destroyed. Just as she would never see the truck stop complete with rows of gas pumps or the crowded convenience store with its tacky gift shop and tasteless restaurant. She would never see what it did to the town her grandmother had loved.

"Forgive me, Grandma," she whispered as she squinted up at the sprawling structure Anna had given her life to.

In its day, the Crenshaw had been a grand hotel with beautiful detailing inside and out. The hotel had hosted presidents, kings and queens and movie stars. There used to be a stable out back that took guests on horseback rides up into the mountains and a huge outdoor swimming pool fueled by a hot spring. It was said that the water could cure anything.

The stables and horses were gone, along with the large pool. Only a few old maintenance buildings remained in the trees at the foot of the mountains.

She blinked and saw the hotel as it was now, its doors and windows on the lower level boarded up, weeds growing high all around it, a look of abandonment in its dust-coated upper windows. Her grandmother had always called the hotel her Old Girl, and now she looked sad and empty after being closed for the past two years. Anna had planned to return as soon as she was feeling better. Her grandmother had never suspected the day she left would be the last time she would ever see her Old Girl.

Casey felt her sun-scorched skin begin to tighten uncomfortably. With a sigh, she put the top up on the convertible, climbed out and opened the trunk. She hadn't needed much in the line of clothing since she wasn't staying long.

Pulling out her rolling suitcase, she stopped to look up at the tower high above the hotel's center structure. It had been her grandmother's favorite spot because of the view. Casey felt her eyes fill at the memory of the two of them curled up in the plush chairs up there. Her grandmother often read to her when she was very young. Later, Anna would always know where to find Casey if she disappeared for very long. She'd be up in the tower with a book, completely lost in another world.

Every June, her mother shipped her off, saying Casey was much better off in Montana than spending the summer with a paid nanny in San Francisco. Her mother was a partner in a large law firm and put in eighty hours a week. Casey seldom saw her, so she much preferred going to Buckhorn. Grandma Anna was always delighted to see her and taught her the hotel business from the ground up.

As she stared at the tower, the sun seemed to wink off the dirty glass of the windows as if the place had been waiting for her return.

She shivered in the heat and hesitated. Was she really up to staying here alone? She considered going to the Sleepy Pine, the only motel in town, two blocks away on the other side of the highway. But she wasn't ready to face any of the locals yet. Then again, who would want to spend any time alone in an abandoned, allegedly haunted hotel? Certainly no sane person, she thought.

It was only temporary, she reminded herself. Once she signed the buy–sell agreement and fulfilled one of the promises she'd made to her grandmother, she'd be gone and so would the hotel and the bad memories along with even the good ones. Her grandmother used to tell her how strong she was. Well, she didn't feel it right now. But it would take all of her strength to get through this, let alone to destroy this once-magnificent hotel, ghosts and all.

As Casey approached the back entrance, she regretted not calling the local handyman to remove the plywood on the boarded-up structure. What if she couldn't get in without tools? She hadn't called because she hadn't wanted anyone to know she was back in town yet. Telling Lars Olson would have been like putting an ad in the local newspaper— if Buckhorn had one.

She told herself that she'd figure it out. It couldn't be that hard to get in, she thought. There might be some tools in one of the outbuildings on the other side of the parking lot if all else failed. As she glanced that way, her gaze strayed to the concrete firepit and the woods beyond where Megan Broadhurst's body had been found. She closed her eyes for a moment, before quickly turning back to the hotel.

As she moved closer, she saw that one of the sheets of plywood barring the entry had been unscrewed from the wall. Someone, she realized with a start, had *already* broken in.

She cautiously stepped through the opening to try the door to the back hallway. Unlocked. The realization that any number of people could have gotten into the hotel over the past two years and destroyed everything inside had her heart pounding again. What if the family items her grandmother had begged her to save were already gone?

For all she knew, teens had vandalized the place with drunken parties. She feared what she would find, unable to bear the thought of her grandmother's hotel being defaced. It was one thing to raze it; it was another to desecrate it.

She hurried down the hall and stopped abruptly, her heart in her throat. The massive main lounge was just as she'd remembered it. The plush inviting furniture, the huge rock fireplace with its dizzying rise up past the mezzanine and beyond. The registration desk with its beautiful mahogany wood inlay, the antique key boxes, the handcrafted wood cubbies and the period wallpaper.

She looked around the huge lobby and main lounge with its stone pillars and high-arched, stained-glass windows, its marble floors and expensive Persian rugs. The lamps and chandeliers were all original from the time the hotel had been built in the late 1800s, as were most of the fixtures. She'd forgotten how beautiful the place was.

Casey felt tears rush to her eyes. Relief swamped her, making her knees go weak. Nothing had been destroyed. She felt the irony soul-deep. She'd desperately wanted— needed—the hotel to be intact and not defaced and pillaged.

But as she looked around, she felt such a sense of history that it filled her with remorse at what she was about to do to it. The quiet took on an eerie feel. She was used to the main lounge being alive with staff and tourists. Not that the hotel hadn't seen hard times before. One year, a wing had been closed and less staff hired as the accommodation lost its allure to the traveling public—until people began sensing the ghosts.

Word had quickly spread, and before long, the Crenshaw was listed among haunted hotels. That was even before people began seeing Megan Broadhurst's ghost—a beautiful blonde in a white dress stained with blood. When the stories were picked up by a San Francisco newspaper and traveled across the region, the hotel was again filled with guests who wanted to spend the night in a haunted hotel in the middle of Montana.

Before her death, Megan had been one of the staff. Anna often hired students from across the country, along with some older full-time staff. Young people had jumped at a chance to spend the summer in Montana with room and board and a job. Plus, they'd loved that the hotel was haunted—and that there were hiking trails up into the pine-covered mountains practically out the back door, and summer street dances where they could meet other young people.

Like Casey, Megan had come all the way from San Francisco to work at the hotel that summer. Casey pushed the memory away as she had for years and headed to the registration desk. As she did, she noticed that the Old Girl had seen better days but was still in remarkably good shape. Yet it could never again be the luxury hotel that had hosted the rich and famous. Not even if Megan's ghost and others were drifting through the hallways, patiently waiting for guests to arrive.

Casey shivered at the thought. Why hadn't she sold the place without setting foot on the marble floors again? Because she'd promised her grandmother. But she would have promised anything seeing how distraught Anna had been the night she died—and she had. She'd made the two promises that night to keep her grandmother from getting even more upset. The first seemed easy enough. She would return and collect some family items Anna wanted her to have.

The second promise, an impossible one, she'd made on the elderly woman's deathbed and had been broken the moment the words had left Casey's lips. But when she'd finally agreed, her grandmother's expression had softened. She'd released Casey's hand and closed her eyes. Anna Crenshaw never opened them again.

Now, forcing away that memory as well, Casey retrieved her key for her room from the antique boxes behind the registration desk and headed for the grand staircase. There'd been a time as a girl when she'd dreamed of coming down these steps in her wedding gown to join her waiting groom. Childish dreams, she thought now as she climbed. Her footfalls echoed around her in the empty vastness.

She fought the urge to look over her shoulder. No one was following her up the steps because there was no one here but her. She told herself not to buy into any of her grandmother's stories of Megan's ghost. Anna clearly hadn't been in her right mind the night she died. Why else would she swear that she'd seen Megan? Why else would she force Casey into a promise she couldn't keep?

Yet as Casey reached the landing, a chill curled around her neck as if something had only just swept past. She cringed at her own foolishness. Even as she did, she was glad that in a few days' time she would be finished here, the hotel also finished, taking Megan's ghost and her unsolved murder with it.

Casey's room had always been the first one down the mezzanine-level wing. Her grandmother had had a suite downstairs behind the lobby. Casey would have preferred to stay on the staff wing. She'd wanted to be one of them, but her grandmother said she was too young to stay on a wing with older girls—let alone boys. Being younger and the owner's granddaughter, she'd never really fit in, even though her grandmother showed her no special preference.

At the top of the stairs, she saw that the door to her room was ajar. In fact, a lot of the guest-room doors down the hall were open. A dozen homeless people could be living here, she realized, having forgotten for a moment that the hotel had been broken into.

With two fingers, Casey pushed the door to her room open wider. Nothing out of place. In fact, it looked as if housekeeping had just finished in there.

She cocked her head at a sound—not in her room, but in the one across the hall. That door, too, was ajar. She frowned. She could hear what sounded like running water coming from inside.

Stepping across the hall, she pushed the door all the way open. The room looked as if her teenage self had just left it. The bed was unmade and clothing was piled on a chair nearby. The table was covered with take-out containers, newspapers and other debris.

She could definitely hear water running from inside the bathroom. She'd recently called to have the water and power turned back on, only to be told it had been on for months. She'd thought her grandmother must have gotten confused and maintained the utility service.

Now she realized that she'd never seen a bill, which meant that whoever had had it turned back on must have paid for it. How odd.

Frowning, she inched toward the bathroom, the splash of running water growing louder. Like the room's door, this one was also ajar. She put a finger to it and pushed. The door swung inward.

Hit by a cloud of steam, she could barely make out the black and white tiles on the floor, let alone the giant clawfoot tub in front of the window or the large glass-block walk-in shower across the room.

But as the steam began to dissipate out the now-fully-opened bathroom door, she saw wet, soapy flesh behind the glass blocks.

Opening her purse, she pulled out her small handgun her grandmother had gotten her for Christmas before advancing to the shower's opening.

CHAPTER THREE

FINN STOOD UNDER the hot spray. He was going to miss this shower when he finally left here. That was about all he could say for the place. The bed was all right. Too large for one person, but the clean sheets he'd found in the laundry were Egyptian cotton, and the down comforter had been like floating in a cloud. He'd discovered everything he'd needed in the hotel once he'd gotten the electricity and water turned back on and had moved in.

He'd expected one of the locals to contact the hotel owner and rat him out. But after the first few weeks, he'd quit worrying about it. As he lathered up with the Swiss soap scented with chocolate and lavender, he told himself his stay here hadn't been all that bad—except for the nights.

Come twilight, shadows began to form. By nightfall, the huge hotel began to make way too many noises that couldn't be explained away easily. Too many nights, fueled by the old ghost stories, he'd heard footfalls out in the hallway, hammering somewhere deep in the building and the distinct sound of someone digging.

Once, he'd seen a blur of white move so swiftly at the end of the hall that he swore he'd glimpsed a woman for just an instant, her long blond hair billowing out behind her. He'd raced down there to find...nothing.

Nope, now that he thought about it, he wasn't going to miss this place.

He turned his face up to let the spray rinse the soap from his hair that he'd trimmed a little—as well as his beard. Once he got to a real city, he'd visit a salon, but in the meantime… The soap ran down his chest to pool on the floor at his feet. As he turned, wiping water from his eyes, he saw her. For a startling second, she was a ghost from his nightmares.

But he was pretty sure that redheaded, blue-eyed ghosts didn't carry guns.

"Mind handing me a towel?" the man drawled as he nonchalantly turned off the shower. Casey watched him shake his dark head of too-long hair like a dog, droplets of water flying through the air.

She took a step back to avoid getting wet. "What do you think you're doing?" she demanded.

He quit shaking off the water to look at her. Water droplets clung to his dark eyelashes, accentuating the deep blue of his eyes. "Taking a shower. I thought it was obvious. A towel, please?" He didn't seem in the least embarrassed to be standing in front of her stark naked. Not that he had anything to be embarrassed about, since she could hardly miss his well-developed body. He was tall, broad-shouldered, slim-hipped and endowed.

She tossed him a towel. "You're trespassing."

He nodded. "And you're early," he said as he slowly dried himself off.

Early? Early for what? She could feel him studying her with his intense gaze, his lashes as dark and full as his hair. He didn't seem at all upset at being caught red-handed, so to speak, and he'd certainly made himself at home, she'd noticed.

"I wasn't expecting you until later this evening."

Expecting her? "Why is it that you seem to know more about my plans than I do?" she demanded. He didn't seem to hear her. Anxious to put even more distance between them, she backed out of the bathroom to let him finish toweling dry. Had Devlin Wright, the agent handling the sale of the hotel, hired this man to keep an eye on the place? Maybe he was here to assess the value of the salvageable furnishings before the building was razed.

As she stepped into the main room, she saw more of the man's clothing had spilled out of a large duffel on the opposite side of the bed. Whoever this man was, he'd been here for a while. "How long have you been staying here?" she called over her shoulder.

"Why? Thinking of charging me rent?" he asked right behind her.

She spun around, startled. But he only walked over to a pair of jeans lying across his bed and let the towel drop. She tried not to watch him pull on the jeans, going commando, before he tugged a black T-shirt over those broad shoulders.

He turned to look at her, and she realized that she'd forgotten to hold the gun on him. She quickly raised it. He had no reaction to the weapon—just as he'd had no reaction to her finding him in her hotel taking a shower as if he lived here. He *did* live here.

The man had maddening gall even if Devlin Wright had employed him, since the sale was far from a done deal until the papers were signed, and Devlin seemed to be dragging his feet.

He settled that deep blue gaze on her. "This was not the way I'd hoped we'd meet," he said in that same lazy drawl.

His grin made him all the more handsome—and clearly dangerous.

"Excuse me? *Who are you?*" she demanded. "What are you doing in my hotel?"

His gaze traveled all five foot six of her, slowing in critical places before finally settling all that heat and intensity on her face. She felt as if she'd just been frisked naked.

"Sorry, it's just that I've heard so much about you, Casey Crenshaw, that I feel as if I already know you." He cocked a brow, deepening that grin to expose two perfect dimples. "Some of what I heard about you was even good." He must have seen that she wasn't amused at his attempt at humor.

He took a step toward her and held out his hand. "I'm Finnegan. Finnegan James. But please, call me Finn."

She ignored his hand as she took a step back toward the open doorway to the hall. "Finnegan James?" she repeated, her pulse jumping in response to the familiar name. It took her a moment to remember where she'd heard it, since that name had been all over the news months ago—and so had a very different headshot of him. She frowned, trying to superimpose the businessman's face from the television onto this wild-looking man's features. In shock, she cried, "You're…*him*."

There was just enough resemblance that she knew this was the same Finnegan James of San Francisco who'd sold his tech business for an astronomical amount of money at the end of last year and, having become ultrawealthy overnight, disappeared. The next headline she'd seen had read *Foul Play? Multibillionaire Bachelor Now Missing.*

"People are looking for you," she said angrily. "What are you doing here in my closed hotel?" At first glance, she'd just assumed he'd been squatting here because he was homeless. Instead, he was some supersmart, very rich man who'd made his fortune before forty. He'd been dubbed *eccentric*, *single-minded*, *brilliant* and *very private* both personally and otherwise. So she figured if he was hiding out here, she could add *weird* and possibly *mentally imbalanced*.

She took another step back, even though she still had the gun trained on him.

"You going to use that?" he asked, motioning to the gun.

"If I have to." She had the barrel aimed at his heart— just above his impressive six-pack. The man was incredibly built. With those long legs, she figured he could reach her and take away the gun before she could pull the trigger.

But if she were him, she wouldn't bet his life on it.

"I asked what you're doing here."

"I thought it was obvious," he said, cocking his head at her.

"Not as obvious as the shower. You're trespassing on private property."

"You've got me there. I definitely have been." He smiled, softening the sharp planes of his face and making her aware of how much more handsome he was now than in the photo she'd seen of him on the TV news. In that photo, he'd looked way too serious compared to the killer smile he was laying on her right now. The smile, though, seemed to make him more of a threat, since it was a little crooked and charmingly disarming.

"If I tell you why I first came here, promise not to laugh," he said almost shyly.

That was a promise she could keep. She was not in a laughing mood.

"I was hoping to see Megan's ghost before you had the

hotel razed. I figured it might be my last chance. And, no, I didn't see her, but there were times when I swear I felt like she was trying to run me off," he said with a laugh. "The banging, the digging, the footsteps in the hall…" He shook his head. "I can tell you think I'm exaggerating, but I'm not. Although actually admitting I originally came here looking for a ghost makes me sound…a little odd."

"No, not at all," she said sarcastically. His answer confirmed what she'd feared. The man was delusional. She really had to get him out of her hotel. If he was telling the truth. "But just to be clear, Devlin Wright didn't hire you?"

He frowned. "Devlin Wright? Why would he hire me?"

To get the price on the hotel down. Devlin had been slow on getting her a definite offer for the place, so she wouldn't have been surprised if the man was trying to pull a fast one. She knew Devlin. He'd worked here the summer Megan was murdered. That was why she'd been suspicious when he'd contacted her about buying the hotel and land for some investors he said that he'd gotten interested in the place.

"You need to leave," she said now to Finnegan James. "There's a motel in town called—"

"The Sleepy Pine. If you'd prefer that, although I wasn't planning on leaving until Monday since…" He cocked his head again. Those midnight blue eyes shone in the afternoon light. She could feel them drilling into her with an intimacy that made her uncomfortable. "You *did* invite me for the weekend."

FINN WATCHED CASEY CRENSHAW's eyes widen in fresh alarm. He'd startled her again. Clearly, she hadn't expected to find him here. He'd thought it was just because he'd obviously arrived early—months early. Now as she took another step back toward the open doorway, he half expected her to pull the trigger on that peashooter she had pointed at him.

"I'm calling the marshal," she said as she reached into her shoulder bag with her free hand and came out with her cell phone. "I hope you enjoy the Sleepy Pine—after you're released from jail for trespassing." She thumbed in three numbers. He'd thought about stopping her but instead crossed his arms over his chest and simply watched her. It would have been so easy to disarm her and take both the phone and the gun from her.

"Yes," she said into the phone moments later. "This is Casey Crenshaw. I own the Crenshaw Hotel here in Buckhorn. I found a trespasser living on my property." Her gaze locked with his. "Yes, I'm in possible imminent danger. He looks *very* dangerous. You're on your way? Wonderful. Yes, I'll do that. I'm on the second floor. Come in the back. It's where he broke in." She tapped the phone.

"Are you finished?" Finn asked. "I could see that you didn't make the call. We both know it would take Leroy longer than twenty minutes to get here since the marshal has to come clear across the county to get to Buckhorn. Also, the last thing you want is people in town to see a cop car come racing into the parking lot of the hotel. Everyone would know that you're back in town, something I'm betting you want to avoid as long as you can, given what they've been saying about you." He took a breath and let it out. "Shall I go on?"

CASEY GLARED AT HIM, hating that he'd seen through her ruse. Worse, he'd seen through her. She hadn't called 9-1-1 because, like he'd said, it could be an hour before the marshal showed up and she didn't want the attention. She'd hoped he would fall for her bluff. He hadn't. How did this man know so much not just about her plans but also think he knew all about her as well?

And he was obviously deranged if he thought she'd invited him for the weekend. There had to be something seriously wrong with him. Why else would a multibillionaire be hiding out here looking for a ghost?

"If you don't leave now—"

He held up both hands. "Look, it seems there's been a misunderstanding. I'll call Shirley at the motel and have her save me a room for tonight, and then I will pack up and leave." She listened to him make the call, talking to Shirley Langer as if they were old friends. Earlier he'd sounded as if he knew the marshal as well. It seemed so strange to her. The townspeople, it appeared, had come to know Finn better than they knew her since it had been ten years since she'd been back here.

He looked resigned as he disconnected and started to load clothing into his duffel bag.

She watched him pack, worried about him. Worried *for* him. He obviously needed help. "Shouldn't you call someone to let them know that you're alive and well and in Buckhorn, Montana?"

"I'd prefer not."

"Isn't there someone who is worried about you—family, friends, financial adviser?"

He cracked a smile before he sobered. "I lost both of my parents last year. There isn't anyone who needs to know where I am." As if on cue, his phone buzzed in his jeans pocket. He pulled it out, checked the screen and quickly declined the call.

"Someone knows you're here," she said suspiciously.

"It was Earl Ray. I'll call him later."

Earl Ray, the local war hero, was calling Finn? Talk about making himself at home here in Buckhorn. Surely Earl Ray had figured out who Finn really was. Maybe he was calling because he was trying to help the man.

"Maybe you should call him back," she said. He'd been missing for months. "Clearly, *someone* is worried about you."

"Earl Ray?" Finn laughed. "He's just looking for someone to play chess with him over at the bakery while he waits for Bessie to finish making..." He seemed to give it some thought. "It's Friday, so she'll be making fried pies, one of Earl Ray's many favorites. He'll be fine without me. But thanks for your concern. As for the rest of the world, I would just as soon keep my whereabouts quiet for a while longer. Unless you plan to tell the media that you've found me."

And bring reporters to Buckhorn in force? Not likely.

"Surely the locals know who you are."

He chuckled. "They think I've been squatting in your hotel for months because I'm homeless. They've been very kind. I'm fine with them not knowing, either. When people know...well, they start treating me differently." He gave her a look as if she was one of them.

"Well, as long as you leave, your secret is safe with me." But she didn't buy for a minute that he was staying in this abandoned old hotel to see Megan's ghost. How had he even heard about Megan? The murder hadn't hit national news. Not even when sightings of her ghost caught the regional media's interest.

But if not looking for Megan's ghost, then what had he been doing here all those months?

CHAPTER FOUR

THIS WAS DEFINITELY not the way Finn had hoped to meet Casey Crenshaw. As he packed, he frowned to himself. There was some obvious confusion, but he decided to let it go for now. Later, he would clear up the misunderstanding.

"Can you at least put that gun away? You're really making me nervous."

She seemed to consider it before very slowly slipping the weapon into her shoulder bag—still within reach if he made any sudden moves.

"I didn't realize what a mess I've made here alone. Or that I'd have company this soon."

He noticed that she was frowning as if deep in thought. She was so damned cute. Not as cute as she was in the photographs he'd seen of her in her grandmother's albums when she was a girl, but still adorable under her strong, sexy-woman exterior. "How did you know I was selling the hotel to a developer who plans to raze the place? Unless…" He saw her eyes darken as her frown deepened. "Unless you're the secret developer who's made the offer on the place."

He stared at her, too startled to speak for a moment. "*Secret* developer?"

"Devlin Wright is the agent handling the sale, but he's been really closemouthed about who the developers are who are interested in buying my grandmother's hotel and land."

That surprised Finn. "You never asked who the developers are? You don't care who it is?"

"Not particularly."

He saw something in her expression just under the surface that he recognized. Pain. The locals were wrong. Casey *did* care about the hotel, about the town, about her grandmother's legacy.

"Sorry, it's not me." Shaking his head, he said, "So Devlin Wright wouldn't tell you who they were?"

"You know him?"

"I've never met him." But he knew the name. "Is he in town?"

"Not yet. At least I don't think so." She was eyeing him even more suspiciously. Clearly this conversation was making her uncomfortable. She pulled her bag closer. Neither of them had forgotten about the gun.

This was definitely not going well. "If you were the potential buyer," she said, "then that would explain what you're doing here." She cocked a brow at him.

"Sorry, I'm not." But now he was curious who was. He could see how anxious she was to make the sale and leave. He met her gaze again. He could tell that she was still more than a little wary of him.

His cell phone rang again. This time when he looked at the screen, he hit Accept. "Shirley?" He listened as she told him the news. "Thanks for letting me know." He hung up. "A busload of tourists just came in. She had to give my room away." He quickly held up his hands at her disbelieving, newly alarmed expression. "It's no problem. I can sleep in the woods. I'll be fine."

She rolled her eyes and groaned. "You think I won't let you sleep in the woods?" One eyebrow shot up into her bangs, giving him again a glimpse of the girl she'd been in this very attractive young woman standing before him. When she'd caught him in the shower, he'd been surprised on numerous levels.

"I was going to let this go, but I can't have you thinking whatever it is I can see you thinking. When you caught me showering, I was getting ready for tonight, when everyone else arrives."

When she spoke, she bit off each word as if talking patiently to a child. "No one is *arriving*. The hotel is *closed*."

Finn realized he was scaring her again, and with the gun within reach, that was dangerous business. "You don't remember inviting the others for the weekend, *either*?" He saw her confusion turn serious. "Wait—you really don't know, do you? Hold on. There's something I think you'd better see." He held up his hands again. "I need to get it out of my duffel, okay, and I will clear this all up."

He moved to the pocket in the side and took out the now-crumpled and discolored envelope. He held it up and then slowly removed the card from inside. As he handed it to her, he watched her face as she read the invitation out loud, her blue eyes widening with each shocking revelation.

"'Crenshaw Hotel ten-year summer-staff murder reunion. A weekend in memory of Megan Broadhurst and her ghost.'"

Casey looked up. "Starting *tonight*?" He nodded and she returned to the invitation.

"'Last chance to put them both to rest before the hotel is demolished. Save the date. Or everyone will know you're the one who killed her.'

"Is this a joke?" she demanded as she tossed the card onto his bed and rubbed her arms as if chilled.

"I didn't think so."

She shook her head, looking dazed. *"Who sent this?"*

"Obviously, I thought *you* sent it. It's on hotel letterhead. Or at least I assumed it was hotel letterhead. I suppose it could have been Photoshopped. But the postmark is San Francisco, where you live, right?"

"I didn't send this."

That much he'd gathered from her obvious shock.

Casey stared at him for a long moment as if trying to catch her breath. "This is why you were so determined to stay here. Why you seemed so…"

"Confused?" he suggested.

"It still doesn't explain what you've been doing here for months, though," she said, narrowing her eyes at him again. "Nor were you part of the staff ten years ago. So why would *you* get an invitation?" She shook her head and waved an arm through the air. "Never mind. It doesn't matter. This isn't happening as long as I own this hotel."

"Hello!" At the sound of a male voice calling from the floor below, they both started.

"I'm not sure you can stop it," Finn said. "I believe the guests are arriving, and there are no rooms in town, as Shirley just told me."

The male voice rose up from the first floor. *"Hello? Anyone here?"*

Casey was within inches of the open doorway. She hurriedly stepped out to walk to the top of the stairs. She felt a shock as she recognized the blond man her sixteen-year-old self had once found handsome. "Jason?" Jason Underwood was the last person she wanted to see. At least she didn't have to ask what he was doing here. It was finally starting to sink in. Everyone from that summer must have gotten an invitation.

"The others are right behind me," Jason called, smiling up at her. *The others.* She groaned inwardly. "Shall I tell them to take their old rooms on the staff floor?" He didn't wait for an answer. "Thanks for the invitation."

"I didn't send it," she called down. "I had nothing to do with this…reunion."

Jason looked surprised before his gaze shifted to the right of her. She caught the scent of hotel soap on Finn's skin as he joined her. "But you brought a friend? I thought it was only going to be the staff and you."

"I got an invitation, too," Finn said and shrugged.

"That's strange. But whoever planned this must have wanted you here for some reason," Jason said.

"I thought the same thing," Finn agreed.

"That means you must have known Megan." Jason turned at the sound of other people entering the hotel. He called back to them, "Casey said we could take our old rooms along the staff wing," as if she'd really said that.

Casey shot Finn a look. *"You knew Megan?"*

CHAPTER FIVE

DR. CLAUDE DRAKE had been thinking of little else but Megan since getting his invitation to the reunion. The day after it arrived, he'd had an early-morning surgery. While he'd made a perfectly clean incision in the anesthetized patient on the table, he'd admitted that as successful as he'd become, Megan had still ruined his life.

Just like the incision he'd made in this patient's flesh, he'd carried the scars Megan had inflicted. That was what the shrink had told him and his parents, anyway. He'd come home a different teenager than the boy genius who'd begged his parents to let him go to Montana for the summer before he had to start medical school. A boy wonder, he'd breezed through college by the time most teens his age were graduating from high school. He'd just wanted one summer before medical school to be like other teens his age.

Then he'd met Megan and ended up working in an old haunted hotel—until her murder.

His parents and the shrink were right. He *was* scarred. But they never really knew how much. He'd shared only a little of his experience with the psychiatrist. Even as he did, he could tell the doctor didn't believe that one teenage girl one summer in Montana could destroy his self-worth so easily. Then again, the shrink and his parents had never met Megan.

He'd finished the surgery and left the closing to a subordinate. The invitation was in his pocket. He hadn't let it out of his sight since he'd received it. He'd wondered if the others would come. Why would they? Megan had been a poison she'd injected into each of them, preying on their weaknesses and then using those weaknesses against them. She'd gone for the jugular and hadn't spared any of them. It was no wonder one of them had finally snapped and killed her.

As he'd stripped off his mask and gloves, he'd considered how many lies he would have to tell to secretly return to Buckhorn and the hotel for this reunion. He'd put off deciding until almost too late. Fortunately, he had his own jet, and Buckhorn wasn't that far from the Billings airport. If he rented a car, he could get there in plenty of time.

But he'd have to lie about where he was going and why. Even though he'd excelled in medical school and was the youngest head of surgery at the hospital, he felt as if his parents were constantly watching him in fear that he was far from okay. They would see the reunion as him regressing. Or worse.

As he'd changed into street clothes, he called his office. "I have a four-day conference coming up. Please reschedule any appointments."

He'd thought about calling his soon-to-be ex-wife but decided to text her instead. The reunion would fall on the same weekend he was supposed to meet with his lawyer and sign the papers ending their marriage. He didn't feel up to arguing about it. That was why he couldn't tell her about the invitation. Or that he was going. Megan had been his kryptonite. Crystal was the only person who knew firsthand the damage Megan had done.

If Crystal still loved him at all, she would beg him not

to go back to Buckhorn, back to the Crenshaw, for any reason, especially this one. As he saw the hotel rise out of the horizon ahead of his rental car, he wished he'd loved his ex enough to have let her talk him out of coming here.

CASEY COULDN'T BELIEVE this was happening. The nightmare just kept getting worse. A murder reunion? Someone had sent out these ridiculous invitations, and now everyone was showing up here, intending to stay in the hotel?

"You can't—" Belatedly, she remembered that there was no place to stay in town. The closest other accommodations were a hundred miles away. As desperately as she wanted to, she couldn't turn them all away this late in the day when there probably wouldn't be rooms in the next town, either. She told herself it was just for one night. She'd put an end to this first thing in the morning.

Jason was calling greetings to the others on the floor below her. "You do realize that the hotel isn't open to guests?" she called down to him before this could go any further.

"That's what makes it so creepy cool," he replied, as if he was still a teen. "Don't worry. Everyone knows we have to make do for ourselves. It's all going to be great." He glanced back toward the rear entrance to the hotel again. "Hey, Claude. Or should I call you Doc?" Then Jason disappeared from view.

She turned to Finn again. "You knew Megan?"

"Let's get out of here," he said quickly. "I promise I'll tell you everything. We'll go to the café and get something to eat."

"You have to be kidding if you think I'm going anywhere with you."

"I'm hungry, and we both have to eat, and I could use the company. I've been eating alone for months. Also, I can tell you aren't anxious to see the old gang." He motioned to the floor below, where they could both hear voices.

She groaned. The man did know her. How was that possible? "Thank you but—"

"Not to mention, I'm interested." He must have seen her moment of bewilderment and quickly added, "In the hotel. I might want to buy it. You haven't signed any papers yet, right?" He nodded as if the idea had just come to him. "At the very least, another offer could get you an even better price from Devlin Wright. Now, about dinner—"

She stared at him. "Are you serious?"

"I'm always serious when it comes to food when I'm hungry," he said.

"About making me an offer on the hotel?"

"We can talk about it at dinner."

She felt on spin cycle. Her sunburn was tightening her skin, and exhaustion was pulling at her after the miles she'd put on earlier today. She just wanted to go to her room, take a hot bath and lie down for a while. But she hadn't eaten since buying some junk food on the trip, and Finn was right: she wasn't anxious to see the staff from that horrible summer and whom she'd tried to forget for the past ten years.

Finn must have seen her weaken because he charged ahead as if he was closing a business deal. "Another reason we should have dinner is that I know you're also anxious about seeing the townspeople for the first time after word got out about your plans for the hotel. Your ears must have been burning when they found out. There was even a group led by Vi Mullen to try to get the hotel into a historical register to stop you."

She felt a moment of alarm. Nothing could hold up the sale. She'd been counting on this.

"Don't worry. They failed. But I would make a great buffer the first time you go into town since some of the residents act like they're afraid of me, except for Earl Ray." He shrugged. "Earl Ray likes me, but I suspect he likes everyone."

"He does." She felt herself giving in. Maybe Finn wasn't as delusional as she'd thought. He'd certainly summarized her situation quite quickly and easily. But then again, she reminded herself, he'd spent months hiding out in a boarded-up hotel in Buckhorn looking for a ghost. That did make him questionable, even if he was rich and eccentric. "I can't believe the locals haven't figured out who you are. Especially Earl Ray."

He shrugged and grinned. "I look homeless, don't I?" She nodded. "They'll be surprised that you haven't had me arrested for trespassing."

"I'm still considering it."

His grin broadened. Dang, but the man was gorgeous. "Their mouths will drop open when they see us together at the café. Plus, it will give me a chance to show you that I'm not dangerous. Nor a crackpot. But the townspeople don't have to know that." He laughed, and she actually smiled.

Still, she couldn't help feeling skeptical as well as wary. The man had sold his business, made a fortune and disappeared, only to turn up after hiding out in this old hotel most of the winter hoping to see Megan's ghost? That would make anyone leery of him. Nor was she sure she could believe him—let alone trust him. And to find out he'd known Megan…

No matter what he said, she sensed he was running from

something. As someone who was doing her own running, she recognized the look. She told herself she should be careful because a man like that, well, he *was* dangerous, especially if a woman let that grin of his get to her.

But danger was relative, she thought as she considered that one of the former staff from ten years ago was probably a killer. Now they were entering the hotel on the floor below with plans to stay for the entire weekend. They'd all been suspects in Megan's murder, her included. Right now, Finn seemed the most normal person here, and she really was hungry. "This dinner you're suggesting... Who's buying?"

"I think I can afford it." His grin really did make him damned irresistible. Right now she would have considered having dinner with the devil if it meant escaping the hotel and this so-called reunion.

JENNIFER MULLEN HAD given little thought to her basic nature—until the invitation came in the mail. She was abrasive, argumentative and had a mouth on her and a questionable past. Enough people had mentioned it that she'd accepted it as true. She also carried a grudge, as any of her exes could attest.

"You're never going to find a man if you don't tone it down," her mother used to tell her. Like Jen wanted or needed a man that badly that she'd been willing to change. Maybe if she ever met a man who made her want to be different...

Then she'd gotten the invitation for the Crenshaw Hotel reunion and thought about the teenage boy who'd taken more than a piece of her heart ten years ago. He'd been the rare one who'd made her wish she were capable of being someone else. Someone who might find herself married to a famous doctor named Claude Drake.

She'd thought that ship had sailed—until she got the invitation. There'd been a lot of other men since then, but Claude had been a real heartthrob. Although, he hadn't seemed to know it. He'd been young and so innocent for someone who was brilliant in other ways. He'd skipped a bunch of grades, graduated from high school and college early and was headed for medical school at eighteen. He'd been inexperienced; that much she knew. Too much book learning and not enough street smarts, especially when it came to girls. He'd been starry-eyed with Jen. His first.

But then Megan had turned his head. Jen hadn't blamed Claude. Megan had a way of getting what she wanted. Clearly she was rich like him and like Jason. So what had she been doing working at the Crenshaw, anyway?

Not that it mattered after ten years. She Googled Dr. Claude Drake. He was famous for coming up with a new surgical procedure. Surely he wouldn't come back to Buckhorn for some murder reunion? What if the invitation was a joke, just one she wasn't getting? Was there even one of them who wanted to spend any time remembering Megan? And yet she'd never forgotten her and doubted the others had, either.

What would Claude be like now? Would he remember the two of them in the woods that night? She felt her pulse tick up at just the thought of seeing him again. If this invitation was real…

She'd studied the invitation as if the answer to her future was subliminally printed on the card stock. Last chance before the hotel was demolished… So Casey Crenshaw really was going to raze the old place, just as Jen had heard?

She'd checked the return address. The postmark was San Francisco. Jen had heard that Anna had died out there recently. So that meant her granddaughter, Casey, must have sent the invitation. She remembered the timid, redheaded kid that Megan had given such a hard time. Why would Casey want to remember Megan any more than Jen did?

She tapped the edge of the invitation card on her front teeth and thought. Did she care who had sent it to her? She cared more about who would be there and what she was going to wear. Pulling out her phone, she called her cousin to tell her.

"That sounds ghastly," Tina Mullen said. "Surely you aren't going?"

"Why not?"

"You hated Megan. You threatened to kill her, as I recall."

"That was just between us. Anyway, everyone who knew her wanted her dead. Besides, remember that boy I told you about?"

Her cousin sighed. "I should have known that's what this is about."

"I'm thinking he might be there. It might be fate." She rushed on before Tina could argue. "By the way, the hotel is going to be razed. It's not just a rumor. That's why the reunion is being held, because it's the last chance before the place is gone."

"Mother is going to have a fit." Jen's aunt, Vi Mullen, had tried to get the locals to chip in to buy the place and failed.

Not that Jen had cared. "I need to borrow something to wear. Since you can't fit into any of your cool clothes…" Her cousin was pregnant and hadn't been able to fit into anything for months. "I need something…sexy." She thought of Megan and felt her stomach roil. "Just in case I run into Megan's ghost, I want to look really good. I have a final score to settle with that bitch."

"I'd be careful talking like that. People will think you really did kill her."

CASEY REALIZED THAT she had needed the fresh air as much as the short walk into town to the café. The hotel was only a couple of blocks outside the city limits. The cool evening spring air felt good against her sunburned face. She caught the familiar scents of Buckhorn. They reminded her of better days when she and her grandmother would wander in on an evening. Anna loved this town, and the residents had loved her.

A few people glanced in her direction as they reached town, but she didn't recognize anyone she knew. The busload of tourists were already scurrying about town as if having money to burn before nightfall. She noticed that the bakery, candy shop and ice-cream parlor were all busy, and so was the general store down the block.

With a start, she saw that they'd reached the café. Like a perfectly normal gentleman, Finn held the door open for her, and she stepped in. She stopped just inside the door. Earl Ray looked up from where he sat at the counter. He was a welcome fixture in Buckhorn and the nicest man Casey had ever met. He'd always been kind to her and her grandmother and was dearly loved by anyone who knew him.

His blue eyes brightened at the sight of her as he got to his feet. At mid-to-late fifties, he was still spry and athletically built with thick salt-and-pepper hair. He was smiling as he pulled her into a hug, saying, "It is so good to see you.

I was so sorry about Anna." As he drew back, he met her gaze. "She will be missed."

Casey could only nod as she looked into the man's open face. There was true caring in his expression.

"If you need anything, anything at all, let me know." Earl Ray shifted his gaze to Finn. She saw the moment of surprise, but Earl Ray hid it well as he smiled and held out his hand to Finn. "Good to see you. Wasn't sure you'd still be with us." The older man's gaze came back to her. "Hope you're staying for a while."

"Thank you." It was all she could say since she wasn't staying. But he and the rest of Buckhorn's residents would know that soon enough—if they didn't already. After all, Finn had seemed to know her schedule.

Finn said goodbye to Earl Ray and then, putting one large, warm hand in the small of her back, ushered her toward a booth away from everyone else. She'd felt an electric shock at his touch and hoped he hadn't felt her reaction. "Nice guy," he said of Earl Ray as they took seats across from each other.

Casey nodded distractedly. What was she doing here with this man who unsettled her? Worse, she hated to admit that he was right. The moment she walked into the café, she could tell that word had gotten out about her—and the sale. While it had been ten years since she'd been here, people had recognized her. Probably the hair. Eyebrows had shot up at the sight of her. The sight of her with Finn added even more disapproval to their expressions.

"This may have been a mistake," she whispered. Of course this was a mistake. Coming back to Buckhorn had been a mistake.

"You have to face the music sometime," he said. "Don't

worry—they've been serving me for months. They'll still feed us."

"And spit in our food," she said.

"Where is your faith in the goodness of humanity?" he joked as a waitress she didn't recognize came over with two glasses of water and two menus.

Casey could feel the locals staring at the two of them. She hid behind her menu until she heard Finn chuckle.

He couldn't have missed the sour looks they were getting and seemed to be enjoying it. "They can't eat you," he whispered, still chuckling.

She peered at him over the top of the menu. "You should know." The items to order hadn't changed in all the years her grandmother had brought her to this café—the only one in town. Only the prices had changed. She closed her menu and put it down, concentrating on the man sitting across from her as a distraction.

"You were going to tell me the real reason you're here, why someone invited you to this…reunion and how you knew Megan," she said quietly. "You haven't been here looking for a ghost."

Finn didn't bother to pick up his menu, just pushed it aside, as he leaned forward and locked gazes with her. She stared into those sparkling eyes and realized he was about to tell her the truth whether she was ready for it or not.

"I grew up mowing lawns." He nodded affirmation as if she had questioned that. "My father owned a landscaping business. I knew I didn't want to do that the rest of my life, so I worked hard in school and college and started my own business."

"That was all in the news after you disappeared."

He smiled at her impatience. "I'm getting there." The

waitress returned. "Want a milkshake?" Finn asked Casey impulsively. "Chocolate?"

She shook her head and turned to the waitress. "Ice tea, please, and I'll take the baked-chicken salad with vinegar and oil."

Her companion looked crestfallen before he ordered a chocolate milkshake and the chicken-fried steak with fries. He grinned over at her. "If you're nice, I'll give you a bite."

Casey shook her head but couldn't help smiling. "You really are incorrigible," she said as the waitress left, taking the unused menus with her.

"But you're glad you came to dinner with me, aren't you?"

She couldn't help but smile and admit she was. With the waitress gone to put in their orders, he continued as if he hadn't been interrupted. "Then I worked more years, nose to the grindstone, to make the business successful. One day I was offered more money than I could count for that business. I took it, not realizing how it would feel when suddenly I didn't have that challenge anymore. I'd worked hard since I was fourteen. Suddenly I didn't have a job. I had so much money that I didn't have any reason to get up in the morning unless I felt like it. I didn't have…a goal. I was questioning everything about my life. My father had died a few months before that, my mother right after him. I was alone with too much money and too much time on my hands."

"I'm sorry about your parents," she said, offering condolences and wondering where he was headed with this discussion and if he would ever get there.

"My father and I were especially close since we used to work together. He and I used to take care of the Broadhurst estate." She felt her eyes widen before he added, "Megan lived there before she took a summer job at your grandmother's hotel. Before she was murdered." He shrugged. His gaze felt electric as it settled on her. "She and I had gotten close for a while back then. So, lost and at loose ends, I decided to solve her murder by coming to the hotel, and if I got to see her ghost, well, that would be something, too, wouldn't it?"

Casey laughed before she realized he meant it. "You're serious."

CHAPTER SIX

"WHEN I WANT SOMETHING, I go after it," Finn admitted, enjoying being with Casey. While he hadn't thought he wanted an old, haunted hotel, he definitely was intrigued by the owner.

"That at least answers one of my questions," she said. "You really thought you could accomplish what the state investigators couldn't? Just like that? You decided to solve the cold case that no one else could. I suppose you thought you'd find the killer hiding in the hotel?"

Finn laughed. It wasn't the first time a woman had questioned what they took as conceit. Except with Casey, he wasn't insulted. "Megan's killer was never apprehended. I thought the answer might be here." He shrugged. "It was worth a try."

Worth a try? "You're telling me you spent *months* looking for clues?"

"I had some time on my hands. Anyway, I loved exploring the hotel, looking in lots of nooks and crannies, learning about the hotel—and you—from your grandmother's journals." She blinked in obvious surprise. "You knew that your grandmother kept journals, right?"

She shook her head as if to clear out the cobwebs. "I knew my grandmother was old-school. She used registration books instead of a computer because she liked doing things the way they'd always been done. But she kept *journals*?"

"There was a journal for every year that she ran the

hotel. And an entry for every day at that. I found a stack of diaries in a cabinet in the office, kind of hidden in the back. It was interesting reading on those lonely nights. Through those, I learned about the hotel, its history, your grandmother's love for it—and about you and her love for you."

"I was wrong. This could get worse," she mumbled under her breath.

He could see that all of this had hit her hard. He didn't know how to soften the impact. She hadn't expected to find him in the hotel—let alone discover the staff from that summer planned to spend the weekend with her.

"The hotel's history is fascinating," he said, hoping at least to prove to her he wasn't a threat. "The more I read, the more interested I became." In the hotel, but mostly in Casey. But he'd also been looking for answers to Megan's murder and some other mysteries that had turned up. "I haven't spent all my time wandering around the hotel looking for a ghost like I first led you to believe. I contacted libraries, museums and historical societies around the area for even more information. The locals provided old newspaper articles and stories." And Megan's ghost hadn't bothered to show herself in all that time. So like Megan, he thought.

Casey didn't look all that relieved by the news.

He thought about the notebook and the other information he'd found. This was definitely not the time to tell her about that—or his suspicions.

During his extensive research on the hotel, he'd found that every few years, a young girl connected to the hotel would go missing in Buckhorn. Megan, though, was the only one whose body had been found.

"You seemed to have attacked this with the same intensity I suspect you had with your business," she said.

He smiled in answer as the waitress brought their meals and drinks. They didn't speak until the young woman left them alone again.

"I'm sorry I scared you earlier." She looked as if she was going to deny it, but he rushed on. "I'd been looking forward to meeting you." He picked up his fork and knife and cut a piece of chicken-fried steak. He took a bite, then cut a piece and slid it onto her plate with a grin.

He knew the smell alone had to have her mouth watering, but she still pretended she didn't really want it even as she picked up her cutlery, cut a piece off and popped it into her mouth. She closed her eyes as she chewed, making him chuckle at her expression.

"It's as good as it smells, huh?"

Those blue eyes flashed open. "This steak is wonderful." He couldn't help but grin. He liked looking at her. She had a very expressive face. He wanted to ask her if she still was interested in art, but then he'd have to tell her that her grandmother had saved a lot of her earlier works. He didn't want to embarrass her.

Casey appeared more relaxed as if actually enjoying herself once she got some food in her. "You really spent a large portion of the winter here?" she asked, as if as curious about him as he was about her. They hadn't talked about him making an offer on the hotel yet. It didn't seem like the time or place. "How was it?"

"Cold, snowy and miserable, but at the same time beautiful in a harsh sort of way. It separates the men from the boys to winter-in, in Montana. I found it rather exhilarating."

CASEY HATED TO admit it, but she found being in his company was both exhilarating—and exhausting. He exuded enthusiasm, charisma and pure, unrelenting male sexiness. For a man who said he'd found himself lost and at loose ends, he'd certainly snapped out of it. She said as much, making him laugh.

"All because of the Crenshaw Hotel and your grandmother. I was lost when I got here but became fascinated with the place." He raised a brow as if seeing her skepticism. "Why do you find that so hard to believe? I was skeptical at first about the place being haunted. Now, not so sure it isn't." He grinned, wanting to lighten the mood. "But if Megan's the one haunting the hotel, I would imagine this reunion will bring her out. Don't you think that's what someone had in mind when they planned this?"

Casey had no idea what the planner had in mind and said as much. She also had no intention of hanging around long enough to find out, but still his words made her shudder inwardly. There'd always been stories of ghosts at the Crenshaw for as long as Casey could remember. The stories were passed down each summer season. The young men on the staff always loved to scare the young women—and even some of the guests until her grandmother admonished them.

But after the murder, more and more guests at the Crenshaw Hotel reported seeing a young woman in a white dress stained with blood. Their stories put the Crenshaw on the map as one of the most haunted hotels in the West.

It amazed Casey, who scoffed at even the idea of ghosts, just as she marveled that there really were people who wanted to spend the night in a hotel with an alleged ghost haunting the hallways. Her grandmother had always smiled good-naturedly when asked about the ghosts.

That was why Casey had been so shocked when on her deathbed Anna had sworn that she'd seen Megan. "It was her," her grandmother had said, gripping Casey's hand so tightly that it hurt. Casey had felt a chill as she remembered the blonde, blue-eyed and sexy seventeen-year-old Megan Broadhurst had been. It was a memory she feared she'd never be able to forget.

"Gram, it was just your—"

"I saw her. You should have seen the look on her face," her grandmother cried. "Such torment. It was as if she were begging me to help her. There was blood on her dress, blood in her hair. Casey, that girl can't rest until her killer is found, and neither can I." Anna's words came out choked. "You can't let that developer who's been trying to buy the hotel stop you. Once the hotel is demolished… You can still get her justice before it is too late. Do it for me."

Casey had tried not to scoff. "I manage a hotel. I'm not a detective or—"

"Casey, please. I know about your nightmares. Her killer has to be found before the hotel is turned to rubble, or none of us will ever be free, especially you. Do this for yourself. Do it for me. Promise me." Her eyes closed, her hand loosening its grip, and for a moment, Casey feared she'd lost her. But then her eyes fluttered open, her hand tightening its hold again. Her grandmother's glazed eyes found hers again. "Promise me. Promise."

And she had. Anna's eyes closed for the last time.

BENJAMIN TRAVERS HAD found his invitation at the bottom of a stack of mail he'd distractedly thumbed through. He'd seen the return address and vacantly thought it was some type of promotion. It wasn't until he went to discard it that the invitation fell out from where his assistant had already neatly sliced the envelope open.

Picking up the card, he saw something about the hotel being demolished and read more. He felt disgusted, unable to imagine anything worse than this proposed reunion. What possible purpose would anyone have to go to such a thing?

But as he'd held the card over the trash can, he'd seen the line about only the killer not attending—as though blackmail would change the murderer's mind.

Maybe the old Ben, as he'd been called back then, would have fallen for that. The geeky teenager with the thick glasses, pimples and skinny limbs. That Ben was gone. Benjamin had spent the past ten years remaking himself, from his body to his place in the world.

He was a prominent scientist, leading in his field of communicable diseases. He'd even been called on during the pandemic. He was currently working on a book when he wasn't being asked to speak around the world on the subject.

If anything, he had Megan to thank for his career choice. They said the best revenge was success. Too bad she wasn't here to see what he'd become—someone who was no longer invisible to people like her.

That old familiar bitter taste had risen up his throat to choke him. He'd swallowed it down, pretending that he'd left behind the bitterness, the anger, the pain of the cruelty she'd inflicted upon him.

He'd looked again at the invitation, wanting to rip it to shreds for even reminding him of that summer. Except he didn't want to let it go. He wanted to show the others how he'd changed, to erase the memory of that summer, to finally put Megan and her ghost long behind him.

He could do that for one weekend, he told himself. He *would* do that.

"How's your salad?" Finn asked, dragging Casey out of her thoughts. As much as she'd adored Anna and missed her dearly, she hadn't come back here to find Megan Broadhurst's killer. Especially since Finn had spent months here thinking he could solve it but had no leads. No, she was only here to have the hotel razed and the land sold, pick up a few things to remember her grandmother by and be gone.

"Not as good as your chicken-fried steak," she answered. But she wanted to hear more about why he was in town. "So you knew Megan and about the Crenshaw and the murder. But it doesn't explain why you got an invitation. Or how the person who planned this macabre reunion knew to send you one." She frowned. "You must have gotten the invitation right after you sold your company. Right before you disappeared."

He nodded. "I have no idea why I got it or who sent it."

"But I can tell you're curious," she said, wondering what he wasn't telling her. There had to be more motivation or she couldn't believe that he would have been invited. "Surely she knew other people? Unless they, too, were invited." She groaned at the thought. Maybe it wasn't just the staff from that summer.

He merely shrugged.

She pushed away what was left of her salad and studied her dining companion. His involvement worried her, just as it bothered her that he seemed to know so much about her grandmother—and her.

"I didn't mean to make you uncomfortable," Finn said. He was more perceptive than she'd thought. Or she wasn't as good at hiding her feelings as she believed. "I was more curious to see how the girl your grandmother described had grown up. Anna was very proud of you."

His words brought tears to her eyes. She quickly looked away and changed the subject. "Are you serious about making an offer on the hotel and land?" Another offer definitely would help get Devlin Wright to quit stalling. She needed this over, even sooner now, with the reunion—and now Finn. She didn't know what to make of him. She hoped to be long gone before she figured it out.

"I *am* serious. When are you supposed to talk to Devlin Wright?"

"In the morning." She realized that he might have planned their meeting to coincide with the reunion, because as a former member of the staff from that summer, he would have gotten an invite.

"I'll have you an offer by morning as well. We should exchange numbers."

She typed his phone number into her contacts and studied him, amazed how this was happening. It seemed... too easy. He met her gaze and held it until she had to look away first.

By the time they walked back to the hotel, the sun had set, leaving Montana's big sky a rainbow of colors over the mountains to the west. A cool breeze stirred the pines and lifted her hair. It felt later than it was. It didn't get dark this time of year until almost ten. With luck, she would be able to avoid everyone until morning, when she'd finish this— one way or another. Hopefully, she'd have an offer on the hotel and land and let the new owner deal with both the reunion and the former staff.

FINN LOOKED OVER at Casey as they reached the hotel. Was he seriously considering buying this white elephant? Why not? He could afford it, although it would mean reappear-

ing, something he wasn't looking forward to. The speculation on what had happened to him had died down. He didn't
want to be the Multibillionaire Bachelor in the headlines
again or involve Buckhorn or Casey.

But he could see that she needed to get the hotel sold.
It was the least he could do, given that he'd spent months
camped out on her property.

As he held the door to the hotel open for her, she said,
"I'll consider your offer in the morning as well as Devlin's."
She sounded all business, those intimate moments in the
café long forgotten.

"Don't accept his until you hear my offer." He liked a
challenge and now didn't want to lose the hotel he hadn't
even considered buying before today.

"What will you do with the Crenshaw?" she asked without looking at him as she entered the hotel and he followed.

Clearly, he hadn't gotten that far. "Truthfully? I haven't
considered that part." She shot him a suspicious look. "But
I am serious. I will make an offer." What he would do with
the place, he couldn't imagine at this point. Tearing down
the building seemed criminal, but to make it viable would
require more than money. It would require a commitment
he wasn't sure he wanted to make. Nor did he think it was
what Casey wanted.

"I get the feeling you want to see the hotel demolished,"
he said, studying her as they entered the main hall and
stopped, neither seeming anxious to go any farther.

She glanced away as if she didn't want to talk about her
reasons for needing the hotel gone. "Why would I care?"

The sound of laughter and raised voices erupted from the
staff wing. Casey headed for the stairs quickly as if hoping to avoid all of it. He followed, wondering if he should

warn her about what he'd found. Not just the notebook and what was written in it, but about the missing young women mentioned in Anna's journals.

If Casey knew what he'd uncovered during his research, how would she take it? Maybe she already knew about the disappearances. Did they have anything to do with Megan's death? Either way, most of the suspects could be in the hotel before the night was over.

They'd reached their floor, and he'd pushed open his door across the hall from hers to retrieve her suitcase for her. They'd left so quickly, she hadn't taken it earlier.

"Thank you for dinner," she said as she took the suitcase handle from him, their fingers brushing. He could see that she felt the electricity. But she had done her best not to show it. "Good night." She sounded tired as she headed across the hall.

"Thanks for not having me arrested. I enjoyed dinner. You're not at all what I expected." He hadn't meant to say that last part. It had just come out.

Casey stopped to look back at him. "If you got your information from my grandmother's journals, then I'm not surprised. Or if you got it from the locals. I'm sure neither version is entirely true."

He said nothing, thinking how she was more than he'd expected, since the first time he'd heard about Casey Crenshaw, it hadn't been from her grandmother. Nor had it been in the least bit flattering. Megan had described Casey as an ugly, spoiled, brainless brat. Casey was beautiful and far from brainless. He could see now how Megan would have been intimidated by Casey, making her dislike her all the more.

As Casey disappeared into her room, he noticed what

he'd missed. A note tacked on his door. *Meet down at the firepit. You won't want to miss the first night's festivities. Bring Casey.*

He chuckled at that. Like he could get Casey to do anything she didn't want to. But as he stared at the note, he didn't like the idea of leaving her alone in the hotel, either.

"WHAT DO YOU MEAN, you aren't going?" Jen demanded when she'd stopped by the Sleepy Pine Motel on the edge of town to pick up her best friend and former coworker.

Shirley Langer mugged a face at her. "I'm not going to some stupid murder reunion. What do you think I am, crazy?" Shirley managed the motel along the two-lane that ran through Buckhorn. She had an apartment in the back and a life even duller than Jen's own.

"You can't *not* go," Jen persisted. "Didn't you read the invitation? Everyone will think that you killed her."

"I don't care." Shirley had turned on the No Vacancy sign hours ago when a busload of tourists had rented all the rooms. Now she wandered back to her apartment, Jen at her heels. With luck, no one would need her assistance until they checked out in the morning.

Shirley opened the refrigerator and took out a beer, handing it automatically to Jen before getting one for herself. "I just want to have a beer, put my feet up and watch something mindless on television. I don't need any more drama in my life. I certainly don't need a murder-ghost reunion."

Jen cracked open her beer and plopped down on the opposite end of Shirley's sagging couch.

"Lars doesn't want you to go. Is that the problem?" Jen said. Shirley's boyfriend—and she used the word loosely— Lars was a point of contention between them. "He has no right to tell you what to do. He needs to put a ring on it before he starts—"

Shirley scoffed. "He doesn't even know about the invitation. I didn't tell him before I threw it away. Anyway, I don't do what he tells me to do unless I want to. Even if he left Tina tomorrow, which he's not going to do until the baby is born and he can prove it is another man's kid, I'm not sure I want him."

It was a small town. Jen's cousin Tina Mullen was Lars's live-in former girlfriend who was pregnant with, Lars swore, someone else's child. "Oh, please, you and your drama." She had it up to her eyeballs with this lovers' triangle. Jen wasn't even sure *Tina* wanted Lars. It would serve him right to lose both of them.

Shirley turned on the television and cranked down the volume as she took a sip of her beer.

"You have to go with me," Jen whined. "I need you there. Think of it as a weekend away. But also you might meet the man of your dreams."

Shirley laughed, looking at her with utter disbelief. "You mean one of the staff who is probably a murderer?"

"Still better than Lars."

"*Away* for a weekend? I can see the hotel across the highway from my front window," Shirley cried. "That's not my idea of a weekend retreat, to go to an abandoned hotel with Megan's ghost sneaking around every corner." She shook her head and shivered.

Jen still wasn't giving up. "Didn't you say one time that you wished you could be a guest in the hotel instead of work there?"

"That was before the summer I worked with Megan." She took a gulp of her beer. "You have to admit, this reunion sounds…stupid. Why would *you* want to go? How do you know that the killer won't be there? We've always known it had to be one of us."

Jen considered that for a moment. "We all had good reason to hate Megan and want her…gone. Who do you think did it?"

Shirley shook her head. She'd put it out of her mind, thinking she would never see those people again. "What makes you think *I* didn't do it?"

ONCE IN HER ROOM, Casey thought she'd feel better, but Finn was just across the hall, and when she looked out the window, she could see people standing around the campfire glowing in the growing darkness. That alone brought back a firestorm of memories, most of them bad.

She counted those gathered around the fire. Five. That meant two hadn't come. At least not yet. She closed the drapes and turned away, her thoughts boomeranging back to Finn. She wasn't sure what to make of him. Would she get an offer on the hotel from him in the morning?

There'd been a couple of times during dinner that she'd thought he might be flirting with her. Clearly, he was a man who'd made his fortune by going after what he wanted. But what did he want with her hotel? Or was he after something else?

The thought surprised and unnerved her. She wasn't what he'd expected? There was something about him having so much prior knowledge of her that made her even more uneasy—and made all of this feel more dangerous.

A murder reunion? Why would someone want to bring murder suspects from that summer back here? She stood in the middle of the room, feeling as lost as Finn had said he was. She'd left the drapes open on the windows facing town. The mountains beyond were a deep purple. Montana's big sky only had a hint of pink as darkness began to descend. The room felt cold. She rubbed her bare arms, telling herself a hot bubble bath was what she needed.

But as she turned toward the bathroom, she caught a flash out of the corner of her eye. Her heart leaped to her throat, pulse taking off at a sprint. She had only an instant to stifle a scream before she realized that what she was seeing was only a white laundry bag hanging on a hook on the bathroom door.

Her pulse began to slow. She blamed Finn. Honestly, between him and the ghost stories and this stupid reunion, she was jumpier than a long-tailed cat in a room full of rockers, as her grandmother used to say. Did Finn really believe that Megan's spirit still walked these halls? Or was he just trying to scare her like all the boys she'd ever worked with here?

"Megan, if you're here, I don't care," she said, her voice seeming unnaturally loud in the empty hotel room. "You made my life miserable when you were alive, and now you're here to torment me? Guess what? I don't care. This hotel is going to be rubble soon. Still want to hang around? Be my guest, but I'm out of here soon, and I won't be looking back."

"I hate to interrupt," Finn said, startling her. She spun around. He stood in her doorway. Hadn't she closed and locked it? Or had she been so anxious that she'd forgotten to close it properly, let alone bolt it? Finn now stood leaning against the doorjamb.

She felt her cheeks flare hot, his look daring her to lie. "I was just talking to Megan's ghost." As if he didn't already know that.

He nodded and grinned. "She say anything interesting?"

"Not that I ever heard." *Just like when she was alive.* "I was getting ready to take a bubble bath and call it a night. I guess I forgot to bolt the door."

"It was open when I came out of my room. Could have been the breeze if you didn't close it securely. My windows are open across the hall." He handed her the note.

She read the neat printing. "'Bring Casey'?" she inquired incredulously as she handed back the note.

"I rolled my eyes at that part as well, but it might be a good idea." She looked at him as if he were joking. Before she could argue the point, he rushed on. "I thought you might like to go down with me. I've had a lot more time to think about this…reunion than you have. Doesn't it make you wonder who's behind it? Someone put this together to get all of us here. Why? What if the reunion is a ploy?"

"What are you saying?"

"That I believe the person behind this got us all here for a reason other than saying goodbye to Megan and the hotel. I'd like to know what it really is."

She rolled her eyes. "Maybe whoever did this saw it as a way to get all the suspects together again. Maybe the person is trying to find Megan's killer. Let's see—who just spent months in this hotel looking for the answers? Oh, what a co-incidence that you just happened to be here doing that very thing *and* got an invitation even though you weren't part of the staff, weren't even here when she was murdered."

He held up both hands. "I know it looks suspicious, but I swear I had nothing to do with this. But think about it. If the person isn't someone determined to unmask Megan's killer, then—" he met her gaze "—it could be the killer has another score to settle. I think we need to figure out why we're all here—and as quickly as possible."

She flinched at his use of *we*.

"I know why I'm here, and it has nothing to do with the reunion or Megan's murder."

"The person who sent out the invitations knew you would be here," he pointed out. "I doubt that was a coincidence."

Casey felt the gravity of his words. She was also a suspect. She thought of the night before Megan had been murdered. They'd all been around the campfire, drinking, talking, laughing and eventually arguing, when Megan pulled her aside and dragged her deep into the woods. Everyone had heard the argument between the two of them before Casey had returned to the fire alone.

She'd stood staring into the flames morosely and drinking too much, furious with her grandmother, with herself, but mostly with Megan, who'd made her summer hell on earth. She should have walked away then and never gone back to the bonfire.

But she'd gone back the next night. Her only other option had been to hide out in her room for the rest of the summer. She refused to let Megan intimidate her. She'd been standing by the fire when she heard the scream in the woods. She'd looked up, startled, and had been surprised to see people rushing into the trees.

She couldn't remember later, when interviewed by the marshal, who'd been around the fire. She herself had gone into the woods to see if Ben, who'd been really drunk, was all right before Shirley's scream. She hadn't found him and had turned back.

But that night she'd rushed in, following the screams, and

found the others. Shirley Langer had continued to scream until Jason put an arm around her and tried to calm her. Shirley said she'd found Megan covered with blood, lying in the dried pine needles. Megan had been bludgeoned to death with a rock, the marshal had speculated, even though no bloody rock had been found.

Everyone had been in shock, maybe especially Claude, who'd told them that he was in medical school, studying to be a doctor. She'd thought that odd since he looked so pale, as if he might faint. He'd leaned against a tree. She realized he must have checked Megan for a pulse, because he had blood on his fingertips that he was trying to wipe off on the bark.

Now some of them had come back and were down at the campfire as if reliving that night. What was wrong with these people? Had they come because of what had been written at the bottom of the invitation about anyone not attending being considered the killer?

Or was Finn's theory not so far out of the realm of possibility? There'd been a lot of hard feelings that summer among the staff because of Megan.

"I don't want to scare you," Finn was saying, "but someone went to a lot of trouble to get us all here."

"This reunion is morbid. Megan's death was a tragedy, not something to resurrect over a campfire. I have no desire to relive the worst summer of my life. If I still own this hotel in the morning, I'm sending them all packing. Now, I'm going to take a hot bath."

Finn didn't move. "I'll buy the hotel for twenty percent more than whatever Devlin offers you."

Casey stared at him. "Just like that?"

"I want to see this through. Someone wanted me here,

and I'm going to find out why. I don't like being manipulated. Just tell me the amount you want, and I'll make the call to have the papers drawn up and money transferred to your account first thing in the morning. After that, nothing will be keeping you here."

Casey felt her heart lift. This was what she'd wanted. Devlin had been stringing her along for months. Finn was giving her a way out. "I have to collect some of my grandmother's things from the hotel before I can leave."

"No problem."

He was serious? "Have you forgotten that I'm one of the suspects?"

"No." He smiled. "I'm counting on you not being the killer. That's why you should leave as quickly as you can. I'm not sure anyone is safe here."

So just take the money and run? Run just as she had ten years ago? Why was she hesitating? This was what she'd wanted. "You really think the killer is behind this?"

"I think it's a possibility I wouldn't discount. Or someone who wants to find the killer even more than I do. Or someone with a grudge to settle. With any of those, it could get dangerous."

"Yet you plan to stay?"

He shrugged as if he had no choice. "I'd prefer you not be here if I'm right."

"This is still my hotel." Why was she arguing the point? He was trying to help her. To give her what she clearly wanted. Or was he trying to help *himself*?

She narrowed her gaze at him. "Why are you so determined to solve the murder of a girl you hardly knew that you would buy a hotel you don't want? You'd risk not only your money but also your life to find her killer because you're at loose ends with nothing better to do?" Casey saw that she'd struck a nerve. "You didn't just *know* Megan, did you?"

He was quiet for a moment as he looked down at the note in his long fingers. "I had a relationship with Megan." His gaze came back to hers. "I was in love with her. Whoever sent the invitation knew about us even though we were keeping it a secret from our parents. It's the only explanation for why I was invited. Which means Megan told someone here about me."

CHAPTER SEVEN

CASEY FELT A CHILL. She finally understood why Finn had spent the winter in the Crenshaw looking for a killer. "You're still in love with her. You're in love with a...*ghost.*"

His laugh seemed to chase away the shadows in the room as he shook his head and locked eyes with her. "I was the same age as Megan, seventeen, when I fell in love with her. I'm not a teenager anymore." He shook his head. "I knew in my heart she and I wouldn't last. The only reason it happened at all was because Megan's parents had grounded her, so we saw a lot of each other for a couple of months before she was sent away." He looked shy. "She was my first love. I'm sure you had one and know how that is."

She had, and she knew that the memory had only gotten sweeter over the years. First love was like that: a fantasy that ended with him moving away before it could bloom. And die. But she had no intention of sharing that with Finn.

"If Megan was grounded," she said instead, "how did she end up working the summer at the Crenshaw? Wait. You said she was sent away?"

"Her father thought it was best if she had a job far away for the summer. He knew your grandmother and asked for her help. He sent Megan out here hoping she would grow up and start taking responsibility for her actions. He'd hoped your grandmother would have a positive influence on her."

"My grandmother never mentioned that," Casey said,

feeling a jolt of surprise and anger. That explained a lot. No wonder her grandmother refused to take sides between her and Megan. Megan wouldn't have been the first young person Anna had taken under her wing. It could also explain why Anna felt guilty about Megan's death, Casey thought, her heart aching. Why Anna was positive that she'd seen her ghost.

"A few nights before Megan died, she called me," Finn said. "She was crying. She wanted to come home, but her parents wouldn't allow it. She hadn't been in Montana all that long and was demanding they let her come home. They weren't having it. She said she was scared. That she didn't feel safe. I was trying to reassure Megan when she said she had to go. Someone was at the door. I heard her say, 'Oh, it's you,' and then the phone was disconnected. I tried to call her back numerous times over the next two days, but each time it went straight to voice mail. I never spoke to her again."

Casey met his gaze. "You shouldn't feel guilty."

"She'd wanted me to go to her parents and plead her case. Like I said, her parents didn't know about the two of us." He shrugged. "I guess I knew they would disapprove of her dating the gardener's son, especially behind their backs. I regret not having the courage."

"You really don't believe that they would have listened, do you?"

"Probably not. Megan had a tendency to overdramatize everything, so I didn't really think she was in danger, either. But I still should have tried. I think I knew that once they found out about the two of us, it would be over. Not that Megan and I could have lasted over the long haul anyway, but they wouldn't have liked that we'd been together while she was supposed to be grounded. I thought it would make things worse for her in the long run."

He felt guilty for not believing Megan was really in trouble. Casey understood the weight of guilt he'd been carrying around. She'd been carrying around her share from that summer for years, too.

The reminder that one of these people was probably a killer made her shudder. "I hope you know what you're getting yourself into."

Finn nodded. "I have some idea. I just don't want anything to happen to you. That's why I want to buy the place. All you have to do is pack up your grandmother's things. I'll take care of everything else."

"You think you know me because of my grandmother's journals, but I'm not that girl anymore."

"I've noticed." He smiled at that, making her remember the way he'd looked at her earlier when he was half-naked. "I wouldn't mind getting the chance to know the woman you are now. But, unfortunately, I don't think this is the right time. I thought you'd sent the invitations and knew what you were getting into. When I realized you hadn't—"

"Hey, you two!" Jason called directly behind Finn. Neither of them had heard him approach. She saw the way Jason was studying the two of them, too inquisitive, too amused, given the smirk on his face. Clearly, he thought something was going on between them.

Casey took a step back, surprised at how close she and Finn had been just a moment before—and not just physically. They'd been looking into each other's eyes. She'd felt something that scared her. He was a stranger she wasn't even sure she could trust. But she could understand why Jason thought he'd seen something…intimate between them.

"We've got a fire going at the old firepit," Jason said. "The beers are on me. Come join us. We're going to be talking old times, and it wouldn't be the same without you, Casey."

She could feel Finn's sharp gaze on her. He'd been watching her and Jason earlier. No way had he missed the look Jason gave her or how uncomfortable it made her.

"If what we have to say about Megan doesn't make her ghost appear, then I don't know what will." Jason laughed. "You won't want to miss this," he said, grinning at Finn as if they, too, shared a secret. She realized they had both been in love with Megan, probably still were.

Jason turned and headed back down the stairs. She and Finn hadn't moved. Neither of them spoke until they heard him on the lower level.

"I wouldn't go down to the campfire if I were you," Casey said. "The things that will be said about Megan…well, they might hurt your feelings."

Finn laughed. "I said I was naive at seventeen. I wasn't stupid. I know she had trouble getting along with people."

"That's putting it mildly. But fine—suit yourself."

"I'll make the call to my bank in the morning," Finn said. "Sleep on it. You might change your mind about selling."

That wasn't happening. But she nodded, not sure she believed any of this.

"I'm going down to the fire, but I can understand if you don't want to."

Her head hurt. She yearned for the oblivion of sleep— as if that would make any of this go away. She thought of the promise she'd made her grandmother—the one she'd had no intention of ever keeping.

"You really think you can solve the murder?" She looked

into his eyes and felt the full impact of them. "Why?" she asked, surprised at the emotion she felt. Jealousy? That a man could care that much this long about another woman? "You said yourself that you knew the two of you would have never lasted."

Finn smiled, almost sadly. "I don't know if you're aware of this or not, but your grandmother always blamed herself for Megan's murder. Maybe knowing the truth will give you both some peace."

She felt tears burn her eyes. Wasn't that exactly what her grandmother had wanted for her? For both of them? After ten years, she'd given up hope that Megan's killer would ever be found. Her grandmother had known that the murder had been like a dark cloud hanging over her and always would as long as it went unsolved.

"If Jason brought enough beer, I just might get some answers tonight," Finn said.

Casey thought about telling him not to believe anything Jason said but saved her breath. She watched him turn back to his room and told herself that she wasn't afraid to go down to the campfire. That she wasn't afraid to relive that summer and Megan's murder. That she hadn't been afraid all these years that the truth would come out.

She nearly laughed out loud. Who was she kidding? She was terrified to even look too closely at the memories. Now someone wanted to dig it all back up, each of them with their own ugly stories and bad memories. Could she trust her memory of the events of that summer night after all this time? Could any of them? Worse, could she trust her own lies to stay a secret?

She stood in the middle of the room, knowing what she had to do. If she didn't go down to the fire, she would feel like a coward who had something to hide. She laughed, since both were true.

Worse, Finn was right. She, too, wanted to know who'd put this reunion together. She feared that person's motivations. Did one of them want revenge? All she knew was her own pain from that summer. No one had saved *her* from Megan. Had the vindictive teenager been tormenting the others—just as Megan had Casey? If that person had felt even more alone and abandoned than she had, would they still be feeling angry enough to kill again?

Or was the person behind this merely looking for the truth?

Either way, Casey knew she had reason to be afraid.

DEVLIN WRIGHT HAD been on the fast track and about to make the biggest deal of his life when he'd picked up his mail and seen the Crenshaw Hotel on the return address. His heart had dropped. He'd been playing it cagey, hoping to stall and get Casey Crenshaw to take less for the hotel and land. What if he'd overplayed his hand?

"This had better not be what I think it is," he'd said and had hurriedly ripped open the envelope.

The invitation definitely wasn't what he'd expected.

He'd stared at the card, turned it over, then finally read it through. For a split second before he'd pulled it out, he'd thought it would be a note from Casey telling him that she'd decided to keep the hotel and land. Or that she'd gotten an offer from someone else.

His pulse had pounded as he'd tried to make sense out of the invitation. Why would Casey do this? Was she kidding? She hadn't mentioned anything about this the last time they'd talked. Why in the world would she send these out—right before they were supposed to finally make a deal on the hotel and land?

He felt sick to his stomach. Did she have some reason she wanted to hold off the sale? Why else would she even bring up Megan's name, let alone get everyone back to Buckhorn, back in that boarded-up hotel for a weekend?

Unless... He'd gone weak at the thought. Unless she was trying to trap the killer. If so, then Casey had lost her mind, and he'd better get her to sign on the dotted line before she was hauled away. Or before she got herself killed and his investors backed out.

PATIENCE RILEY HAD laughed when she'd gotten the invitation. Of course it was a joke. A bad joke at that. She'd turned away from her massive desk to look out over the city of Manhattan. From the wall of glass that was her corner office, she admired the view—and her reflection.

Tucking a lock of hair behind her ear, she didn't look much different than she had ten years ago. Slim, petite and cute with her short dark pixie cut that accented her big gray eyes, she'd kept in shape. She'd always looked young, something she'd used to her advantage. Ten years ago, she'd looked even younger than Casey—and Anna's granddaughter had been merely a child.

Looking young and naive had always served her well, but she had been neither. Just as she hadn't had the luxury of growing up like most of the staff that summer. Rich, privileged, spoiled rotten, it had angered her that Megan, Claude and Jason had taken jobs that kids like her really needed—not to mention Casey, whose grandmother owned the place. Jen and Shirley had been the exceptions. Local girls with no big plans for the future, they'd at least had a roof over their heads their whole lives. Patience hadn't been so lucky.

But her upbringing had given her a kind of strength that the others lacked. She demanded more of herself, while hiding that raging desire inside her. That was why Megan had underestimated her time and time again. Megan hadn't seen what was really inside her, or she would have run for her life while she could.

As Patience had turned back to her desk to peruse the invitation again, she was sure that Casey hadn't sent it. That would have been completely out of character for her. But one of the others? She could believe that. They probably had nothing better to do.

Or maybe one of them had an agenda. Nothing good, of that she was sure. She'd had no desire to attend. Did she care if she looked guilty?

"Excuse me," her assistant had said as she'd stuck her head in the door. "They're ready for you downstairs."

"Thank you." The editor of one of the leading women's magazines in the country, Patience wasn't easily intimidated anymore like she'd been ten years ago when she'd been nothing more than one of the hotel staff.

She'd tossed the invitation into the trash and risen from her desk. She'd said goodbye to Megan ten years ago. She saw no reason to repeat herself.

Pushing out the door of her office, Patience had smiled to herself at the thought of the staff huddled around the campfire again behind the hotel telling ghost stories. Did they really think they could call up Megan's ghost? What then? Ask her who'd killed her?

Or was it more about assuaging their guilt? None of them had stood up to Megan even as they'd watched her tear apart one staff member after another. They'd been a bunch of cowards, afraid they'd be next.

If they were looking for absolution, good luck finding it. They were all guilty, herself included. But Casey Crenshaw the most. She could have gone to her grandmother. She could have stopped it. If anyone was to blame for what had happened, it was Casey and her grandmother.

Megan and her mind games, she'd thought as she'd headed to Paste-Up. Megan had spared no one, except Ben, who she'd simply pretended didn't exist, and Patience, whom she fawned over like she was her pet. Patience had smiled bitterly at the memory. Megan had known better than to try to torment her. Instead, she'd made the rest of the staff mistrust Patience and treat her as an outcast by simply sparing her alone.

Oh, yes, Megan loved mind games. Right until she took her last breath.

ACROSS THE HALL, Finn was pulling on a hoodie sweatshirt, his door still open. "If you give me time to change, I'll go with you," Casey called.

He looked up in surprise and maybe concern.

She hurriedly closed the door before her good sense returned—or he could talk her out of it. She had to face them at some point. As tired as she was, she wanted to get it over with. Would they all show up? Had they all arrived?

She could imagine the speculation down there around the campfire. Like her and Finn, they would wonder who'd sent out the invitations and why. By now Jason would have told them that Casey denied doing it. But would they believe him?

Her fingers trembled as she dressed. She pictured each

of them—Ben, Claude, Devlin, Jason, Shirley, Jen and Patience—as they'd been as teens and wondered if they'd changed as much as she felt she had. Why did she fear that one of them had been waiting for ten years for her to return here?

Clothes changed, she grabbed a jacket and left her room.

Finn stood in the hallway waiting for her, his door closed. "You sure about this?"

She nodded, lifting her chin in almost defiance as she locked her door, then checked it, still wondering why it had come open earlier. She felt scared and more than a little paranoid. But she wasn't sixteen anymore. The woman she'd become could do this.

He gave her a look like one her grandmother would have, as if proud of her for facing her demons. It made her want to laugh. She was trembling in her sneakers. But then Finn had no idea what she'd been hiding all these years.

They took the staff stairs at the back, just as she'd done as a kid. She'd spent one summer looking for secret passages. She knew they had to exist in the rambling hotel, but the back stairs were the closest she had come to finding any.

The moment she and Finn stepped outside, she smelled the pine smoke and was hit with the memory of the night Jason took her into the pines after everyone else had left the fire for the night.

"You all right?" Finn asked.

She nodded. She hadn't realized that she'd stopped and now stood staring at the dark silhouettes standing around the orange crackling blaze fifty yards away just inside the trees at the foot of the mountain.

This was probably a mistake—just not as large a mistake as she'd made ten years ago, she told herself. "You're a lot stronger than you think you are." She heard her grandmother's voice so clearly that the woman could have been standing next to her. Casey smiled, realizing it was true. She wasn't that shy girl Megan had manipulated. Nor would she be manipulated now by whoever had sent out the invitations.

As they neared the gathered group, she could see Jason with his back to them and heard him talking. She couldn't make out his words, but suddenly he broke off in mid-sentence to look over his shoulder. Someone had warned him of her approach.

"Are your ears burning?" Finn whispered to her. "Mine are."

Casey didn't answer. She was looking at the familiar faces around the campfire and remembering. They were all looking back at her.

Except for Patience Riley. She was looking into the woods as if she'd heard something, an odd smile on her face.

CHAPTER EIGHT

THE FIRE GLOWED bright orange in the growing darkness as Casey and Finn reached the group. Jason hurried to the cooler, coming back with two beers. He handed one to her and one to Finn. Several of the others had been talking among themselves but now stopped to listen.

"This reunion was a great idea!" Patience said, lifting her beer can in a salute. "I didn't think you had it in you, Casey."

"I didn't send the invitations. I had nothing to do with this. In fact, I can't imagine why anyone thought this was a good idea." She looked around the campfire. They'd all changed little except for Ben. It could have been ten years ago, the campfire, the beer, almost all of them gathered out here.

Ben rushed forward to hug her. Casey was surprised by the gesture and shocked by how much he'd changed. "It's good to see you," he said. "I'm so sorry about your grand-mother." The others quickly added their condolences. "I knew this wasn't your doing." All she could do for a moment was nod and smile. "I'm glad you're here."

"Good to see you, too, Ben," she said lamely, since who in their right mind would want to be a part of this?

"It's *Benjamin* now. I'm a doctor. I specialize in viruses. You probably saw me on the news during the pandemic."

"Of course," she said quickly. She had seen him, but

she hadn't recognized him nor even put the name together with the Ben from that summer. "I always knew you would do well."

"Thank you." He smiled, reached for her hand and squeezed it before going back to his spot by the campfire.

The roar of a car engine made them all turn. The sound was followed by the flash of headlights as a vehicle sped into the parking lot behind the hotel. The lights blinked and went out, and moments later Shirley Langer and Jennifer Mullen stumbled out, laughing. They walked up carrying a bottle of wine, sharing a joke.

"You started the party without me?" Jen demanded loudly, verifying what Casey had suspected the moment they'd driven up. Both had already had a few drinks. "Wow, you really did all come back to Buckhorn," the attractive brunette said as she looked around the campfire. Her gaze stopped on Finn and she frowned. "Who are *you*?"

"Casey brought a date," Jason said.

Before Casey could correct him, Finn said, "I received an invitation, like I suspect the rest of you did."

Jen's gaze swung to Casey for clarification.

"Casey didn't send out the invitations," Benjamin hurriedly told her. "It seems she isn't any happier about this than some of the rest of us."

"Does it really matter who invited us?" Jason demanded. "We're all here. Why not make the best of it? I, for one, plan to have a good time."

FINN DISAGREED. It *did* matter who had invited them. It mattered a whole lot.

While the atmosphere around the fire had a party look to it, he picked up on the tension. None of them trusted each other, he realized, and probably with good reason. Not only was Megan's murder unsolved, but also these people had been the last to see her alive. All were suspects.

He found himself studying their faces, wondering if one of them was responsible and what that person hoped to accomplish by being here, even if they hadn't sent out the invitations. He couldn't help worrying that the one person who didn't get an invitation—Casey—might be the target.

"So, Casey," Jason said, "I've been catching up with everyone else. Claude's a famous surgeon, Ben's some kind of scientist—"

"Infectious disease specialist," he interrupted. "And it's Benjamin, not Ben."

Jason continued as if the man hadn't spoken. "Patience is a fancy magazine editor, Devlin is a real-estate agent… So what about you, Case?"

Out of the corner of his eye, Finn saw Casey flinch at the nickname. "She's a hotelier at one of the finest hotels in San Francisco," he said. Casey shot him a surprised—and not necessarily appreciative—look.

"What is a *hotelier*?" Jason asked with a laugh. "It sounds…dirty."

"She runs the entire hotel," Finn snapped, hating that he was letting the man get to him. "I would think someone like you would already know that, since don't you live in your father's hotel?"

Jason nodded. "You got me there. In the past ten years, I've accomplished nothing. If I wasn't overeducated and not nearly as smart as the rest of you, I would have known Casey couldn't have put this together. Because if she had, I never would have been invited. Isn't that right, Case?" Finn wasn't about to touch that remark as Jason turned back to the others. "Who needs a beer?"

"I believe you left out a couple of people, *Jase*," Patience said and motioned with her head in the direction of Jen and Shirley.

Jen tilted her wine bottle at Patience. Her smile was venomous as she looked at Jason across the campfire. "I work in my aunt's antiques barn, but I'm sure you already know that. Shirley manages the local motel. Any of you have a problem with that?"

"Easy," Jason said, holding up his hands as the tension around the fire rose to a new pitch. "No bloodshed, already. Also, no judgment, especially from me. I would have gotten to you, but I got distracted."

Finn knew what was coming. Patience slowly turned her gaze on him and tilted her head. "Who exactly is Casey's date?"

"Not one of the staff," Finn said. "That's why I was surprised to receive an invitation."

"Oh, come on, Finn," Jason said. "I heard around town that you've been living in the hotel for months. Odd, to say the least. You must have some connection to Megan or you wouldn't have gotten an invitation. You wouldn't be here now."

Finn chuckled. "You're right. Seems everyone here knew Megan, myself included. I came here a few months early to solve her murder." He turned to look at Jason. "What's your reason for being here, Jase?"

"Me? Like I said, I just came to have fun." He laughed and looked around the group before returning to Finn. "But I suspect there's more to your story."

"You got me there," Finn said. "I've since decided to buy the hotel and the land."

Out of the corner of his eye, he watched Casey as the news swept around the fire. Like him, she had to have seen everyone's surprise, especially Jen's and Shirley's. Being locals, they knew that he'd been squatting there a good portion of the winter and early spring and had assumed he was homeless and broke.

But it was Devlin's openmouthed reaction that pleased Casey the most, he saw. "What's this?" Devlin demanded.

"I'm making an offer and taking care of the paperwork in the morning," Finn said.

Devlin shifted his gaze to Casey. "I thought we had a deal."

"Not hardly. I kept waiting for a formal offer, and you kept making excuses and putting me off, trying to get a better price," she said, returning his glare.

Finn could feel Jason's gaze on him. Speculating? Or had he already figured out who he was? Either way, Jason was enjoying this. Finn thought the man would like to see them all at each other's throats. Finn wondered how long Jason had been in town. Long enough to hear about Finn spending months in the hotel, which meant he'd been here for a while.

"Finn? Finn *what*?" Devlin asked, also turning to look at him.

He'd known it would be out once he contacted his lawyer, accountant and banker in the morning. "Finnegan James."

Devlin's gaze widened in shock as he recognized the name. He swore under his breath and kicked a rock into the firepit. Finn saw Jason smile. He really was enjoying himself. Maybe too much.

"Let's not argue." Jen took a drink from the wine bottle and passed it to Shirley, who simply stared into the fire as if she wished she were anywhere but there.

"So we have no idea whose brainchild this was," Jen said, looking around at them all. "Kind of macabre and ghoulish, just like Megan." Most everyone laughed. "But no one is going to take credit for this reunion?" She searched the group speculatively, meeting with only silence. "If none of you invited us all here," she asked, "then who did?"

"That's the million-dollar question," Jason said, grinning. "Someone wanted to get us all back here awfully bad. Got to wonder why, huh?"

"That about sizes it up," Finn said, seeing how quickly things could get out of hand.

CHAPTER NINE

BENJAMIN RATHER LIKED watching the others squirm. They were all terrified—even of Megan's ghost. It amazed him how much the young woman had affected all of their lives.

She'd ignored him as if he were nobody. He'd worked hard to prove to himself that she was wrong, which was silly. There was no proving anything to her. She was dead. Her body was slowly decaying in her dark, cold coffin.

He looked around the campfire, wondering why the others had come back. Were they that afraid that if they hadn't, someone would think that they really had killed Megan?

He scoffed at that as he watched them all trying to have a good time, drinking too much, looking warily at each other. They really didn't know who killed her—or if they were next.

Ten years ago, he'd watched them play games, stabbing each other in the back, being tossed away like trash when Megan was done with them.

Benjamin tried to gauge which one of them had hated her the most. It was difficult because any one of them had wanted her gone, himself included.

He noticed, though, that no one seemed leery of him. What fools they were.

CASEY FOUND HERSELF watching Finn out of the corner of her eye. He was holding his own, which didn't surprise her. He had just let the cat out of the bag, as her grandmother would have said. It wouldn't be long before the press picked up on it and he was making headlines again. She was surprised that he'd given up his anonymity for her.

She could see him studying the people around the fire, questioning each of their motives. She wondered about *his*. Was he really going to make her an offer on the hotel and property in the morning? Why was he doing this?

Looking around the campfire, she couldn't understand what they were all doing here. Were they really that interested in Megan's murder after all this time? If one of them were the killer, wouldn't they be glad to hear that the hotel was going to be razed? Any evidence would be gone. Or would it? Was the killer afraid something would be uncovered?

They really didn't look as if they had changed, except for Ben. *Benjamin*, she corrected. Patience still wore her dark hair in a pixie cut and looked younger than a woman hugging thirty. A curly brunette, Jen's hair was shoulder-length and jagged as if she had taken scissors to it herself. Shirley's long brown hair was pulled back in a ponytail that stuck out the back of her baseball cap. Jason looked exactly the same, same smirk, same shiftiness in his gaze. Devlin appeared to be getting a little bald. He kept brushing his brown hair back as if to cover the sparsely covered spot.

She watched them all share a look around the campfire and felt the atmosphere change as if they were finally starting to question why someone had wanted them here. One of them had purposely gotten the others back here. Finn was right. Someone had an agenda. But what?

Jen laughed as if wanting to ease the tension. "Interesting that we all came back." She took the wine bottle from

Shirley and took a drink. "So you're all good with this? It's really happening? Three nights, two days, here in a supposedly haunted and now-abandoned hotel." She looked at Casey. "You are going to let us stay, aren't you?"

"I only came here to sell my grandmother's property," Casey said as she felt everyone waiting for her reply.

"That doesn't exactly answer my question," Jen said, looking from her to Finn. "On the invitation, it said we were all to stay in the hotel for the weekend."

"Casey said she is fine with it, but we all have to fend for ourselves," Jason said, again as if she'd really said that.

"Like you've ever had to fend for yourself," Benjamin mumbled under his breath.

She'd been determined to throw them all out in the morning. But by morning, she hoped that she no longer owned the hotel and it was someone else's problem. "That will be up to the new owner."

"But you're taking part in the festivities, right?" Jen said, her focus still on Casey.

Festivities? "No, I'm just picking up a few things of my grandmother's, selling the place and leaving. Like I said, it will be up to the new owner as to how long you all can stay."

"*What?* You have to take part in the reunion," Jason said, reaching into a cooler to get another beer and toss one to Devlin. "You're a part of all this, just like the rest of us."

Claude hadn't spoken until now. He'd been staring into the fire but clearly following the conversation. "We haven't even talked about Megan yet." He brushed a lock of surfer-blond hair back from his forehead and looked at each of them around the campfire. He was like her, younger than the rest. Megan had called him the boy genius, but when she'd said it, there was mocking in her tone. He hadn't looked like a medical genius. He looked like the surfers at the beach back in California.

"That is why we're here, right?" Claude asked. "To talk about Megan?"

"That and an excuse to drink," Jason said and laughed. Clearly, he'd already had a few. "I'm thinking games, truth or dare, and how about a Saturday night reenactment—just like old times?"

Casey felt as if he'd hit her in the chest with a baseball bat. "You can't be serious." She couldn't imagine anything worse.

"Who gets to die this time?" Jen asked, as if getting into the chilling suggestion.

"No one's going to die," Shirley said as she took the wine bottle from Jen and took a gulp.

Claude was shaking his head. "I didn't sign up for fun and games. I thought we were going to deal with our feelings about Megan and the effect she had on us."

Gone was the party atmosphere from earlier, as if a gust of wind had blown it away. The campfire flickered.

"'Feelings'?" Jason said, scoffing. "You can't be serious. We all know how we felt about her."

"I think what Claude is getting at is that it's high time we got to say out loud here in this place how we felt about Megan," Benjamin said. "What better place than among people who also hated her?"

"Except not everyone did. Right, Jason?" Claude said, glaring across the campfire at him.

"If you think I'm going to wax poetic about her, you're wrong," Jason said, sounding petulant. "You think you were the only one she twisted into a pretzel?" He shook his head and took a gulp of his beer.

"Go ahead, Claude. You should go first since you were her first," Jen said with a chuckle. "But she wasn't your first, was she." The last was tinged with bitterness.

The doctor's jaw tightened as he looked into the fire. "We all let Megan manipulate us. Why did we do that?" He shook his head. "We have only ourselves to blame for not standing up to her. She's still manipulating us, or we wouldn't be here."

The group let out a roar of dissent, Jen's voice rising above the others. "Come on. She was a miserable bitch who enjoyed making the rest of us miserable. Stand up to her?" She scoffed. "She would have made us pay, and we all knew it."

"That's putting it mildly," Shirley said and looked at the ground again as if embarrassed to be speaking of the dead. "We probably shouldn't even be talking about her like this. If she's really still here…"

"What? Her ghost?" Benjamin demanded. "Megan's gone. She isn't here. So admit it. No one here was sorry when she died."

"She didn't die," Jen said. "She was murdered."

Casey couldn't help being surprised at how vicious they all sounded. It must have shown on her expression, because Jen said, "What, Casey? You thought you were the only one who hated her? Nothing could protect any of us from Megan. Isn't that really why we all came back? To show her that we all survived and she didn't."

"Casey could have gone to her grandmother," Patience said quietly.

"No, she couldn't," Finn said. "Megan was at the hotel because her father had asked his friend Anna to see what she could do with her."

"You know this how?" Patience demanded while Casey cringed that he was taking up for her.

"Anna left a journal," Finn said. Casey could see how reluctant he was to explain all this because it would seem as if he were taking up for her—which he was.

She quickly interrupted. "My grandmother couldn't do anything with Megan any more than the rest of us. She hoped that it would work itself out over the summer."

"Oh, it worked itself out," Jason said.

"Anna blamed herself for not sending Megan away," Finn said.

The only sound for a moment was the popping and crackling of the fire. Claude kicked at one of the logs sticking out of the fire ring. Benjamin stared down into his beer. Devlin drained his can and helped himself to another one from the cooler.

Finn was the first to speak. "I'm surprised you all felt this way about Megan. I remember reading the things that you all said printed in the newspaper after her death."

"Lies," Benjamin said. "We just didn't want the cops thinking we killed her. She treated me like I was gum stuck on the bottom of her shoe."

"She enjoyed hurting people," Jen agreed quietly. "But, ultimately, she paid the price for it."

"You all hated her?" Finn asked. There was general agreement around the campfire. "So why come back for this…reunion?"

"Maybe we need closure," Jason said.

Claude broke the long silence that followed. "You all seem to be forgetting that the marshal still thinks that one of us killed her and got away with it. This will always be hanging over our heads until the killer steps forward."

The breeze stirred the flames. Casey felt fatigue settle deep within her. It had been a really long day with way too many surprises.

Jen let out a nervous laugh. "We all had our reasons for wanting Megan dead, that's for sure. The question is…is she still here?"

Jason made a scary ghost sound, apparently going for the laugh. The joke fell flat.

"Is it just me, or does this feel like a bad idea?" Shirley said, her face glowing in the firelight. "Whoever got us all back here might want…not just a confession but revenge."

"Seriously?" Jen shook her head. "*Revenge?* But we didn't do anything."

"Exactly," Benjamin said. "We did nothing to stop Megan."

"Until one of us killed her," Jason said.

"Not revenge for killing Megan," Patience said, speaking up. "Revenge on the people who didn't try to help us." Her gaze went to Casey.

She suddenly felt all eyes on her. "If you must know, I went to my grandmother several times, even though I knew better. She told me to make the best of it and learn from the experience." There was surprise around the campfire. "She never treated me any different than the rest of the staff. So keep me out of this."

Jen shook her head. "Sorry, Casey, but you're neck-deep in this. Megan treated you abominably. She seemed to make it her mission to come between you and your grandmother. That's more unforgivable than anything she did to the rest of us. If anyone wanted her dead, it had to be you."

Casey could feel everyone's gaze on her, suspicion adding to the flames. She shook her head, threw her half-finished beer into the nearby trash can and headed for the hotel. She hadn't wanted this. She hadn't ten years ago, and she sure as hell didn't now.

"You going after your girlfriend?" Jason asked, sounding drunk and mocking.

Finn wanted to punch him. Instead, he simply finished his beer, threw the can away and excused himself. "Casey!" She kept walking. He caught up to her, grasped her arm and brought her to a stop just past the parking lot.

"I'm sorry. I shouldn't have encouraged you to do this. I didn't know how bad Megan had been to all of you, especially you."

She looked up at him, her face illuminated in the hotel's exterior lamps. "You were in love with her. Yet you really had no idea what she was like?" she demanded in disbelief.

He sighed. "I saw it. I didn't want to admit that there was a vicious meanness in her. I blamed it on her being unhappy because she was grounded. I wanted to see good in her because she was nice to me."

"Of course she was. Look at you." She broke free of his hold and continued toward the hotel.

"Will you please stop?" He caught up to her at the back door of the main building. When she turned to face him, he could see how close she was to tears. "I hate her for hurting you."

She let out a laugh that sounded more like a sob. "She tormented me for a few weeks one summer when I was sixteen. Then she died. End of story." He watched her look away from him toward the campfire, knowing there was much more to it. He could see the others silhouetted around the fire. "To think that I just wanted to be one of them. I didn't want to be the owner's granddaughter. I didn't want to be the youngest. I kept telling myself that soon I would be eighteen—legal age—the same age as most of the staff. But it wouldn't have made a difference." She fell silent for a moment. "Why do they want to relive that summer? Why do they want to feel such awful emotions?"

He wished he knew. "Maybe they think it will be cathartic."

She shook her head. "They're down there celebrating her death, each of them probably wishing they'd been the one to have killed her. And I know how they feel. That's one reason I feel so guilty."

Her words rose up from a well of pain. He reached for her. She started to step back, but he was faster. He pulled her into his arms. At first her body was stiff, unforgiving. As he rubbed her back, she began to melt against him.

"I hated her." The words were muffled against his chest. "I wanted her to suffer. I wanted her gone forever." She pulled back a little to look at him. "But I didn't kill her."

"I never thought you did." He drew her in again, his gaze going to those gathered around the campfire. But one of them *did* kill her. He felt it at gut level. The same one who had gotten them back here under the pretense of a reunion to say goodbye to her ghost?

At least now he knew that his fears had been justified. They blamed Casey for not getting her grandmother to stop Megan's abuse of them.

CHAPTER TEN

DEVLIN SWORE UNDER his breath as he watched Casey leave and Finnegan James go after her. Finnegan James? What was he really doing here? Why would he want this run-down old hotel? It made no sense. And how did he know Megan?

Not that any of that mattered. Devlin needed the Crenshaw. He'd promised the land to his clients. He'd told them he could get the hotel and land for a song. He'd been so sure he could get Casey down on the price. He already had a hard-luck story to tell her about his investors. He knew how desperate she was to unload the place.

So what had happened? Finnegan James had happened.

Devlin frowned as he stared into the fire. The man looked like he was homeless. Yet he was that wunderkind who'd made a fortune on the first company he'd started? If he had such a head for business, what did he want with the Crenshaw?

Devlin tried to calm down. There was still time. He'd talk to Casey first thing in the morning. He'd make her an offer. But how much? Maybe she was only trying to get more money out of him with this Finn character.

He looked up, realizing that everyone was staring at him. "Sorry?"

Jason smirked. "I hope you didn't want this place too badly. Sounds like she's gotten a better offer." He howled with laughter.

"What makes you say that?"

"He's better-looking than you are," Jason said, as if Devlin just wasn't getting the joke. "And he has a lot more money."

"Who is he, anyway?" Jen asked.

"You don't know?" Jason shook his head. "You've never heard of Finnegan James, the Multibillionaire Bachelor?"

"You have to be kidding," Jen said. "I thought he was joking about buying the hotel. He's *rich*?"

"Richer than Midas," Jason said.

Devlin swore under his breath again. "I thought he disappeared and was presumed dead after all this time."

Jason nodded sagely. "Look where he turned up."

Devlin felt sick to his stomach. Who was he kidding? He was totally screwed. What was he going to tell his investors? "He's not serious about buying it. He's just trying to get into Casey's pants. What would Finnegan James want with the Crenshaw?" he said, sounding more confident than he felt.

There were chuckles around the fire. "I agree that he seems more interested in the owner," Jason said. "But a man like him? He can have both."

CASEY WIPED HER eyes and pulled free of Finn's arms after a few moments, feeling embarrassed. Megan had loved making her cry, and here Casey was ten years later, in tears over the same hurts. She'd thought she'd put all of this baggage behind her. Or at least tried. But she hadn't, and neither had her grandmother. Why else would Anna try to force her into a promise she couldn't possibly keep?

"Everyone down at the campfire thinks we're intimately involved," she said as she glanced in that direction and realized they'd all been pretending not to watch the two of them.

"Seems a shame we aren't, then."

She knew he was joking, but still she felt a flutter at even the idea. It was nice being in his arms, even as she'd at first resisted it. It was only too easy to imagine the two of them in that big shower, their skin soapy and wet. She could almost smell the chocolate and lavender on their slick flesh… She shivered and shoved the image away. "Be serious," she said.

"I am serious. It isn't like the idea hasn't crossed my mind."

"I'm sure it has," she snapped.

He merely grinned. "Guess it hasn't yours, then?"

She side-eyed him for a moment before she had to smile. He knew darned well that it had crossed her mind. "Why do I bother talking to you?"

"Better than talking to yourself. Or Megan's ghost."

Casey could only shake her head. The man wasn't going to let her forget what he'd overheard. How could he find humor in it, though? "This is not what I had planned when I came back here."

"Meeting me?"

"Definitely not meeting you."

"I was joking about us being lovers," he said. "Well, kind of joking." He cupped her cheek with one of his large, warm hands. "Your grandmother wrote so much about you… I'm sorry, but I feel as if I know you. I forget that you don't know me. Yet. I wish we had more time. You might come to actually like me."

I can't do this, Casey thought, feeling as if the ground under her feet was no longer solid. She pulled away from his warm, inviting touch. Finn threw her off balance. He might think he knew her, but she definitely didn't know him. Sure, she'd seen him naked, and most anything she wanted to know about Finnegan James she could find online. But she didn't know if she could trust him yet.

This entire situation made her question everything, especially what she was doing here. Maybe even more what *he* was doing here. She turned and pushed her way into the hotel's lobby.

He said nothing as he followed her in. She started up the stairs, Finn right beside her. It wasn't until they reached the top that she looked over at him. "I don't need you to babysit me."

"You have a probable killer staying here in your hotel. Like it or not, I'm going to be keeping an eye on you. It's what your grandmother would have wanted."

She groaned but was too tired to put up a good argument. "I just hope you're serious about buying the hotel so I can get out of here."

"I am. First thing in the morning."

Casey nodded. "Then I'll collect my grandmother's things and be gone."

"Agreed. You should get as far away as possible."

She met his gaze. The way he looked at her warmed her to her toes. All her instincts told her that Finnegan James was a good man. So why did she keep pushing him away? Because he was in love with a ghost.

"You're still determined to find her killer." Even after seeing how everyone felt about Megan, he was still in love with the woman. Or at least the idea of the woman. That should tell her everything she needed to know about why she was keeping him at arm's length.

"I told you it isn't about Megan for me, but it is for you, isn't it?" He rushed on before she could interrupt. "You came here to destroy the hotel and put an end to all of this. But even if I buy the hotel and raze it tomorrow, a killer will still be out there. The past won't be gone. Neither will the suspicions. Can you really say you don't care?"

"Yes," she said with more force than she felt.

He eyed her. "Who are you trying to protect? You or your grandmother?"

She felt as if he'd punched her. "What?"

"Remember, I've read your grandmother's journal from that summer. She suspected Megan was mistreating you. She wanted to protect you, wished she had. I suspect you're doing the same thing."

"You can't really believe that my grandmother killed Megan."

He shook his head. "Your grandmother's guilt was from not stopping it before it happened. I'd put my money on someone down at that campfire, someone who's come back to the scene of the crime. I have two days. If I'm right, the killer will show themselves before it's over."

She stared at him for a moment before she shook her head. "I'd be careful if I were you. A lot can happen in two days." *And three nights*, she thought.

But she wasn't sure if she was warning him—or herself.

CHAPTER ELEVEN

JEN HAD HOPED that Claude would make the first move. When he hadn't, she decided she had to. "Smoke," she said as an excuse to move over by Claude. "It was in my eyes." He didn't look up as she joined him. All his attention seemed to be on the fire. He looked as bored as she felt. She wondered what he was thinking about. Was he remembering that summer? Did he remember what they did back in the woods that first night? Or was he thinking about Megan?

"Hey," she said and gave him a nudge with her hip, thinking maybe she could get his mind off the woman.

He looked over at her in surprise as if he hadn't noticed her join him. He blinked now as if trying to place her, his brow furrowing, his eyes a little unfocused. She didn't think he was drunk. More like lost in his own dark well of thoughts.

She felt her confidence spring a leak when it became clear that he didn't remember her. She'd given herself to him. She'd been his first, and he didn't remember her. "Jen. *Jennifer*, if you prefer." Which he had, ten years ago. "Mullen."

Recognition came into his eyes, and he quickly looked away as if wanting to forget her. Why had she thought what they'd done ten years ago had meant something to him just because it had her?

Her punctured ego deflated like a burst balloon. She

raised the nearly empty wine bottle to her lips and fought tears. She'd always sold herself short. She had the gall to give Shirley a hard time about Lars. They were both losers. That was why Jason had left them out when he went around the campfire telling how everyone else had become successes.

"Looks like you could use a beer," Jason said, suddenly beside her. He took the empty wine bottle from her and handed her a beer can. She felt his other hand rest gently on her shoulder. "There's something you have to see," he said and drew her back away from the fire, away from Claude, away from the others and her embarrassment.

He led her into the woods, and she followed, too shattered to resist. She just assumed he planned to take advantage of her. She realized that she would let him, and that made the tears come again.

They'd gone just far enough into the woods that they couldn't be heard or seen when he turned and looked at her. "You okay?"

She realized she was sobbing silently, tears streaming down her face. Jason Underwood had come to her rescue? She'd never thought of Jason as the least bit heroic. She'd always thought he was a jerk. "I think I've had too much to drink. It's making me melancholy." She swallowed, the sobs juddering to a stop. "Or maybe it's Megan's ghost screwing with me." She made a swipe at her tears and tried to smile.

"This is hard on all of us," he said, and she laughed.

She hadn't meant to and quickly added, "Not you. You're in your element."

He looked back toward the fire. "Don't fool yourself. I'm just good at not showing any real emotion. Don't you wonder why everyone came back?"

She shrugged. "They didn't want the rest of us to think that they killed her."

He shook his head. "Would you really care if we all thought you'd killed her?"

Jen considered that for a moment and then laughed. "You're right. I wouldn't care."

"Obviously some came back to show that they'd not only survived but also thrived in spite of what happened that summer," Jason said.

She followed his gaze back toward the glowing fire, thinking about that. She knew her reason for wanting to come to the reunion. It had nothing to do with Megan. "What about you?"

"Me?" Jason continued to stare in the direction of the campfire and the dark silhouettes of the former summer workers that could barely be seen through the pine boughs. "I just came back to see what happens next." He finally looked over at her. "I suspect for most of them, Megan's just an excuse. Except maybe for whoever killed her. I would imagine that person wants to make sure no one ever knows the truth."

She hugged herself against the growing chill in the dark pines. "Or maybe that person has put it behind them and just didn't have anything better to do."

He looked over at her. "Maybe. I came also because I felt sorry for Megan."

She shot him a disbelieving look. "You really were in love with her, proving love is deaf *and* blind."

"We had a lot in common—controlling parents, too much money, too much privilege. Her parents had forced her to come out here, and she was miserable." He met her gaze. She could see the shine of his eyes. "She was scared that someone out here was going to hurt her."

"Because she was such a bitch."

Jason shook his head. "More like revenge. She confided in me that she'd been grounded for several months after getting in a car wreck. She was driving too fast. Several of her friends were hurt. One was killed. She'd lied about being the driver and had blamed it on the girl who was killed."

She looked at him openmouthed. "Was this true?"

"She was in a wreck, and according to the news reports, the other girl had been driving her car, had taken the keys and insisted on driving, even though she was drunk. There were two other girls passed out in the back. Why would you think she'd tell me if it wasn't true?"

"Seriously? For sympathy, as an excuse for her behavior."

Jason sighed. "She'd been getting death threats before she came out here. She didn't tell anyone but was glad when her parents sent her away from San Francisco. When she got here, though, she was still scared and miserable and didn't feel safe. Then things started happening, she said. Someone started stalking her. She couldn't sleep or eat toward the end."

Jen laughed. "She sure hid all of that well while she was busy terrorizing the rest of us. You really don't believe any of this, do you?" she asked, getting anxious to return to the fire. "A friend of a friend came to work here to kill her? That sounds like bull."

He shrugged. "Well, she was right, wasn't she? She's dead. Someone killed her. Truthfully? I didn't believe her. I felt just like you do. Until she was murdered. Now I think there might have been something to it. She really thought that one of you was after her."

Jen scoffed again. "I think she just pushed one of us too far." She glanced back at the campfire and shook her head, bored with the conversation. Megan was dead, and she wasn't sorry. She let her thoughts return to Claude. She felt injured by his snub, and now that she'd gotten past the tears, she was angry. Who did he think he was? He'd been glad enough to fall into her arms that first night ten years ago. Just because he was now some famous doctor—

"I thought I could do this," Jason said, interrupting her thoughts. "But—" he met her gaze "—I might lose it."

"*You* might? We all might."

"Especially whoever killed her," he said.

It was getting colder and darker in the pines. She realized that she'd finished the beer Jason had brought her and now chucked it into the woods. She preferred the second cheap bottle of wine she had in her car. She thought about going to get it. Or maybe she would just leave for the night. She wasn't sure if she would be back, though.

A sick part of her wanted to give Claude another chance.

"I'm cold. I'm going back to the fire," she said to Jason and touched his arm. "Thanks for getting me out of there." He nodded mutely. She could see that he was still lost in his memories, but there was nothing more she could say without hurting his feelings. He'd brought her back here to talk about Megan. Of course he had. She knew it shouldn't, but it hurt her feelings that he hadn't even tried to make a pass at her.

"Be careful," Jason called after her, as if he thought there might be something in these woods she had to fear.

Jen laughed to herself as she headed toward the warmth of the campfire. She wasn't the one who needed to be careful.

CASEY FELT IT the moment she stepped into her room. That sense that something was wrong. She'd turned up the heat earlier. Spring in Montana often teased. One day the temperatures would leap, only to fall just as rapidly come nightfall because Buckhorn was in the mountains.

A numbing cold breeze curled around her neck, sending a chill through her like the one she'd experienced earlier coming up the stairs.

But that wasn't all that had stopped her just inside the door. At first she didn't know what had sent her heart plummeting and made her freeze in midstep.

Nothing looked amiss, and yet she sensed it. Someone had been in her room. She smelled the scent still in the air. Megan's perfume. Megan's signature perfume was so distinctive that Casey would never forget it.

"She's dead," she whispered to herself. "She isn't wearing perfume where she is." Casey closed her eyes and took a deep breath.

"Don't let her get to you," Anna had said ten years ago. "Be the better person. You need to learn to deal with this sort of thing. Someday this experience will serve you well."

Opening her eyes and letting out the held breath, Casey wanted to laugh. She'd let her imagination run away with her. No one had come into her room. Hadn't they all been down at the campfire? She tried to remember. People often would walk into the woods to pee after too many beers. But one of them could have doubled back to the hotel. Or come to her room while she and Finn were talking at the back door.

The wind blew the drapes aside. She rushed to the window to close it and shut out the cold night air, recalling that it had been locked when she'd left earlier. She was sure of it.

That was when she saw it out of the corner of her eye and felt her stomach knot. She turned slowly to look into the bathroom to the words written in lipstick on the mirror.

I know what you did

The letters were half scrawled, poorly shaped. But with a shudder, she knew exactly what the person wanted.

A confession.

CHAPTER TWELVE

As FINN CAME out the back door of the hotel again, he studied the figures silhouetted against the firelight at the edge of the woods. He'd felt the tension around the fire earlier. It was as if everyone was trying too hard to get into the party mood, while all the time knowing that there was a probable killer among them.

He'd read the marshal's report on the murder. No one else had been seen in the area that night. No tracks had been found other than those down by the firepit and Megan's. Nor were any vehicles seen around the time of the murder. The pit was far enough away from the hotel that it was only used by the staff and always had been. The marshal had concluded that one of them had probably killed Megan. The question had always been which one. Because of a lack of sufficient evidence, no arrest had been made.

"Casey not coming back out?" Jason asked, a smirk on his handsome face.

"She's had enough for one day," Finn said.

"But not you." Jason handed him a beer.

The talk around the campfire was hushed as the cold night hunkered just outside the flames. Patience was visiting with Jen and Shirley. Claude and Benjamin stood apart, both silent. Devlin stayed close to the cooler full of beer, looking sour and still upset. Clearly Jason wanted a party, but he wasn't getting it.

"Claude, you should have brought your guitar," Jason said.

"I don't play anymore."

The tension was as thick as the smoke rising into the air. As Finn looked around the group, he realized that Casey wasn't the only one he had to keep an eye on. Jason was at the top of that list. He'd seen the tension between him and Casey. She'd tried to hide her dislike of the man, but, given what Megan had told him and what he'd read in Anna's journal, he already had a pretty good idea why she couldn't stand Jason.

There'd been something sparking between Casey and Jason before he'd hooked up with Megan and doused that spark before it ever had a chance. Megan, of course, had told a slightly different story, saying that Jason had begged her to save him from Casey, who he said had a schoolgirl crush on him. According to her journal entry, Anna had seen something entirely different but had been caught in the middle.

But Finn suspected Jason, at least, was still interested in Casey. He just wasn't sure what that interest was.

"So you dated Megan?" Patience asked.

He nodded. "Just for a few months before she came out here."

"Now you're looking for her killer," Jason said. "How's that going?"

Finn smiled and took a sip of his beer. He pretended he'd never heard of these people and wasn't biased, but he'd already learned about them from Megan's phone calls and Anna's journals. There'd been a time when he would have trusted Megan's word about what was going on at the Crenshaw. But no longer. He'd known about the ugly side of her that struck out when she wasn't happy. He'd heard enough around the campfire tonight to leave little doubt. Megan had gone after Casey because she'd been young and vulnerable.

He thought of Megan's phone calls complaining about the way she was being treated. He remembered her contempt for the owner's granddaughter, who she said was snotty and always tattling on her. Another lie. He'd felt guilty all these years because he hadn't helped Megan. He'd thought she was the victim even before she was murdered. He'd put her on a pedestal, making her into someone who'd never existed—and certainly not someone to look up to, let alone love.

Finn still wanted to find her killer, but for Casey and her grandmother, just as he'd told Casey. He tried to imagine what could have happened to push one of those people around the fire into bludgeoning her to death from behind. Had Megan trusted the person? Was that why she'd turned her back on her killer? Or had they sneaked up on her?

"I think it's time to play truth or dare," Jason announced. There was a general groan around the fire. "Let's start with Patience. A truth or a dare?"

Finn listened as the game moved through the group. He suspected none of them would tell the truth. Just as he suspected things had heated up over the weeks that awful summer before boiling over that night in the woods.

The lack of evidence still bothered him. Head wounds bled. The killer should have had blood all over him or her. The marshal had speculated that the person could have thrown the murder weapon into the nearby creek and then rinsed off the blood and buried the stained clothing in the rocky shoreline along the creek, since no bloody clothing was found in the area.

Had the killing been planned? Or was it spur of the moment? There were plenty of rocks around. He realized as he studied those around the fire that it was easier to think of the killer as a male. A man was stronger and taller and more likely to take a rock to someone's head. According to the books he'd read, women were more apt to push the intended victim down a flight of stairs or resort to poison. But not always.

Casey had been the number one suspect because she'd had a very vocal and angry argument with Megan away from the campfire in the trees that night. Megan's body was later discovered in those same woods.

She was still a suspect. He couldn't imagine something like that hanging over his head. Another reason Finn wanted to find the killer. What confused him was Casey's reaction earlier. She really didn't seem to care if the killer was ever caught. More than that, she seemed almost discouraging when he'd told her his plan.

Until this moment, he hadn't considered that she might have something to hide. He should have. She'd been coming to the hotel every summer for years—until the murder. That summer, when she was sixteen, was the last summer she would spend here with her grandmother. He'd thought she had just outgrown summers in Montana.

But what if she hadn't returned until now because she knew something about Megan's death, something she'd been hiding all these years? Was she protecting herself? Or someone else? His first thought was her grandmother.

What if it had been someone from the staff that she'd covered for out of fear—or love? But enough to lie for, if that person was here at the reunion and afraid she might still talk?

It would explain why she'd been so shocked and upset

by the invitation—let alone the arrival of the staff from that summer. It might also explain why she was hell-bent on selling and having the hotel razed. Could Casey have kept the killer's secret all these years?

He felt his heart begin to beat harder. What if the killer feared that she'd sent out the invitations because she could no longer keep his secret?

Finn knew that whatever he sensed she was hiding was going to come out. Was that why she was so determined to sell and get out of here? His head hurt. He found himself running scared that Casey was somehow involved. His gut told him that the killer had come back to finish things, and Casey might be at the top of that list.

Two days and three nights. Finn could feel the clock ticking. He looked around the campfire. If he was right, one of them had killed Megan and would kill again. But which one?

TRUTH OR DARE? Seriously, Jason? Devlin refused to play, even though Jen had taunted him. Jen. She hadn't changed. He knew that even before she made a move on Claude. Then she'd let Jason take her into the woods. He could guess what the two of them had done.

He mentally shook his head. It was only a matter of time before Jen hit on him—just like ten years ago. Except he wasn't that desperate anymore, and if she pushed it, he'd let her know right quick.

"Did you hate Megan enough to kill her?" Jason asked Shirley.

Devlin listened to them spewing out the truth about Megan without a second thought to the fact that they were still murder suspects. It was none of their business how he'd felt about Megan. He wasn't like the others. He'd wanted her beauty, her money, her position in life. He would have done just about anything to be her in male form—even though he couldn't stand her.

He had dreamed of success—money—since he was a boy lying in bed listening to his parents fight over it. He'd learned early on that money was all that mattered. People who didn't have it suffered. He'd been determined not to be one of them.

Megan must have seen the burning desire in his eyes. She knew what he wanted, and it wasn't to grope her in the woods. "Dev," she said, knowing he hated the nickname, "you need a woman like me on your arm, along with my family connections and their money. You and I could conquer the world because you get it. All the others want love—and, of course, sex with me. But not you."

She'd played him, teasing him with a picture of what his life could be like with her. He'd felt like a fish on a hook. If he tried to pull away, seeing that she was only teasing him, she'd reel him back in.

Until she didn't.

She'd dangled the carrot in front of him and then laughed when she'd finally grown tired of the game. "Dev, you'll never have me or anyone like me. Sorry, but it's true. I can see your future, and it isn't pretty."

It was the last thing she'd said to him the night she died. She'd been laughing. "Did you really think you were good enough for me? I don't mean to hurt your feelings, but, Dev, you'll always be a loser who thinks he deserves better." She'd made a sad face as she'd patted him on the cheek and turned to walk away, leaving him gutted and homicidal.

It had stayed with him the past ten years, her voice mocking him even as he'd tried to become the wealthy man he'd always dreamed of being. He realized now, standing around this campfire, that Megan had been right. He was a loser.

So what was he still doing here? He'd come here to make money on this deal. But he'd blown that, too. He'd been avoiding the investors' calls and texts all day. They'd been anxious for him to close on the purchase.

He needed this money desperately since he'd already spent most of what he thought he was going to make. When this was over, he'd be worse than broke. He'd be in debt to the wrong people.

What a fool he was. He'd come here thinking he was the one who was going to have the last laugh.

Then again, I kind of did have the last laugh, didn't I, Megan?

I KNOW WHAT YOU DID

Casey had scrubbed the words from her bathroom mirror and then taken a hot shower, too impatient to soak in the tub. Her sunburn ached. What had she been thinking?

Now she lay in bed listening to the old hotel moan and groan and creak. She told herself the noises had gotten worse over the past ten years. Either that or she was too aware of who else was here at the hotel. Supposedly they were all still outside. But how easy it would be for one of them to sneak away. Just as they had done to leave the message on her mirror.

She closed her eyes, trying to pretend that the hotel was full of real guests just like in the old days. The place would ring with the joyful sounds of people on vacation, laughter and music and children running down the hallways.

Back then, the hotel had felt alive in an entirely different way than it did tonight. She'd felt safe here—until Megan and the murder. Tonight the hotel's moans and groans made her feel as if it knew what she planned to do with it. She knew it was ridiculous, but if buildings could have feelings, the Crenshaw would be one of them.

She was on the edge of sleep when she heard the footfalls. She tensed as they approached. Probably just someone coming back from the campfire. But if true, the staff would be on the lower level. Only Finn would be on this floor. He couldn't be coming to her room. They'd said all they had to say for the night.

The footfalls stopped outside her door. She froze as she waited for a knock. Her breath caught in her throat as she saw the knob move. Someone was trying to open the door.

She lurched up and out of bed, afraid she hadn't locked the door even when she knew she had. Her cell phone ringing made her jump. Who could be calling her this late? Finn? They'd exchanged numbers earlier, but she didn't recognize the incoming number. She looked from the phone to the door and back before she answered.

"Hello?" she asked in a whisper. Of course it wasn't Finn. Why would he call if he was standing right outside her door? She could hear the sound of muffled voices in the background. "Hello?" she said a little louder. It was probably a robocall.

She tried to call the number back, but it went straight to an automated voice mail.

She disconnected, her gaze going to her door. She moved toward it, debating what to do. She hadn't heard whoever had been outside leave. She thought about grabbing the straight-backed chair and shoving it under the knob.

Whoever she'd heard coming down the hallway, whoever had tried to open the door, whoever it had been was now still standing just outside. She moved to her purse on the entry table. Slipping her hand in, she closed it around the gun handle. Flipping off the safety, she stepped to the door, listening the whole time. Could she hear someone breathing on the other side? Or just feel them out there?

Quietly, she unlocked the door, grabbed the knob and flung it open, gun ready.

It took an instant for her eyes to send the message to her brain. The hand holding the gun trembled. The hallway was empty.

She felt a cold draft curl around her neck. Heart hammering, she stepped back into the room and closed and locked the door again. She stood for a moment, telling herself that she'd only imagined the footfalls in the hallway. Only imagined someone standing outside her room. Only imagined that cold gust of air that had circled her neck almost…teasingly.

Then she pushed the chair against the doorknob and took the gun with her back to bed. She knew she wasn't going to be able to sleep a wink.

SHIRLEY HAD DRAGGED Jen away from the fire more easily than she'd expected. But Jen was determined they were going to stay at the hotel, so they'd gotten the extra bottle of wine and their overnight bags from the car and headed inside to find a room for the night.

Once in bed, Shirley had tried to relax. She had no desire to see Megan's ghost, she thought as she lay in bed listening to Jen snore. She'd spent that summer steering clear of Megan. After growing up with eight siblings, she'd learned to disappear when possible. If not that, then how to duck and weave when one of her brothers or sisters was on the fight and looking for someone to take their anger out on.

She'd recognized that mean streak in Megan right away. It was hidden under a thin veneer of smiles and small kindnesses. She knew better than to take the bait. Owing Megan would be very costly.

Because she steered clear and declined even the smallest of seemingly nice gestures and presents, Megan eventually came hunting for her. Like the cat who'd mangled all the other mice and needed a new toy, Megan came after her with a vengeance. The more Shirley hid, the more determined Megan was to corner her.

It became a game, one Megan had clearly relished. She would go out of her way to do something nice for Shirley in front of the others to force her to accept. Shirley would decline, saying that brand of lotion made her break out, she couldn't eat candy because of a tooth that had been bothering her, she couldn't take that expensive blouse Megan no longer liked because the color was all wrong for her.

Pretty soon everyone was watching—waiting and watching. By then they all knew how treacherous Megan could be when she wasn't getting the satisfaction she demanded.

Shirley had known it would end badly. There was no way it couldn't, she'd learned from experience. The harder Megan tried to get to her, the more frustrated she got. Megan had grown tired of tormenting the others. There was no one left but Shirley.

One of them was going down.

CLAUDE STOOD WATCHING the flames die to embers, knowing he should leave. Coming here had been a mistake, he thought as he glanced at the dark, hulking form of the hotel beyond the faint firelight.

Most everyone was probably in bed already asleep by now. Only a few lights glinted from inside. The structure had taken on an eerie, skeletal look that would have frightened him ten years ago. Nothing could scare him now, he told himself. Not even Megan's ghost.

He studied the backlit windows and saw no faces. No one cared enough to watch him. Everyone had left the fire earlier, ignoring him as they walked away and disappeared inside. He glanced toward the woods. He had to go back in there. As he slipped away from the fire, just as he had that night, he thought he might have forgotten how to find the exact spot where Megan had died. Bludgeoned to death with a rock. At least that was the theory, since the rock had never been found.

But even in the pitch black inside the pines, he made his way to where he'd last seen her. It was his amazing brain. It could hold unreal amounts of information and not explode. He could remember everything, which in this case was a curse.

Standing where her blood had drained into the soil, he was reminded of the scrap of paper he'd picked up when no one was looking. It had Megan's blood on it. He had stared at it for a moment before pocketing the note.

It wasn't until later that he'd read the words that had been printed on the paper. *Meet me in the woods.* It hadn't taken all that much effort on his part to connect the handwriting to the person who had written it. But like his pocketing the scrap of paper, he hadn't told anyone, especially the marshal.

Until he'd returned here, he wasn't sure he'd planned

to do anything with what he knew. He stared down at the ground, remembering exactly what she'd looked like lying there. Often when he couldn't sleep, he imagined her eyes, unfocused, her slack face, her skin already draining of color. He'd memorized her dead face and put it in a special place in his brilliant brain.

Instead of haunting his dreams, the image gave him peace. Death didn't scare him. Megan didn't scare him. Nothing did anymore.

That young boy he'd been hadn't feared Megan. It was what she'd unlocked in him that terrified him. His parents had seen his genius and ignored the rest. They knew there was something inherently wrong with him. He'd seen the alarm at what they realized they had created. Megan had brought out a dark side of him, and he'd liked it.

At the sound of a twig snapping somewhere in the darkness, he turned. For a moment, he couldn't make out the approaching shape, but he didn't have to. He knew exactly who it was. Like him, this person knew where to come. The scene of the crime.

"I was beginning to wonder if you would show up," Claude said, even though he couldn't yet see the killer in the deep shadow of the trees. He could feel Megan's twisted malevolence in him, thrumming in his bloodstream, just under his skin. He hadn't been able to handle it as a teenager. It was too powerful. But he was ready now. He heard another twig break, off to his left, but he ignored it. He felt invincible and realized that, right now, he was actually glad that he'd come back here. This was where it had to end.

THE BIGGER THEY ARE, the harder they fall. The words came out in singsong bursts on hot, hurried breaths as, deep under the hotel, the explosives were placed in the boreholes along the structural outer walls for maximum effect.

Dynamite was the explosive of choice. Simply absorbent stuffing soaked in a highly combustible chemical, once the chemical was ignited, it would burn quickly, producing a large volume of hot gas that would expand and apply immense outward pressure.

The powerful shock wave would bust through the columns at supersonic speed, shatter the concrete into tiny chunks. The secret was spreading the explosive devices throughout. Then setting them off like knocking over dominoes. *Boom...boom...boom* as the explosions raced around the hotel's footprint, and the building imploded.

It had taken some calculation. A person had to be smart when working with this much firepower. One wrong move and it could blow up too soon. But if done correctly, the explosions would accomplish what had to be done.

The hotel wouldn't just be brought down; it would be turned to dust—including anyone in it. Ultimately every secret would be erased. Nothing could come back to haunt the guilty or destroy the innocent. The Crenshaw Hotel would be gone and eventually forgotten.

Just like misdeeds.

The bigger they are, the harder they fall. Soon. Very soon.

CHAPTER THIRTEEN

Saturday

WHEN FINN WALKED into the hotel kitchen the next morning, he overheard Jen telling Shirley about Megan's car wreck that Jason had related to her the night before. The story shouldn't have shocked him, given what he now knew about Megan.

The two women left as he entered. But he'd heard enough that when Jason came in right behind him, he demanded, "Is it true? Megan killed someone?"

Jason rolled his eyes. "I knew I shouldn't say anything to Jen, of all people."

"How do you know Megan was driving the car?" Finn demanded.

Jason sighed. "Because she admitted it to me. She was really drunk and scared, and she told me about the car wreck. Some of her friends were hurt, and one of them was killed."

"Megan swore she *wasn't* driving. That's what she told the cops. She said her friend had taken the keys from her. The one who died was driving."

Shaking his head, Jason helped himself to a cup of coffee and took a seat at the table. "Megan lied. She was really upset because she'd lied to everyone, including the police, and had gotten away with it, except now she believed that someone was stalking her, determined to make her pay for what she'd done."

Finn stared at him, feeling the truth at gut level. "She *was* driving."

He nodded. "She was apparently upset and driving too fast after a party. Two girls were in the back, passed out. The girl who died was in the front and trying to get her to slow down. Holly, right? Holly had unsnapped her seat belt and was trying to get out when she thought Megan was going to stop at an intersection. Instead, Megan sped through it and then missed a curve in the road. Megan was upset over some boy she'd wanted to hook up with at the party, but he was with some girl who'd gotten to him first."

Finn took a breath and let it out slowly. He poured himself a cup of coffee, his hands shaking. Megan had lied. Not just to him, but the cops, her parents, everyone. "Surely, if that's true, the cops would have realized who was driving."

Jason shook his head. "None of them were wearing seat belts. After the car rolled and some of them were thrown clear, it was hard to tell who was driving. Holly was dead and couldn't deny the story. The two in the back couldn't, either. Megan said she was lucky she hadn't been killed herself. I guess they all sued the dead girl's family."

Only because they believed Megan's story. Finn shook his head, wondering why Megan had confessed to Jason, of all people, instead of him. He hadn't wanted to believe it, but he could practically hear Megan saying the words. It sounded just like her. She hadn't been sorry that she'd framed her dead friend. She was sorry that someone knew and was after her.

"She thought one of the staff was, what, a hit man?" he asked.

Jason shook his head. "More like a friend of a friend who wanted justice for Holly and her family. Someone was definitely messing with Megan, from what she told me. I just thought it was Casey trying to get back at her, you know, moving things around in her room, turning the heat way up or way down, leaving windows open when a storm blew in, that sort of thing. Just silly, vindictive things." He chuckled. "The same things Megan had been doing to Casey."

Megan, Finn thought with a sigh. She'd been so busy making enemies here that it was hard to know who had wanted her dead. Someone after her because she'd lied about the car accident? Or one of the staff members she'd pushed too far?

"She said someone had stolen her diary, and she was worried they would send it to her parents. Apparently she'd confessed everything in the diary. I didn't even know she kept one," Jason said.

Finn only knew because he'd seen it once at her house in California. "She said she'd confessed in the diary about the car wreck? Did she also mention that she'd written down who she thought was stalking her?"

Jason shrugged. "She might have. She wanted me to help find the diary, terrified of who might read it. The night she told me, she was scared and drunk. The next morning she tried to avoid me. I figured she'd found it and regretted opening up to me. When I got the chance, I tried to tell her that I'd keep her secret, but she said she didn't know what I was talking about."

"You *didn't* keep her secret," Finn pointed out.

"I did for ten long years. I figure the statute of limitations on secrets is probably up. Anyway, isn't this reunion about telling the truth?"

"I don't know. Is it? I thought you were here just for the fun?"

Jason chuckled. "Right." He turned as Casey walked in. "Morning."

"Morning," she said with a nod and headed for the coffee as Jason rose, finished his and, leaving his cup on the table, started toward the door.

"A bunch of us are going into town for breakfast. You're welcome to join us." When neither Finn nor Casey responded, Jason simply nodded and left.

DEVLIN HAD AWAKENED to his worst nightmare. He realized in the light of day that things were much worse than he'd realized. He'd been so convinced that he could get the hotel at a cheaper price… He'd bragged at length to the investors that he knew Casey Crenshaw and that she was a pushover. That she wanted to dump the hotel so badly that he'd get them a deal they would be talking about for years.

The memory of how arrogant he'd been made him sick to his stomach, but that wasn't the worst of it. He needed to call them and give them the bad news, softening the blow by telling them that the person who was making an offer would unload it soon if they wanted to wait.

The investors would squawk. They'd already paid his expenses to come out here on numerous trips where he'd padded his bill. When he got them an amazing deal, he'd figured they wouldn't mind the huge amount he'd run up.

Now he was screwed. They would be furious. The word would spread, and his career would be ruined. No one would trust him. It was why he hadn't called them, why he'd hung out around the campfire pouring down Jason's beer until he couldn't take any more of Jason or Claude or talk of Megan before going to bed.

Megan was the last thing on his mind. She was dead. Good riddance. Why dig her back up at all? His phone vibrated as a text came in. He looked, even though he already knew it was from one of the investors wanting an update.

He swore and put his phone away. He blamed Casey for this. Clearly she'd fallen for Finn and his good looks and his money. Who would have known that Finnegan James would end up in the Crenshaw Hotel? That Finn had a relationship with Megan? That he'd be here now, acting like he had to protect Casey from the rest of them? It was as if Finn knew that one of them was a killer. It wasn't something Devlin had forgotten.

He thought about last night when he'd left the campfire. All who had been left around the fire were Claude and Jason, and even Jason was clearly tired of Claude.

"Wait up," Jason had called as Devlin had left the golden aura of the campfire to wade through the dense darkness of the parking lot toward the hotel.

Devlin had pretended not to hear him. He kept thinking that anything could happen this weekend. Any one of them could die.

The thought had perked him up as he reached the lights of the hotel back entrance. If he were dead, the investors couldn't destroy his career, his life, his future. He'd pushed open the door, letting it slam, still pretending he hadn't known Jason was right behind him.

This morning, he knew he had only one chance to save himself. Somehow he had to have this hotel and land. Which meant he had to convince Casey to take his offer. Otherwise, he was a dead man.

CASEY FELT THE tension the moment she walked into the hotel kitchen. Jason had made a quick departure, leaving her alone with Finn. "Was it something I said?" she joked, then saw his face. He looked as if someone had punched him in the gut. "Or something *you* said?"

Finn groaned and raked a hand through his dark hair. He didn't look as if he'd gotten any more sleep than she had. She listened as he filled her in on what Jason had told him.

"Wait—what?" she said.

"Megan lied. If someone knew she lied, that she'd been responsible for the car wreck and gotten away with it, then she could have been right. Maybe someone *was* stalking her. Someone could have gotten a summer job here planning to make her pay."

"That's kind of a long shot, isn't it?" Casey said. "But if true, then her death might not have had anything to do with what happened among the staff. Or it could have been Megan's guilt just making her paranoid."

"That's what I would have said, if someone hadn't killed her."

"I've never considered that Megan's murder might have been premeditated," Casey said after a moment. "It wasn't like the killer brought a weapon."

"Everyone thought that the killer saw an opportunity when he found Megan alone in the woods. So he picked up a rock and caved in the back of her skull. It had been a spur-of-the-moment decision. She never knew what hit her."

"Or *who* hit her," Casey agreed with a shudder. "It sounds like Megan had a lot of reasons to feel guilty. No wonder you didn't believe that her life was in danger. You didn't know the truth about the car accident or what was going on here at the hotel."

"If that's what got her killed," Finn said with a shake of his head. "The guilt could have been getting to her. Or it could be one of the staff with their own reason for wanting her dead," Finn concluded.

Casey questioned whether Megan could feel guilt: she had so much of her own. She told herself that she wasn't getting involved in finding the killer. That she didn't care. That she just wanted to get as far away from all of this as possible. "Either way, you have a lot of suspects. Unless…"

"Unless I try to find out which of the three girls in the car might have a connection to someone who worked at the Crenshaw that summer," he said, finishing her thought.

She wanted to smack herself. *Don't get involved. Don't let him pull you in.* And yet her mind was already working. "If someone killed her because she lied to save her own neck and got her friend killed, that would make more sense than murdering Megan over some silly squabble here at Crenshaw."

"Jason said that she admitted in her diary that she'd been driving the car," Finn said. "I'm wondering what else she might have written down—maybe who she thought was after her. Someone has that diary."

Casey had just taken a sip of coffee. It went down the wrong way, making her choke. She couldn't seem to get any air into her lungs. She fought for her next breath as Finn hurried over to her. She held up a hand to ward him off.

"Are you all right?" Finn asked.

The concern in his eyes was so caring, so trusting, that she had to look away.

"I'm okay," she managed to say around gasps. That Megan might have told the truth in her diary, that she might have also written down the name of the person she thought was stalking her… That had never dawned on Casey. Until now.

"I looked all over the hotel and grounds for her diary." He shook his head. "The killer must have taken it. I guess we'll never know what she wrote in it. Unless it comes out this weekend."

"Probably just more lies," she said, finally breathing a little easier. "I'm sure it would be worthless, especially now."

As if sensing she'd had enough talk of Megan, Finn reached into the hip pocket of his jeans to pull out some folded papers. "I'll get these typed up, but for now, here's my offer. It will all be legal and done once we both sign."

She took the folded sheets from him and spread them out on the table, glad to have a distraction. The offer amount jumped out at her. Her gaze shot up to him. "Are you serious? This is way over what Devlin offered."

He shrugged. "Mine's a fair offer based on the land value and the hotel's worth. I did my homework."

Casey stared at him. "You plan to run the hotel?"

"That isn't necessarily an option, but I took into consideration the value of the furnishings and materials that could be saved before demolition. Trust me, I don't make deals that don't benefit me."

She didn't doubt that, but she also couldn't help being suspicious. Like he'd said, he was doing this for her and her grandmother. So why did she think he wanted more than the hotel?

"All you have to do is sign the buy–sell agreement," Finn said. "I'd have your lawyer check it over first, though. You're welcome to take a photo and email it if you're still in a hurry to get this over with."

"I wouldn't sign anything until you hear what I have to say," Devlin interrupted as he stepped into the kitchen. "You owe me that much."

She might have argued that, but Finn quickly agreed with him.

"He's right. You should hear him out. I have some business to tend to," Finn said to her as she folded up his offer and set it aside. "I'll talk to you later."

Devlin came over to the table as Finn left. "I'm sorry you feel that I stalled and led you on."

She said nothing, simply waiting. She was still shaken from what Finn had told her about Megan and that damned diary. She just wanted to get this over with so she could get on with finding the things on her grandmother's list and be done here.

"You need to at least *consider* my offer."

He took a chair across from her. "I've been on the phone all morning with my investors." He pulled out a yellow notepad and pen from his battered briefcase. She watched him tear out a piece of paper and write down a number on it before pushing it across the table to her.

She glanced at the figure, then at him. "This is less than you originally offered."

"That's because the cost of demolition and construction has gone up in the past six months. My investors—"

She rose from the table, picking up Finn's offer as she did. "You're wasting my time."

"Wait." He tore another sheet from the notepad, scribbled on it and seemed to hesitate before he wrote down another figure and slowly shoved it across the table in her direction. "That's the best I can do."

She glanced at the number. "Sorry."

"*Seriously?* You got a higher offer than *that*?" Devlin sounded astounded. "Well, I suppose Finn is in a position to lose money to get what he wants." He met her gaze, the accusation clear in it. "You have to wonder what he really wants out of this deal."

Casey had wondered the same thing, but it made her angry that he would suggest it. "Devlin, the way you stalled, I would have taken less from anyone as long as it wasn't you."

"Casey, I had to talk to all the investors and—"

"You thought you were the only buyer and you could get the hotel and property for nothing. That's on you, Devlin. I'm sure your investors will understand."

"I wasn't stalling. I knew I was coming for the reunion. I just thought we'd do it then. I didn't see what the urgency was."

"I would imagine you wouldn't." No one knew why she wanted the hotel sold so badly. But she feared they would find out. She started out of the kitchen.

"So what's Finn going to do with the hotel?" Devlin called after her.

"I don't know, but then again, I don't care."

That wasn't true, Casey thought as she headed for the stairs. When she'd come here, she'd only wanted the place sold and the hotel razed. At the time, she'd thought it would wipe out all the bad memories. No more haunted hotel. No more thoughts of Megan.

That was before she'd met Finn. Before this reunion that brought everyone back. Before Casey had begun to realize that her grandmother had been right. She wouldn't be at peace as long as Megan's killer was still out there. As long as she was under suspicion. As long as she had something to hide.

She hated feeling so off balance. She'd been sure of what she wanted when she'd come here. Now... Last night as she'd showered, standing under the warm spray, she'd finally felt herself relax for the first time all day. She'd tried to forget everything, especially Finn. Never had she thought she'd find a man like him in one of the hotel showers.

Was she really up to facing the past? Facing Megan's ghost? This was what her grandmother had wanted and what she'd forced Casey to promise. Because her grandmother had known she was hiding something?

If Anna Crenshaw could have, she would have conjured up Finn, dangling him in front of her, tempting her, seducing her into doing exactly what she had wanted. Even from the grave, she felt as if her grandmother was still guiding her to do the right thing.

Did Finn suspect that she wasn't telling him everything? The worst part was that she liked him. He was true to his word, giving her an offer first thing this morning—just as he'd promised. She'd enjoyed their dinner together. She'd found that she enjoyed him in spite of originally thinking he was delusional and dangerous. She still thought he was dangerous—but only because she could see how easy it might be to fall for him. The man was so darned likable.

Finn had spent months in an abandoned hotel trying to solve his old girlfriend's murder. What woman wouldn't find that strange but also charming? The man had his... attributes, that was for sure. She'd seen them, and her body had responded against her will.

The thought sent a shiver through her. It had been so long since she'd met someone who'd spurred anything close to desire in her. But she was human. And Finn was all wonderfully male. She couldn't banish those thoughts any more than she could thoughts of Finn out of bed as well.

While searching the hotel for clues to Megan's murder, he'd found Anna's journals. What he'd really been looking for, though, was Megan's diary. He'd obviously been hoping that Megan would provide the answers he'd needed. He still did.

Megan's diary had haunted Casey for ten years. At sixteen, all she'd wanted was to find it and destroy it—to protect herself. Back then, she hadn't been able to imagine anything worse than someone finding the diary and reading the lies Megan had written about her. Megan had taunted her with the awful things she'd said she'd put in that diary about her. Now she wondered if Megan had lied. What if there had been nothing about her in it?

That had never crossed her mind, not ten years ago, not when Megan had seemed hell-bent on destroying her.

Now she felt sick. What if Megan had written about the car wreck, written the truth? Or realized who it was who was stalking her? The name of her killer could have been in that book. If the diary had been found, all of this could have been over years ago, the killer caught and behind bars.

Her heart banged against her ribs. Any chance of finding those answers was lost. No one would ever know what Megan had written. Because the diary was gone.

Casey swallowed, remembering the terror she'd felt the day she'd found it. She knew what would happen if she got caught in Megan's room—let alone with her diary.

She hadn't had much time. Maybe if she had, she would have read some of it. Probably not. She'd been too scared she would get caught. Even if Megan hadn't killed her, she would have gone straight to Anna. Casey knew what her grandmother would have said about her taking the diary—let alone what she planned to do with it.

She'd hurried out of the hotel, running across the parking lot to the outbuilding where they kept the charcoal lighter fluid to start the nightly staff campfire. Everyone else was busy in the kitchen getting ready for the evening meal. If any of the guests saw her at the firepit, they wouldn't think anything of it.

Dousing the diary with the fluid, she'd then hurried to the pit. Pulling out the matches, she'd struck one and dropped it and the diary in. Flames had erupted at once, rising bright orange and emitting a cloud of dark smoke. Even knowing she would be missed in the kitchen, Casey had stood watching the diary burn until nothing but ashes remained. Sixteen and foolish, she believed she was saving herself from Megan and her lies.

The memory turned her stomach. She'd known Megan would throw a fit when she'd found her diary missing. She'd also known whom Megan would accuse. The staff quarters had been searched. Everyone had been questioned. Everyone had been under suspicion, especially her. Each staff member had sworn that they hadn't seen it, hadn't taken it, hadn't even known she kept a diary—Casey among them.

But Casey had always feared that her grandmother had known, because Anna knew her too well. But no one could prove a thing. Megan had only become worse after that, as if terrified that the diary would be found before she could get her hands on it. What *had* she written in it?

Megan was the only one who knew. A few days after the diary went missing, she was murdered. That argument in the woods? That had been Megan accusing Casey of taking it. After Megan's body was found, after the marshal arrived and began questioning everyone, Casey told herself the diary wasn't important. So she'd lied by omission.

Later when there was a search for the book, she'd lied about not seeing it. She'd lied to her grandmother. To the marshal. To everyone. Now she was lying to Finn, who'd just spent months looking for it within these walls.

She couldn't bear to think of what he would say if he knew what she'd done. But she might find out soon, she realized. *Someone* knew. The person who'd written on her bathroom mirror knew. It was only a matter of time before they told. Or were they still hoping she would confess?

She told herself to accept Finn's offer, pack up her grandmother's things and leave. If she was lucky, she could get away before whoever had left the message on her mirror told the world.

I know what you did

But even as she thought it, she knew that she wasn't the same woman who'd arrived here. That woman had a plan to get out of here as fast as possible and take her lie with her. The woman she was now wanted to confess—to Finn.

She felt she owed him at least that. Admitting what she'd done with Megan's diary wouldn't help Finn find her killer, but it would let her leave here without the guilt she'd carried for years.

But first she would deal with at least one of the promises she'd made her grandmother.

CHAPTER FOURTEEN

AFTER FINISHING HER COFFEE, she pulled her grandmother's list from the pocket of her jeans and unfolded the sheet of paper. Seeing her grandmother's neat script hurt her heart. She missed Anna. Even after she'd quit coming to the hotel in the summers, they had remained close. Closer than she had ever been with her mother.

Casey tried to concentrate on the list. It was longer than she'd expected. She shook her head. What was she supposed to do with these items once she found them? She knew her grandmother wanted them kept in the family. But Casey lived on-site at the hotel. She had no place to store them.

For a moment, she felt overwhelmed with loss and grief and the weight of the one promise she'd meant to keep.

After a moment, she studied the list again, noting that her grandmother had suggested where a few of the items might be found in the huge hotel. So at least it wouldn't be a case of looking for a needle in a haystack. But the list did make her wonder if the elderly woman had been in her right mind. Or was the list long and involved because Anna was determined to keep Casey in this hotel as long as possible? So long that she faced the past and her part in it? It wouldn't have been unlike her.

She decided to start with one item that was supposedly in the tower. It had always been her and her grandmother's favorite spot in the hotel. For a moment, she considered taking the elevator, but she decided to walk.

Taking the stairs, she quickly climbed. The last part of the stairwell to the tower was narrow and steep. She was glad when she finally pushed through the door, breaking out into the bright light of the circular tower with its walls of windows.

The glass was dusty, and the room needed to be cleaned, but she'd forgotten how wonderful the views were from here. She opened one of the small windows to let in some fresh air. A gust of warm breeze rushed in. She breathed in the sweet scent of a Montana spring morning.

Every breath was a reminder of what she'd done and what she was about to do. Her grandmother had wanted this place to stay in the family as it had for almost a century and a half, but she also knew how impossible that was for her granddaughter. As much as Casey loved the Crenshaw, it wasn't something she wanted to take on. Especially after Megan's murder.

She walked around the tower, admiring the different views and feeling her grandmother in the room. Anna had always had afternoon tea up here. "Everyone should get to spend time on the top of the world, don't you think, Casey?"

She'd chuckled. "I doubt this is the top of the world."

"It is for us, and that's all that matters."

Soon Anna's top of the world would be nothing more than rubble to be hauled away. If she sold to Devlin. Who knew what Finn would do with it? Could she sell to him with the contingency that he must destroy it?

Either way, her grandmother's Old Girl would be gone.

"I'm sorry, Gram." Tears burned her eyes as she turned away from the view and saw other footprints in the dust on the floor. She wasn't the only one who'd been up here recently. Finn. She could see where he'd walked around. She could imagine him standing at the windows, looking at the varying views.

The footprints ended at the large, overstuffed chair—her grandmother's. The knitted throw still hung over one arm, and a book lay open facedown on the small table next to it, along with a cup that Casey knew had held tea.

The scene looked as if her grandmother had been interrupted and had stepped away to tend to hotel business but would return any moment. The feeling was so strong that Casey thought she could hear her grandmother's tread on the stairs.

She turned, half expecting to see her, and felt the loss with an intensity that brought more tears to her eyes as Finn filled the doorway.

"Sorry. I didn't mean to startle you," he said.

Turning her back, she moved swiftly to her grandmother's chair as she tried to hold back the tears. She picked up the book and, placing the bookmark between the last pages that had been read, closed it. There was a dark stain at the bottom of the cup from the tea that had never been finished. She snatched up the throw and held it to her chest and was rewarded with the scent of Anna's rose perfume.

"The view from up here is incredible," Finn said behind her. She heard him move to the windows to the west. "You can see snowcapped mountains miles from every window. I understand why it was your grandmother's favorite room." She knew he was giving her time to pull herself together. She took a breath, dashed her tears with her sleeve and turned to look at him.

He still had his back to her. "She mentioned it numerous

times in her journal. She wrote about how she used to read books to you up here when you were little, how you had tea parties and invited your dolls." Casey felt her heart bump in her chest. "You must have such wonderful memories."

He turned to look at her and must have seen how close she was to breaking down. He switched to business as if knowing that would help her. "I have made all the arrangements for a contract to be drawn up the moment you accept my offer for the hotel and land." She nodded, afraid her voice would crack if she tried to speak. "I also made a few calls on that other matter we discussed. If there's a connection between that car accident and someone on the staff from that summer, my PI will find it."

She stepped to the window next to him and tried to concentrate on the view to the north. From here, a person could see the entire town of Buckhorn nestled between the pine-covered mountains. A dark two-lane strip of pavement cut right through the middle and kept going.

"You can change your mind."

She glanced at him, gave a shake of her head, knowing he meant selling the hotel. But it was the news he'd given her this morning that had shaken her. What if Megan's murder could have been prevented if only Casey had looked in the diary? If only she hadn't destroyed it? The killer could be in prison now and not possibly inside this hotel considering their next victim. "It's just...difficult to let go."

"I'm sure it is." His look was so sympathetic that she knew if she didn't drag her gaze away, she would start crying again. Her loss was so fresh, and being here in the place her grandmother had loved so much was wrenching at her heart. She turned away.

"You're buying an old hotel on a whim, and I'm guessing you still don't know what you're going to do with it."

"You're right about that," he said behind her. "What would you like for me to do with it?"

She swallowed. Did she really believe that she could put all of this behind her if the hotel was razed to nothing but dust? Would it help her sleep any better? "Whatever you want."

Retrieving the tiny china tea set on the shelf behind her grandmother's chair, she stepped past him, avoiding his gaze. She'd taken but a few steps when she remembered the cup she'd left behind. Her grandmother would have wanted her to return it to the kitchen.

She knew it was silly. The entire place might be gone in a matter of weeks, but she stopped to turn back. When she did, though, she collided with Finn. He caught her with one arm to steady her, and she saw that he had picked up the cup before leaving the room.

The gesture touched her so deeply, making her realize that he really had come to know her grandmother over the months he'd been staying here. She met his warm gaze and saw in those breath-stealing seconds that he also knew her more than she had wanted to admit. The intimacy of it made her skin dimple with goose bumps.

His gaze locked with hers. She felt heat rush to her center. Her knees went weak with a need that made her tremble inside. If he touched her now—

"Casey?" The grating female voice called up the stairs. "*Hello?* Are you up there?"

The last thing she wanted to do was answer Vi Mullen. Especially right now. But she also knew that the woman wouldn't go away until she did. She could hear Vi starting to climb the stairs.

"I'm coming down!" Casey called and dragged her gaze from Finn, the moment gone. She still felt weak with need but also with relief. The last thing she needed to do was complicate this already-confounding situation. Not to mention that she was lying to him. That didn't make her any better than Megan.

"I'VE BEEN LOOKING all over this place for you," Vi said disagreeably as she glanced up the stairs as if searching for something. Or was it someone? Had she heard Casey and Finn talking up there?

Finn was nowhere to be seen, as if he'd guessed that she didn't want Vi seeing them together. Or had that moment they'd had together affected him the way it had her, and he wanted some time before facing anyone?

"Well, now you've found me." Casey could just imagine what this was about. She'd expected Vi would come by as soon as she'd heard she was in town. She guessed she was lucky it had taken the woman this long.

"Let's go down to the main hall," Casey said. "It's not as dusty down there." She would have preferred the stairs, the way she'd come up, but for the older woman she pushed the elevator button, and the two of them rode to the ground floor.

The woman had some papers she was holding and a determined look on her face. Casey hoped this wasn't about trying to get the hotel on the historic register and stopping the sale. She motioned to one of the Victorian couches and excused herself to put the tea-party set away in her grandmother's office.

When she returned and had taken a seat, Casey began. "Vi—"

"Coffee," the woman interrupted.

"Coffee?" Casey realized it wasn't an offer; it was a request. "I'll see if there is some in the kitchen. Let me check." She got up and walked down the staff hallway to the kitchen. Finn had apparently made another pot. There were also pastries with a note saying he'd picked them up at the bakery and to help yourself. She was touched by his efficiency and his thoughtfulness.

Casey felt her stomach growl as she poured herself and Vi a cup of coffee. She put the cups on a tray along with some pastries. She thought about bringing out a carafe for refills but was determined that, whatever Vi wanted, it wouldn't take that long.

The woman's eyes widened as Casey put a cup of coffee and a turnover in front of her. "Are these Bessie's?" Vi asked and took a large bite. "Oh, they are. She does make the best pastries."

Casey sat down and picked up her cup. She cut off a forkful of one of the turnovers. It was sweet, buttery and flaky, the berries inside bursting in her mouth. No one baked like Bessie.

"Aren't they heavenly?" Vi said as she devoured hers and then slurped most of her coffee. "I can imagine how much you must miss Buckhorn and Bessie's sweets and your grandmother. This old place has to remind you of her." The woman shuddered. "It must be so hard for you, staying here all alone."

"I'm not alone," she said, as if Vi didn't already know that.

"Oh, yes, that...that man who's been staying here."

Another shudder conveyed what Vi thought of Finn. "He seems...dangerous, don't you think?"

Vi had no idea what having such a man like Finn around was like—let alone a half-dozen murder suspects.

"I heard some other people have moved in as well," Vi said. "More homeless?"

She hurriedly changed the subject. "I'm sure that's not why you're here."

"I don't want the hotel destroyed," Vi said, putting down her cup a little too hard.

Casey shook her head. "Why?"

"Because it's a local landmark. I can't bear the idea of someone tearing it down. Half this town worked here at some point in their lives. All of us in town are a piece of it."

The woman was right. A lot of the locals had been a part of the hotel, not to mention all the teens who'd worked at least a summer here. It had almost been a rite of passage to work at the Crenshaw. Now it was the end of an era.

Vi cleared her voice, finally getting to business. "I want to buy the hotel." She tossed the papers in Casey's direction.

Casey gathered them up, shocked. She'd wanted to sell the hotel and grounds for months. Where had Vi been all this time?

"What would you do with it?" Casey asked without looking at the papers.

"Does it really matter to you? Isn't my keeping the Crenshaw better than razing it and building a truck stop?"

"I think a truck stop would be more useful," she said honestly. Picking up the offer, she saw that it was ridiculously low. "This is generous of you, Vi, but I'm sorry—the hotel is already sold."

"What? But Devlin told me—"

"I didn't sell to Devlin."

"You can't have sold it that quickly. You have to give me a chance. At least consider my offer."

"I'm sorry. I've already agreed to another offer." She tried to hand back the paperwork, but Vi refused to take it.

"Think about what your grandmother would have wanted."

After being in the tower, sensing her grandmother there, Casey felt too vulnerable to have this conversation right now. If there were any way to keep the hotel, to make it viable, she would know. She'd been in this business for years. Vi had no idea how to run a hotel or what was involved. It wouldn't be a year and the place would be closed again. How long would Vi hold on to it before she sold the property just as Casey planned to do?

"Look at this place," Vi said, taking in the huge main hall. "You can't destroy it. It would break Anna's heart."

"Vi, the answer is no. The deal is done." Which wasn't quite true, but close enough. "I'm sorry. My grandmother knew I had to sell it."

"Not to have it torn down."

Casey shook her head. She needed to know that she'd taken care of things and not let the hotel limp on as something it wasn't or couldn't ever be again.

Vi pursed her lips, reached for her napkin and wiped her mouth. "You're making a mistake. Your grandmother will be rolling over in her grave when the bulldozers start taking this place down."

"My grandmother was cremated."

"You know what I mean. I'm offering to save the hotel."

"If there was a way to save it, I would do it myself." Casey pushed to her feet.

"At least let me send Emery over to get the boards off the

windows so you can enjoy it while you're here," Vi said in a change of subject that practically gave Casey whiplash.

"Not necessary." Vi's brother Emery had to be in his early sixties by now. He had no business up on a ladder. "Finn will handle it once he's the legal owner."

"Finn? You can't mean that man who's been living here as a squatter?" Vi cried. "He doesn't have a penny to his name."

"He must have rich friends," Casey said, not about to reveal Finn's identity to this busybody. Vi would find out soon enough. "But thanks for the offer," she added, remembering her manners.

"Emery told me to mention that he was worried about the old boiler downstairs," Vi said. "He was trained in boilers, you know. They can be dangerous, he told me. He wouldn't mind checking—"

"I'm sure Finn will deal with it," she said.

Vi's face wrinkled in a frown. "Emery gave his life to this place," she said stubbornly.

Casey thought that was a bit overly dramatic. She remembered how her grandmother had kept the man on years after she should have. Casey had often found him napping in one of the rooms when he wasn't hiding out in the maze of pipes and equipment under the hotel.

She suspected that some years he'd lived down there, even though her grandmother had forbidden it. But when she'd offered him a room in the staff quarters, he'd declined.

"I thought Emery retired to Arizona after my grandmother closed the hotel?" Casey asked.

"He did for a while, waiting for Anna to return and reopen the hotel. She'd told him she would hold his job for him." Vi seemed nervous. Casey noticed how her hand shook as she picked up her cup and finished her coffee. "The new owner should hire him, just for his peace of mind. Emery could use the money. He's been staying with us, but I know he wants to get a place of his own. Or he could stay in the hotel once it's up and running again."

So that was why she was pushing this. Emery was living with her and Axel. "I really doubt Finn will be running the place as a hotel. I would imagine he'll raze it and build something else."

Vi looked like she might cry. Did she really love this place that much? She did own an antiques barn. Maybe she had real feelings for old things.

"I'm sorry, Vi. It's for the best."

"Is it?" Her gaze swung to Casey, her look cold and brittle. "You have no idea what you're about to do." Vi stood awkwardly, clearly upset.

Casey began to load the tray with their empty plates and cups. All of this was hard enough without Vi trying to make her feel guilty. "I really need to get back to what I was doing."

"Tina also worked at the hotel, you might remember. And Jen." Vi suddenly shuddered, rubbed her arms with her hands as if feeling a draft. "This place is haunted, you know." Vi looked as if she'd felt Megan's ghost or one of the others said to cruise the place. "You can stop this before it's too late," she said as she picked up her purse to leave. "I'd hate to see the community turn against you. They loved your grandmother so much."

Casey again tried to hand back the paperwork, but the woman pretended to ignore her. "Let me walk you out."

"Don't bother," Vi snapped. "I know the way." With that, she turned and left.

"We really need to start locking the doors," Finn said as he came into the kitchen, where she was cleaning up the dishes only moments later. She wondered how much of the conversation he might have overheard.

"Thanks for the pastries."

"No problem." He seemed to hesitate. "She's right, you know. It isn't too late to change your mind." Well, that answered the question of how much he'd heard.

She shook her head. Nothing could change her mind about selling the hotel. "But it's strange that suddenly someone else wants to buy it."

"I think all of it is strange as hell, especially this reunion. That's why I plan to keep an eye on all of them. I just added Vi Mullen to my list."

CHAPTER FIFTEEN

At breakfast in downtown Buckhorn, Jason realized that everyone thought he was the organizer of this reunion. He wished he had been. Unfortunately, he wasn't that creative.

But taking it over? He had no problem with that. Besides, everyone had let him. Even the person who'd planned this, which seemed odd. Not that he gave it much thought. His life of privilege had always afforded him pretty much anything he wanted. He knew he intimidated those who had grown up without it. That was why this group so easily followed him, he was sure. Not that he was much of a leader—just ask his old man.

But he could handle keeping the conversation lively around the campfire, he could afford to buy the booze and he would come up with games for them to play until they found out why they were all here. This might be the only thing he was really good at. He could handle this ragtag group. His thoughts clouded as he thought of Megan. She had been a whole different story.

Remembering came with a niggling worry that whoever was behind this reunion was just giving him enough rope to hang himself. If the person knew him, then that person would know he would take over. That person might sit back and let him think he was in charge of the weekend. But in truth, he was being manipulated just like the others were, only they didn't realize it.

He hated the feeling that someone was pulling his strings as well as everyone else's here.

AFTER BREAKFAST, SHIRLEY headed back to the motel while everyone else headed deeper into town. Buckhorn was so small that it wouldn't take them long before they would all be at Dave's bar. She found herself getting ticked off at her best friend. Jen had talked her into this. Twisted her arm was more like it. Jen never took no for an answer. That was probably one reason her relationships with men never lasted. That and her mouth. Jen would cut a man with that tongue and make him bleed.

Right now, Shirley wasn't sure why Jen was her best friend. She'd felt left out last night at the campfire—just as she had ten years ago when she and Jen had worked at the hotel together. It was depressing reliving that summer.

When Jen had made her move on Claude and then gone into the woods last night with Jason, that had felt like the last straw. She'd thought about texting Lars, seeing if he wanted to meet up at her apartment at the motel.

She hadn't gotten the chance before Ben had moved over beside her at the campfire and tried to strike up a conversation. Shirley wasn't interested but tried not to be rude. She pretended to get a text and pulled out her phone. In the process of sending a text first to Jen to tell her she was leaving, she really did get a text.

From Lars. Shirley had felt her heart do that little dippy-do—a little more dippy-do than usual. She knew it was because she'd been so miserable by the fire with these people she liked just a little better than she had Megan, whom she'd despised. Seeing a text from Lars made her feel better. She had a boyfriend, a job, a place to live. Her life wasn't so bad.

She opened the text and read.

WTF Shirley? You said you weren't going to that stupid reunion with people you can't stand. I stopped by the motel and was told you wouldn't be back until Monday. WTF?

Shirley had felt her face heat from more than the fire. Lars had obviously stopped by for a booty call, and she wasn't there waiting for him like she always was. She never knew if he could get away from his live-in supposedly not-girlfriend who was pregnant with someone else's baby, and now he was angry. Boo-hoo.

The text had set her off. She knew exactly what Jen would say. "Serves him right for taking you for granted. This is good for him. Might make him appreciate you more. Might even get him to leave Tina and commit to you. If that's really what you want."

Was that really what she wanted? If he ever did get off the fence and leave Tina, would she feel trapped into living with him or, worse, marrying him? Did she ever want to get married again after two strikes out? She didn't think so. The truth was, most days she wasn't that unhappy with the way things were now.

She'd started to text Lars back but was interrupted. "Thought you might like another beer," Benjamin had said next to her at the fire. He'd gone to the cooler and come back with a cold brew just for her. He'd smiled as he handed it to her. It was so thoughtful that she'd tried to remember the last time—or any time—Lars had done something thoughtful for her.

Looking at Benjamin, she'd seen that he'd been flirting with her. Or at least trying. She'd recognized the smile. Let Lars stew in his own juices. She'd put her phone away and smiled back.

Now at the motel, she checked to make sure everything was running smoothly. It was. Her friend appeared to be doing a fine job of taking care of the motel in her absence. It really was a no-brainer.

But she busied herself double-checking to make sure the register was up to date. She was at the desk when the door opened, and her lover's baby mama walked in.

HER GRANDMOTHER'S LIST in hand again, Casey wandered through the hotel, feeling as if she was on a scavenger hunt. More and more, she suspected her grandmother had planned it this way. At the end of the wings of each floor there was a small garden room. She couldn't remember what room had the antique Tiffany lampshade as per the neat script. *You'll know it when you see it*, Anna had written.

Casey started on the north-wing ground floor, going through each garden room. Each had its own colors and designs, each more lovely than she remembered. Her grandmother had loved selecting fabrics and patterns over the years, keeping with the character of the hotel. She would spend months looking for a certain fabric or lamp or vase.

Casey had never appreciated how perfect each room was until now. It hurt to see that most were in excellent shape. She knew that all of the furnishings would be sold along with the kitchen equipment, which was nearly brand-new. She couldn't bear to do it and was happy when Finn had added an amount to his offer for the contents of the hotel— minus the listed keepsakes.

She found the Tiffany lampshade late in the afternoon.

The hotel had already filled with evening shadows. The hallways were dim. Some of the wall-sconce bulbs needed to be replaced. Not going to happen, she reminded herself. This was no longer her responsibility—as soon as she signed the papers to sell it.

It was no wonder that she'd lost track of time. She found herself pausing in each sunroom, taking in the decor, feeling her grandmother's hand as if seeing each room through her eyes.

As she headed back with the lamp, she looked up and let out a startled cry. Lost in thought, she hadn't heard anyone approach. She took an instinctive step back as, out of the shadows, an older, gray-haired mountain of a man appeared.

"Emery." Her voice broke. It had been years since she'd seen him, but she recognized him at once. He had a craggy face and blue eyes that seemed bottomless. She'd heard her grandmother describe him as an overgrown kid more than once.

He smiled, clearly amused that he'd frightened her, even as he said, "Didn't mean to startle you." His hair was longer than she remembered but just as disheveled. He'd aged but still looked strong and fit.

She remembered all the times as a girl that he had sneaked up on her, laughing when she'd jumped. She'd told her grandmother about it.

"Emery has to have something to do," she'd said and chuckled. "I clearly don't keep him busy enough. He doesn't mean anything by it. He just likes to get a rise out of you."

"Emery," Casey said now, "what are you doing here?"

"Heard you were back and that you had guests. Thought I might be of help. Didn't Vi mention I'd be stopping by?"

"It must have slipped her mind," Casey said, groaning

inwardly. "Thank you, but we're fine. I've sold the place. I believe everyone is leaving by Monday."

"Is that right?" He rubbed his gray-stubble jaw and looked around with those watery, pale eyes. "Heard you were selling. Wouldn't mind working part-time for the new owner. Maybe you could put in a good word for me."

She noticed the man's gnarled hands, his worn canvas pants, his faded flannel shirt. She wondered if he had fallen on hard times and that was why he'd come back from Arizona to live with his sister.

"I don't think the new owner will be keeping the hotel open. I expect he will demolish it and do something else with the land."

Emery didn't look any more glad to hear that than his sister had. "Shame. Damn shame. I thought this building would always stay in the Crenshaw family. I know that's what Anna always told me."

"Times change."

He nodded, those eyes on her. "I really should check the boiler while I'm here."

"Not necessary, but thanks for asking," she said. "If you'll excuse me, I have things to do. I believe you know your way out." She turned and walked down the hall. She could feel that gaze boring into her back.

Her grandmother would have let him check the boiler and then written him a ridiculously large check to cover his thoughtfulness. Casey felt for the man and his situation.

At the end of the hall, she didn't have to look back to know he was still standing there. She could almost hear her grandmother saying *What would it have hurt to let him check the boilers?*

CHAPTER SIXTEEN

SHIRLEY TRIED TO hide her shock at seeing pregnant Tina pushing open the motel-office door. The woman looked as if she might deliver right here, right now. Shirley had heard that Tina had gotten big, but that, too, came as a shock. It probably wasn't that surprising, as small as Buckhorn was, that she and Shirley hadn't crossed paths before now. The two of them didn't travel in the same circles, even though the circles were very small in this Montana town.

She could see that her surprise gave Tina some satisfaction. What if she'd come here for some kind of confrontation? As she watched Tina reach into her purse, Shirley froze. She'd expected the woman to pull out a gun, point it at her head and fire.

"I was hoping you'd be working," Tina said cheerfully as she pulled something out of her purse. "I wanted to give you this." She held a small envelope and waddled forward to hand it to her. "It's an invitation to the baby shower." Was the woman joking? "My mother and my friend Sunny are handing them out all over town, but I wanted to bring you yours personally." She smiled as she said it, even though it looked like it hurt her face muscles to do so.

Shirley and Lars had been having an affair ever since Tina had walked out on Lars and then come back allegedly pregnant. Or maybe, Shirley reasoned, Tina had come back to him because after she'd left she'd realized she was pregnant with his baby. The affair had continued. Just as Lars hadn't moved out of the apartment he'd shared with Tina—and still shared.

So she'd been expecting Tina to confront her ever since. It was a recurring waking nightmare. But even in it, the name-calling and accusations led to violence with hair-pulling, head-banging and ultimately lost blood.

Shirley had expected some kind of ending when Tina had returned. But nothing had happened. Tina had to have known about Shirley and Lars, and yet she seemed to have just ignored it.

Or maybe she thought that Lars's preoccupation with Shirley was only temporary—just until the baby was born.

"The shower is next Saturday," Tina was saying in a too-sweet voice, like some rich drink that was laced with poison. "Sorry for the short notice." She patted her belly. The baby must have moved, because it seemed to give her a twinge. "Please, baby, just wait a couple more days," Tina pleaded and laughed. "I knew putting off the shower was a mistake. I hope you can come."

Shirley realized she was still holding the tiny envelope. Was this Tina's way of telling her she knew and that it didn't matter? It was a message, of that Shirley was sure.

"Please don't feel you have to bring a gift," Tina said. "Your attending will be gift enough." She smiled and headed for the door.

Shirley hadn't said a word, had barely taken a breath. She watched Tina go before she tore open the envelope. She wasn't sure what she'd been expecting. It was just a baby-shower invitation.

But she knew it was a lot more than that.

Shirley tossed the invitation in the trash, then dug it

out and ripped it to the tiniest of pieces. The gall of the woman. "'Please don't feel you have to bring a gift,'" she mimicked in Tina's too-sweet tone. "'Your attending will be gift enough.'"

Seriously? Most people in Buckhorn just put an announcement in the local shopper flyer when they were having an event. Since everyone in town knew everyone else and a lot were related, anyone who wanted to come could and would.

But not Christina Mullen. She had to make a big deal out of this with a party so big it required cute little baby invitations.

Shirley hadn't realized that she was crying. She brushed angrily at her tears. What if Lars was wrong? What would he do if the baby was his? What would he do if it wasn't? Was it even about the baby?

She realized that she no longer knew what she wanted. But she suspected a man who couldn't make up his mind wasn't one of them.

WHILE CASEY HADN'T seen Finn since the tower earlier, she'd gotten a text that the paperwork would be ready soon.

Seeing the text had sent a tidal wave of emotions that had threatened to swamp her. Relief and regret turned in a deep sadness as if she was experiencing her grandmother's death all over again.

She told herself that she was only doing what she had to. She couldn't afford to keep the hotel. Now the deal was nearly done. She had no idea what Finn would do with the Crenshaw. Soon it would no longer be any of her business.

But even as she tried to convince herself that this was what she'd wanted, it still hurt. The pain made her all the more anxious to finish this, which meant getting the other things on her grandmother's list as the first step. One promise at a time, she told herself.

At her room, she saw a note taped to her door. *Need your help on the staff wing. Finn.*

She couldn't imagine what he would need her for, but after dropping off a few items in her room, she took the back stairs to the staff wing. Pushing open the door as she came out of the stairwell, she saw that the hallway was empty.

"Finn?" She started down the hall when she caught a sweet and almost cloying scent that made her stumble to a stop. It was so familiar that it blindsided her—just as it had last night in her room. She tried to catch her breath, but each brought more of the overpowering scent. This time, there was no doubt about it.

Gasping, she turned as if expecting to see Megan standing behind her. *Surprise!* But the hallway was empty. That was when she saw where she'd stopped in the hall. Her heart dropped. She stood in front of room 33. Megan's old room.

Even as her rational brain argued that ghosts didn't wear perfume, she rubbed the back of her neck and looked behind her, unable to resist making sure she was alone. The smell wasn't her imagination. It was strong enough to turn her stomach. Her heart pounded as she tried the knob, but unlike most of the other hotel-room doors, this one was locked.

SHIRLEY WAS GOING out the back door of the motel apartment, anxious to meet up with Jen and tell her the news, when Lars drove up.

She couldn't believe his nerve. Did he not know that Tina was going all over town handing out baby-shower invitations? Had he dropped by just minutes earlier, he would have run into her.

"What are you doing here?" she demanded as she stomped out to his pickup. He had the window down, his arm resting on the frame. She noticed the hole in his shirt at the elbow. Something about that hole annoyed her about him. Didn't he own a decent shirt?

"Tina was just here in the motel office," she said, sounding as upset as she felt. Buckhorn was way too small to keep living like this.

He didn't seem all that surprised. "What'd she want?"

"To invite me to her baby shower."

Lars made an angry face. "Why the hell would she do that?"

"Maybe to poison me."

"I don't think she'd do that." He actually sounded as if he meant it.

"It's obvious, dummy. She wants to remind me in front of all her friends and this town that you're still with her and that she's carrying your baby."

"I already told you that the baby isn't mine."

Shirley shook her head. "I have to go."

"Wait. Can't we—"

"No. I'm busy."

Lars let out a curse. "At that stupid reunion everyone in town is talking about?"

She couldn't argue that it wasn't stupid, so she merely stormed off. She'd told Jen that she hadn't mentioned it to Lars. She knew what Jen would have said, so she'd lied about it. She'd been lying about more than some stupid reunion.

Down at Vi Mullen's antiques barn, she found Jen and

Benjamin apparently enjoying themselves, digging through dusty junk.

"I need to talk to you," Shirley whispered. "Privately."

"Whatever you have to say, you can say in front of Ben, here," Jen said.

Benjamin didn't correct her on his name. He merely smiled.

"Tina invited me to her baby shower."

Jen raised a brow. "That's pretty bold of her. Her mother will have a fit." She laughed. "Sounds like the shower is going to be a lot more fun than I thought it would be." She turned to Benjamin and gave him a short explanation of why.

"What if it's his baby?" Benjamin asked.

Shirley just shook her head, but Jen piped up. "It's more complicated than that. The baby is like a line in the sand. Once that little one comes into this world, well…" She raised her gaze to her friend's. "Well, someone will finally make a decision."

"I need a beer." Shirley looked at the two of them and saw that she wasn't going to have to go to the bar alone.

MEGAN WAS DEAD. There was no ghost. But someone wanted Casey to believe that Megan's ghost roamed these halls wearing her signature perfume. That was why the door was locked. Casey felt anger replace that earlier moment of shock and fear. Whoever was behind this, she was going to find them.

Turning, she ran down the hallway to the registration desk. She was only mildly surprised that the keys to room 33 weren't in their slot. She rushed into the office for her spare passkey. It was gone. Finn probably had it. That was an unsettling thought. It meant he could get into any room at any time.

Where was he? In his room? She headed for the stairs. As she climbed, she realized that Finn must have smelled Megan's perfume in the staff hallway. Why else had he left the note to meet him down there? He would know Megan's perfume. But if he had the passkey, then why hadn't he opened Megan's old room?

Casey swore under her breath. She was going to put an end to this as soon as she could get into that room. If she got there in time. She feared that with all this wasted effort, any evidence in the room would be gone.

Storming up the stairs, she was almost to the top of the staircase when she looked up and saw Finn. Startled, she heard him say "Where's the fire? Sorry, bad joke, and not funny in an old hotel like this."

Her head had jerked up and, taken by surprise, she lost both her momentum and her balance. As she began to fall backward down the staircase, she'd grabbed for the railing, but it was too far away to reach. Her arms windmilled as she frantically tried to grasp anything to stop her from falling.

Suddenly Finn's warm, strong hand closed over her wrist. For a few seconds, the two of them were suspended on the top edge of the towering staircase before he pulled them both up and onto the landing.

"What the hell, Casey?" he demanded, breathing hard as if his heart was drumming like her own. She could hear the fear in his voice. That had been too close. Had she been any more off balance, they both would have been plummeting down the stairs at this moment.

FINN'S BLOOD WAS pounding in his ears. He could see that Casey was visibly shaken as well. He drew her away from the stairs, trying to slow his thundering pulse. Gripping both of her upper arms in his hands, he turned her to face him. "What is going on?" he demanded.

She blinked, looking even more upset than she'd been when he'd seen her on the stairs. "Your note."

He stared at her as if she were speaking a language he didn't recognize. "What note?"

She reached into her pocket and shoved the note at him. Taking it, he unfolded the paper and read the words, then looked up at her, his gaze meeting hers. "I didn't write this. This isn't my handwriting."

"You weren't on the staff wing? You weren't in room 33?" she demanded.

He let go of her. "No. Why would I have gone—" He stopped and sighed. "Megan's old room?" He knew it was her room, and she knew he knew. "What happened?" His voice came out a little high, the scare on the stairs still fresh.

"I...I smelled her perfume." He didn't have to ask. He remembered Megan's signature perfume. She wore it all the time. That smell had haunted him many a lonely night as a teenager. "If you didn't leave the note..." He could hear the doubt in her voice.

"Someone did who knew you would come down there if I asked you." He saw that his words hit home. She would have come because she trusted him. Because she had every reason to trust him. "Where were you headed in such a hurry?"

"I was looking for you. I assume you have my grand-mother's passkey. I want to open the door to that room be-fore anyone destroys any evidence they might have left behind."

He looked at her, remembering the creepy things that had happened in the months he'd been here alone. "I have the passkey in my room. I didn't want to leave it at the main desk." He sighed again and raked a hand through his hair. "You can't think I had something to do with this."

They'd reached his room. He stepped inside. It took him a moment to locate the key. He turned to her, holding the passkey on the once-red, now-faded ribbon that her grandmother used to wear around her neck. "Let's go check room 33. Unless you don't trust me to go with you."

"I don't know what to think right now."

He handed her the passkey. She put it around her neck. It upset him that she didn't trust him. "Good idea keeping it around your neck," he joked. "What are the chances I would ever get it off you?"

She shot him an unamused look. "Yes, what are the chances?"

He walked with her down to number 33. He'd gone to the room when he'd first gotten to the hotel. He'd had the crazy idea that he'd pick up some vibe, some sense of Megan. It was ridiculous. For years after her death, other staff had lived and breathed in that room after it had been fine-combed by the cops and then cleaned hundreds of times. He hadn't found Megan in there any more than he'd found her anyplace else in this hotel.

Casey used the passkey to open the door. As it swung open, he caught the once-familiar scent. His reaction was like a punch to the gut. He stood frozen in the doorway as Casey entered the room and began to search it.

No wonder she'd reacted the way she had. The perfume was so Megan. He could picture her, all confidence and defiance. Poor little rich girl. Wasn't that what someone on the staff had called her? While she'd complained about her life, he'd always thought that she didn't have a care in the world. How little he'd known.

Casey stopped at the small table next to the window. She bent down, running her finger over what appeared to be a mark on the carpet.

As she slowly rose, he saw her touch the top of the table with a finger and then hold it up to her nose. The movement had dispersed the scent into the air again. He breathed it in, assaulted with memories, all bittersweet. He'd never known Megan. He wasn't sure anyone really had.

"Someone dragged this table over by the door," Casey said. She pointed to another spot on the carpet, this one closer to the door.

"They probably used some kind of spray device to disperse the perfume into the hall." Had whoever had done it been waiting for someone to come by as they hid behind the locked door? Or was this just for her—the reason they'd left the note for her?

Finn felt a draft and quickly stepped to the window. He shoved aside the drapes and could see where the screen had been bent when it was shoved aside. He looked for tracks in the soft dirt outside, but there were none. There was a rock ledge along the exterior. It appeared someone had been coming and going from an adjoining room.

Turning, he met Casey's gaze. He doubted that the two of them were the only ones who remembered Megan's perfume, but whoever had left the note had been targeting her. Targeting them both. "The person could have gone out the window. Or wanted us to think they did."

"I'm sorry I thought it was you," she said.

He nodded, still upset that she didn't trust him. "Whoever did this might have wanted to come between us. Isn't that what Megan had done with you and your grandmother? If so, it almost worked." He raked his fingers through his hair again. "This could be all for the reunion." But even as he said it, he remembered those sleepless nights when he'd heard things and been convinced he wasn't alone.

"If they did it to scare me, they're wasting their time. I'm leaving as soon as I can." She met his gaze. "Maybe I'm not moving fast enough to suit them."

"I think they don't want you to trust me," he said, holding her gaze. "We both know who might benefit from that."

CHAPTER SEVENTEEN

"DEVLIN?" CASEY SHOOK her head. "He knows I'm selling the hotel to you. Let me see the note." She'd barely glanced at it before, but now she felt a start as she recognized the handwriting. It was the same as the message that had been left on her bathroom mirror.

She felt Finn's gaze on her.

"Casey? Is something wrong?"

It was on the tip of her tongue. *Tell him. He isn't going to stop until he learns the truth.* "I don't think it was Devlin." She thought of the offers he'd made her just that morning. Not his handwriting.

"Maybe it's someone who doesn't want the truth to come out," he said.

Maybe. What if the person who left the message on her mirror believed that she'd read the diary and that Megan had named her killer? Was the perfume stunt just another warning? Except, this time, whoever had written the note had involved Finn. To make her not trust him so she wouldn't tell him?

For ten years, she'd lived with her secret. But she couldn't keep lying, especially to Finn. She opened her mouth, the words just lying there on her tongue. Releasing them seemed so easy.

But they weren't what came out. "You're the only one who still cares what happened to Megan." The words were tinged with bitterness and jealousy and anger and, of course, guilt. Look at the trouble he'd gone to for Megan. Months in this old hotel.

And he still wouldn't let it go. It made her angry that anyone could care that much about Megan, especially Finn. Especially since Casey had nothing but contempt for her.

Finn looked as if she'd slapped him, and then, slowly, he nodded. "You're right. In all these years the killer hasn't been caught. The marshal who got the call that night has retired, and while the case might still be open because there's no statute of limitations on murder, no one is actively looking. Except for me. You're just wrong about why I'm doing this." He settled a look on her that sent shivers down her spine.

Stepping to her, he took her shoulders in his big hands. "I might be the only one looking for the truth, but someone sure is going to a lot of trouble to make us think Megan's ghost is in this hotel. I'm afraid it's a distraction for what's really going on behind the scenes. Whoever is behind this, they don't want you and me together. Why is that?"

FINN LOOKED INTO Casey's blue eyes. She couldn't have been more beautiful right now, her cheeks flushed, those blue eyes glittering bright, her bow-shaped lips slightly parted.

She looked so damned kissable. He felt that pull again— just as he had in the tower earlier. "Why would anyone care about keeping us apart?" she asked.

Their gazes locked, and it was as if all the air in the room had been sucked out. "They're worried that we know more than we do." But at this moment, he didn't care what their motives might be. That alone was sending up a red flag. *Abort! You can't get involved with this woman. Not now.*

"The person must know that you're determined to find Megan's killer," she said.

He swore under his breath. She still thought this was about Megan. He ignored the warnings flashing in his brain as he drew her to him. There were no words that would convince her he'd gotten over Megan a long time ago.

Casey Crenshaw? That was a whole other story, and one he wanted desperately to delve into. Her eyes widened as he pulled her to him, needing to hold her, to taste her, to show her how he felt—even knowing that the timing couldn't have been worse.

She came to him, her body molding against his. He could feel the thunder of her pulse so like his own. He wanted this woman with every fiber of his being. He looked into her eyes. She wanted to trust him, but even though he could see that she was afraid she shouldn't, desire flamed in those blue eyes.

If she kept looking at him like that, he was going to sweep her up in his arms and carry her to his room and ravage her. The door to the room slammed closed as if caught by the wind.

Casey started and pulled free of his arms as a cold breeze stirred her hair and then his own. He felt the chill all the way to his bones. It was as if Megan had brushed past them both, coming between them.

CASEY COULDN'T BELIEVE how close she'd come to surrendering to the powerful desire Finn had lit inside her. She felt shaken as she stepped back to rub away the cold chill that had circled her neck.

"It seems I need to check the windows around here," she said as she shivered. She knew she hadn't fooled Finn. He'd felt it, too. She wondered how many windows in the hotel were open, causing the drafts. In a few days, it wouldn't be her problem.

She could feel Finn looking at her. He must be thinking the same thing she was: how close that had been. "That wasn't Megan. There are no ghosts."

"Just keep telling yourself that," he said and chuckled softly. She could hear the desire still thick in his voice. He cleared his throat. "Bad timing."

She nodded. They stood almost awkwardly now. She still felt an aching need inside her, a raging desire that he'd set ablaze. If he touched her right now... "So who do you think it is, the person trying to come between us?"

From his smile, she knew that he'd thought of Megan when the door had slammed, when that cold breeze had brushed past them. "Not a ghost."

"No," she agreed, even though if the door hadn't slammed when it did, she could very well have been in one of these rooms naked in Finn's arms. Just the thought sent a tremor through her. It would have been just like Megan to keep them apart. If Casey believed in ghosts.

DEVLIN COULDN'T REMEMBER the last time he'd drunk this much or been this sick. "Just shoot me," he said to the empty hotel room. He'd opted for his own room without a roommate and was glad of it now. He thought he might die as he lay half-naked on the bathroom floor waiting to heave again.

Why had he drunk so much?

The answer came back to him in a wave of nausea: the conversation at the bar earlier about who'd been in the woods the night Megan died. Jason had been going around the table trying to remember the timeline they'd told the marshal.

"Devlin," he'd said as if forgetting for a moment that he was even there, "what were you doing in the woods that night?" The way Jason asked it, the words intimated that he was a loser who wasn't out there with a girl, so what did that leave?

"I was taking a whiz," he'd said and motioned to the bartender for another beer since, after all, Jason was buying.

"Oh, right, sure," Jason had said, making it sound as if Devlin had been lying. "And Benjamin—"

"I'd stepped away to do the same thing," Benjamin had said quickly.

"Amazing that you two didn't piss on each other," Jason had said and laughed.

"So Jen and Shirley had gone to get more beer. Megan and Casey had been at the fire. Jen and Shirley returned. Shirley…" He'd stopped and looked over at her.

Shirley had been staring down at her beer as if knowing he would be coming to her soon. She'd told him the same thing she had the marshal ten years ago, she'd said. "I was sick in the car coming back with the beer. I didn't want to go all the way back to my room, so I went through the trees down to the creek and washed up as best I could. I was on my way back, turned around and a little lost, when I found Megan." Shirley had looked relieved when Jason took her at her word and moved on.

He looked at Jen. "I was at the fire. Casey was there. Maybe she saw Megan wander into the woods. I didn't really notice."

Jason nodded. "Now, if we just knew what Claude had been doing."

"I think we already do," Patience had said and ordered

another round. Shirley had said she needed food, and the others had agreed.

Devlin left them to hit the bathroom. When he returned, he noticed that his cell phone was lying on the bar but not where he'd left it. He picked it up, feeling as if someone had opened it. Anyone at the bar could have seen him put in his passcode.

"I'll buy the ingredients for taco salad," Jason was saying magnanimously as Devlin had looked around at the others. Only one met his gaze: Jen. She smiled as if everything was fine. Or was it a knowing smile?

"Just tell me what to buy," Jason said as he borrowed a pen and pad from the bartender and began to make a list. "Who's up for making it back at the kitchen?"

Devlin ordered another drink as Jason and Patience climbed off their bar stools to head to the store, with the others following shortly after them.

That had been hours ago. Why hadn't he left the bar with them?

FINN STILL FELT shaken because he'd almost kissed Casey, something he'd been wanting to do since the first time he'd laid eyes on her. He'd come so close. And then that damned door had slammed.

He shook his head. Not even Megan's ghost was going to keep them apart. But, given the note, someone was certainly trying to come between them, someone human and alive. He had to question the person's motive—and how far they would go.

For months, he'd believed he was alone in the hotel— just him and the ghosts. It hadn't been his imagination that he wasn't. Had someone been trying to chase him away?

Failing that, were they now trying to do the same with him and Casey?

"Whoever is behind the note and the perfume, they're after something," he said and saw that he'd hit a nerve. "They're clearly trying to divide us." Divide and conquer, he thought as he realized that the person's agenda could quite possibly be at cross-purposes to his own. He'd been looking for Megan's killer. "If the killer thought that you knew something that could help me..." He saw the color drain from her face for a moment. "Casey?"

"I can't help you," she said a little too quickly. "Nor can I imagine why anyone would think that." She looked nervous and upset.

He swore under his breath. Shit, she did know something. Or at least the killer thought she did. "If Megan's killer even thought you had information—"

"I don't." She took another step back. "I really need to get back to what I was doing."

Finn nodded, angry at himself but even more angry with the situation. Whoever wanted to come between them, it was working. He could feel her pulling away. Worse, he had no doubt now that she knew something. He just worried it could get her killed.

She started to turn away, but he put his hand on her arm to stop her. "Casey, we have to pull together. You can trust me."

CASEY MET HIS GAZE, furious with herself. Finn knew that she was holding back. She saw it in his eyes. Someone knew she'd taken the diary. If Megan suspected who had wanted to kill her and had written it down... If the killer thought Casey had read it… Was the killer worried that the one person she might confess the truth to would be Finn?

Then the killer would be right, she realized.

She stared into his handsome face and knew that he was right. They needed to stick together—and she did trust him. Someone wanted her to think she couldn't trust him because of the note. It made her angry that she'd played right into the person's hands.

"There's something I need to tell you." But even as she said it, she knew that telling him about the diary could be the one thing that could divide them.

She felt a tug at her heartstrings. She didn't want to see his disappointment when she told him. How could he ever trust her after she'd lied to everyone about the diary? He'd saved her, by being here when she needed someone desperately. He'd done nothing but help her. He was buying the hotel and land, paying her more than Devlin had offered. He'd provided a barrier between her and the town and the reunion staff.

If there was one person here she could trust, it was Finn. Except maybe not with her heart.

"I did something I've regretted—"

Patience's voice startled her and Finn as well. They both turned to see her coming toward them. From the look on her face, she'd heard at least some of what they'd been talking about.

CHAPTER EIGHTEEN

"WE WERE LOOKING for you two," Patience said when she reached them. She had a quizzical expression on her face, making Finn wonder how much of their conversation she'd overheard. "Dinner's ready. Taco salad. We set a place for both of you. Now we're just trying to find Devlin. Jason went to his room, but he wasn't there."

"Haven't seen him," Finn said, his thoughts more with Casey. She'd just been about to tell him something. From her tone, it was important. "Is he missing?"

Patience shrugged. "He was hitting it hard at the bar, and now nobody can find him. Oh, well, more food for us." Finn noticed that she seemed jittery, revved up somehow. She was fingering the necklace at her throat.

Finn shot a look at Casey. He could see relief on her face as she said, "Taco salad sounds good." Whatever she had been about to tell him was going to have to wait. She'd just found an excuse to put it off. He didn't want to push it, not now, not in front of Patience, but he wouldn't let it go.

"New necklace?" Casey asked.

Patience let go of the turquoise charm at the end of the chain. "You like it? I found it at the antiques barn. Jen said it's supposed to ward off evil."

"Some people will believe anything," Jason said as he found them. Finn saw the exchange between Jason and Patience. Something was definitely going on there. "No Devlin, though. I'm sure he'll turn up."

"Well, Shirley's dishing up, so we'd all better get in the kitchen," Patience said and led the way in, Jason behind her and Finn and Casey bringing up the rear.

"Just like old times," Jen said when she saw them. "Except the food is better than what we used to make ourselves. Wish I could say the same for the company," she joked and smiled across the table at Benjamin.

"Didn't know I could cook, did you?" Patience said, giving Jason a hip bump before taking a seat at the table.

"You're full of surprises," Jason said as he sat down next to her. "I never know what to expect."

Casey moved to one of the four empty seats, and Finn joined her. Patience was toying with the turquoise charm at her neck again and clearly flirting with Jason and vice versa. Finn didn't like the weird vibe in the room.

As he looked around the table, he could see that everyone appeared tired, some a little sunburned from their day exploring town and most a little tipsy. Jason looked as if he was feeling no pain. Finn suspected he'd spent more time at the bar than even the others.

"So what's everyone been up to all day?" he asked. Someone had come back to the hotel to not only leave the note but also set up the perfume stunt.

"We took in Buckhorn," Patience said. "That took us, what, ten minutes?" She laughed a little too hard and exchanged a grin with Jason.

"Oh, come on. It took longer than ten minutes," Jen said. "Stop bad-mouthing Buckhorn."

"It only took longer than ten minutes because of the ice-cream shop," Jason said.

Patience chuckled. "I *did* love the ice-cream shop and sitting outside watching the early tourists. That was fun. Then we shopped some at the antiques barn and general store, before meeting up with everyone else at the bar and having a few beers," Patience said, possibly explaining why she was so talkative.

The taco-salad bowl came to him. Finn let Casey take some before he helped himself and passed it on.

"What about you?"

Casey looked up as if surprised Patience had directed the question at her. "I spent the day collecting a few things of my grandmother's."

"You could have come along," Jen said. "We needed someone who could beat Patience at pool. She and Jason hustled up all the old men in the bar."

"We made eighty dollars." Patience pulled out a wad of money from her jeans pocket. "Not bad for a day on the town."

Casey's smile never reached her eyes, Finn noticed. "So you two are pool sharks?" He got the feeling that she'd noticed Patience fingering the necklace and had picked up on her odd behavior.

Patience shook her head and finished chewing the bite she'd taken. "We have a pool table in the man cave at home."

"You're married," Finn said, realizing for the first time that she was wearing a wedding ring. He'd just assumed they were all single or divorced.

"I'm practically a newlywed."

"You didn't bring your husband," Casey said.

"Gracious, no," Patience cried. "He'd be bored to tears. Anyway, it was only for the staff…" Her gaze landed on Finn. "And Finn," she added quickly and then frowned.

"You never really explained why you were invited, though, did you? Or did I miss it?"

"He knew Megan," Jason said between bites.

Patience mugged a face at him. "I'm sure a lot of people knew Megan, and they're not here."

"My father and I worked for her family, landscaping, so I knew Megan that summer before she came out here." He shrugged. "But as it turned out, coming here was the best thing I've ever done."

Both Jason and Benjamin guffawed at that. "Yes, aside from making your fortune before forty."

Finn ignored them. Instead, he looked over at Casey. "I met Casey and am buying this hotel and property—once we sign the papers."

"I guess that's why Devlin was knocking them back at the bar," Jen said.

"Probably also why he isn't here," Jason added.

The room grew uncomfortably quiet for a few moments. "So you all went shopping?" Finn asked, looking at Jason.

"Yeah, right. Devlin and I drank and played pool at the bar until the girls showed up and showed us up." He laughed at his play on words.

Finn looked to Benjamin.

"Patience and I prowled around in the antiques barn until Shirley dragged us to the bar."

Shifting his gaze to Shirley, Finn hated that she seemed to realize that he was interrogating everyone. But his instincts told him that one of them had come back here to write the note to make Casey not trust him. He really wanted to know who it had been—and why.

"Me next? I had to check in at the motel. Some of us still have jobs," Shirley said, sounding defensive.

"What's with all the questions?" Jason asked, frowning down the table at him.

"Just curious what you all found to do in Buckhorn," Finn said, realizing Jen hadn't weighed in. Also, Devlin wasn't the only one missing, he realized. Claude wasn't here, either.

But before he could ask, Jason stopped eating to look at him and asked, "What did *you* find to do?"

"I spent most of the day making the necessary calls that go along with buying a hotel," Finn said. "The rest of the day I did more exploring—which reminds me," he said, turning to Casey. "I couldn't find a key to get down to the basement."

She frowned. "I can look later," she said and pretended interest in her dinner plate. "This taco salad is delicious."

"Okay, truth? Shirley did most of the cooking part," Jason said. "The rest of us just did some of the chopping, at least the ones who hadn't had too much to drink."

"Claude's not joining us?" Finn asked.

"The last time I saw him was at the campfire last night," Jason said and shrugged.

"That's right. He wasn't at breakfast," Jen said. "Or at the bar."

"Anyone see him in town?" Finn asked. There was a general shaking of heads. "No one has seen him since last night?" He shifted his gaze to Jen.

"Don't look at me. I left him at the campfire when Shirley and I came into the hotel to find a room. We never left the room after that."

He turned to Shirley, who didn't look up from her plate, which told him everything he needed to know. Jen had just lied about staying in all night. "What was Claude driving?" Jason told him. Getting up, he excused himself to go down the hall to the service door where he scanned the parking lot.

"His rental car's gone," Jason said, suddenly next to him, startling him. "But Devlin's rig is still here, so he couldn't have gone far, although he's not in his room." Finn let go of the door and turned back toward the kitchen.

"No one saw Claude leave?" he asked when he and Jason returned to the kitchen. There was general agreement around the table that no one had seen him drive away last night.

"I left him down at the campfire," Jason said. "Everyone else had already gone in. Devlin was right in front of me. Claude was saying he wished he hadn't come back, didn't know why he had. He kept saying the poor little rich girl had ruined his life. Given the mood he was in, I guess I'm not surprised that he left."

If Claude was the last one around the campfire, then it had to have been late. Also, Claude had appeared drunk. "I hate to think he was on the road in the middle of the night driving after drinking," Finn said. But if Claude had been in an accident, they would have heard by now, wouldn't they?

The room had gone quiet again. "Sounds like he bailed on us," Patience said.

"Well, look at the bright side," Jason said. "If Claude killed Megan, now he's gone."

"Why would you even say that?" Jen demanded.

"Because we all kind of had to show up, didn't we? Claude shows up and leaves right away. Seems like a no-brainer to me," Jason finished.

"Don't you think that's kind of a leap?" Shirley asked.

"She's right, but if it was Claude," Patience said, "well,

then, I'm glad he's gone. You have to admit, he was acting oddly."

Jason nodded in agreement. "Clearly, he's never gotten
over Megan, that's for sure."

"Unlike the rest of us," Benjamin said sarcastically.

"I suppose if he killed her, that would explain it," Patience said.

Jen made a disgusted sound and shoved away her
almost-empty plate. "His leaving doesn't mean that he's the
killer." But she didn't put up much of an argument. None of
the others joined in. If anything, they all seemed relieved
that Claude was gone.

DEVLIN WOKE ON the bathroom floor in the dark. He pulled
himself up and grimaced at the smell. How long had he
been lying here? A long time, since it seemed to be dark
outside. Through the open doorway he could see shadows
filling the room.

Getting to his feet, he turned on the light and blinked.
This wasn't his bathroom. A shot of adrenaline rocketed
through him, chasing off the hangover for a moment. Where
the hell was he?

He stumbled into the adjoining room, turned on a light
and looked around. This wasn't his room. Except it looked
enough like it that he figured at least he was still in the
Crenshaw Hotel, although he had no idea how he'd gotten
here. He must have only thought he was drunk and sick
and full of regrets in his own room.

The regrets were still there, but he was no longer drunk
and, for the moment, not feeling that sick. He looked down,
surprised to find himself dressed. Had he gone out some-

where after passing out earlier? He'd never been blackout drunk before. Until now.

He moved to the door and opened it to peer down the hallway. The hotel seemed unusually quiet. It felt really late. Since he didn't seem to have his phone, he had no idea how late. He noticed the room numbers. Apparently he hadn't gone far. He was still on the staff wing.

Devlin could hear voices in the kitchen. As quietly as possible, he tiptoed down the hallway to his room. The door was ajar. He looked in, wondering if anyone had come looking for him. The overhead light was on, but he could have left it that way.

Everything seemed to be where he'd left it. He stepped in, closing the door quietly and locking it before leaning against it for a moment. Through the open window he could smell the scent of rain. The wind lifted the drapes. In the distance he could see storm clouds. A thunderstorm was on its way.

Spying his cell phone, he stepped to the bed and picked it up. More messages and calls from the investors. For a moment, he just stared at it. Then he checked his bank account and swore. He had enough that he could run. Not far, but maybe far enough that he could start over somewhere. Do something else. Be someone else.

The lease at the apartment was in his girlfriend's name. There was really nothing tying him down anywhere. He doubted she would be surprised when he didn't return. It was one reason she'd wanted the lease in her name. She hadn't trusted him even when things had been going well between them. Not that he could blame her.

He'd never felt more like a loser. It made no sense. In high school he'd been voted most likely to succeed. He was smart, got good grades, had his whole life ahead of him the summer he'd taken the job here at the hotel before he planned to head to college.

He thought of Claude and some of the others. They blamed Megan for their failings. Devlin scoffed at that. Even with her head trips, she hadn't been what had led him to this point. He'd just assumed he would succeed, as if it was written in the stars.

Now he could see that he'd been waiting the past ten years for it to happen. Not that he'd been doing badly. He had a degree in business, drove a nice car that would be paid off in four years and still had most of his hair.

Who was he kidding? His life wasn't supposed to turn out like this. He'd thought he'd be like Finn, rich by forty. He wished he could blame Megan. But she'd spotted him for the loser he was and called him on it. He'd been angry. Who wouldn't be? Once she was dead, though, he'd put her behind him.

Just like he would put all of this behind him and move on. It was something he was good at. Maybe the only thing.

Which meant he had no intention of being here in the morning. He'd just started to pack when he heard a sound and turned to see that someone had shoved what appeared to be a note under his door. He listened but didn't hear anything before he moved to pick up the piece of paper.

Written on it were the words *Meet me in the woods—now*.

He realized with a start that someone knew about the note he'd seen lying on the ground next to Megan's dead body. He'd stupidly started to pick it up but had quickly dropped it when he saw the blood on it. He'd stepped away from it as the others had joined them.

Someone must have found it, must have seen him pick

it up and drop it, and now they were thinking they could blackmail him? He laughed. "Can't get blood out of a turnip." His head hurt too much to try to make sense of it. For years, he'd lived in fear that the note would turn up—with his fingerprints and Megan's blood on it.

All he knew right now was that he had to get out of here. He wadded up the note and shoved it into his pocket rather than leave it in the trash. He hurriedly packed, already thinking that he would reinvent himself once he left Montana.

His phone dinged as he got a text. He ignored it, figuring it was one of the investors. It dinged again. And again.

With a curse, he pulled his cell from the pocket of his jeans and read I'm waiting. He didn't recognize the number, but he did the photo that accompanied it, even though the snapshot was grainy and dark—except for Megan's white dress and long blond hair. Still, there was no doubt about who was with her—a younger version of himself. He had his hands around her neck as he forcefully held her backed up against a tree. She looked as if she was fighting to pull away.

In truth, she'd been laughing, her head thrown back. She'd been literally asking for it, but whoever had taken this didn't know that. So maybe it wasn't about the note. Either way, they had something they thought they could hold over him.

He stared at the photo for a moment and then finished packing and sneaked out of the hotel, taking his suitcase down to his car before he headed into the woods. Best end this before he left.

POOR LITTLE RICH GIRL? Jen scoffed silently at that. Everything about Megan smelled of money, from the way she looked, to her clothes, to her perfume. Especially her perfume. Jen had never forgotten that scent. The scent had reached her long before Megan had that first day. She remembered breathing it in as if it were rarefied oxygen. In one whiff, it had embodied everything Jen wasn't and never could be.

She had yearned for Megan's carefree confidence, the way she went through the world as if nothing could touch her up there so high above it all. Above the rest of them.

Jen remembered the day Megan's perfume order had come in at her aunt's general store.

"Don't touch that," Vi had barked. "That little bottle is worth more than you make in a year."

It wasn't quite that expensive. Jen had had to use all of her savings, though, to buy a tiny vial of it. She still took it out sometimes and put it on, closing her eyes and pretending. All it took was just a drop of it—the perfume was that potent.

The fantasy lasted only moments, though, leaving her feeling gutted, because as soon as she opened her eyes, she was faced with the truth. Not even Megan's perfume would make Jen Mullen special.

Wasn't that exactly what Megan had told her when she'd caught Jen in her room wearing not just her perfume but her white sundress—the same one Megan had later died in?

CHAPTER NINETEEN

CASEY STAYED BEHIND to clean the kitchen after everyone had an excuse to leave earlier. Jen had excused herself to go to the bathroom, no doubt an excuse to get out of dishes since she hadn't come back. Shirley had said she didn't feel well and was going to her room. Patience said there was something she had to do as well, and the guys had all left to look for Devlin—at least, that was their excuse for getting out of chores.

She didn't mind doing dishes, actually. It was mindless work that let her sort out her thoughts. She'd picked up on whatever was going on with Patience and Jason. It made her think of the expression *Misery makes strange bedfellows*. She knew that Finn had noticed, too. It bothered her that Claude had left, though. Now everyone was thinking he was the killer and for no real reason. What would they say when *she* left?

She was through cleaning up the kitchen when Jen returned. "You going down to the campfire again tonight?"

Casey shook her head. "I have too much to do."

Jen laughed. "I don't blame you for not wanting anything to do with this reunion. Bad memories, huh?" Casey said nothing, concentrating on folding up the dish towel in her hand. "Patience and Jason have come up with games, they said. Probably more truth or dare. Like anyone tells the truth."

Casey was straightening up the condiments on the table when she saw the scrap of paper someone had stuck under the ketchup bottle. As she pulled it out, she froze. It was a list of ingredients, she saw, for taco salad. She recognized the handwriting—the same as the writing on her bathroom mirror and on the note that was supposedly from Finn.

"Looks like someone's grocery list," she said, holding it up.

Jen glanced at it and laughed as she took the list. "Jason's. He misspelled *chipotle*?" She shook her head as she wadded up the list and tossed it into the trash. Turning on her phone, she began to dance to the music as she checked the refrigerator and then the cupboards. She found a bottle of hotel wine and held it up.

Casey nodded her assent. She still owned the hotel, so she guessed it was hers to share. She noticed how at home Jen seemed here in the hotel. She'd found the corkscrew on her first try.

But then again, she lived in Buckhorn. She might have spent a lot of time in the hotel over the years that Casey had been gone.

"I think I'll take this with me, then," Jen said and left.

When Casey had begged off the campfire, saying she still had a lot to do, she'd been telling the truth. She wanted to find a few more items on her grandmother's list before taking that hot bubble bath she'd been dreaming of and turning in early. It still hadn't sunk in that with the stroke of a pen she would have sold the hotel. And the Crenshaw would no longer be hers.

She wondered if Finn had found Devlin. She knew he wanted to question him about Claude. It did seem odd that Claude would have left without telling anyone.

As she started to leave the kitchen, she saw Jason and Patience going down the hallway. Jason whispered something and reached for Patience's hand. She quickly closed her palm as if to hide a note he gave her.

Casey watched as the young woman waited until Jason left before she opened her palm and took out the note. Patience smiled as she quickly read it and pocketed the scrap of paper before she headed toward the back door.

Of course it had been Jason who'd written the messages. But why? Maybe just to keep things interesting for him. Like Megan, it amused him to cause trouble.

As for Patience and Jason, what were those two up to? Probably just hooking up, but still, Casey was curious. Hadn't Patience said she was practically a newlywed? Casey watched her exit the back door and run across the parking lot, past the firepit and into the woods. It seemed odd that anyone would suggest meeting in the trees after what had happened to Megan.

Letting the door close, Casey started to go up the back stairs when she heard someone coming. She froze, just out of view, not wanting to get caught snooping.

Jason seemed to be in a hurry as he rushed out. She didn't need to go to the back door to see where he was headed. But she did anyway. He crossed the parking lot, hurried past the pit and disappeared into the woods—only minutes behind Patience. Why meet in the woods when they had a hotel full of empty beds?

She remembered that Patience had been almost giddy at dinner. Casey had assumed she'd had too much to drink and that had explained both her actions and the flush to the young woman's cheeks.

But now she recalled ten years ago when Jason had put

a flush in her own cheeks—before he dumped her. The thought made her turn back to the hotel and the list. She needed to get away from here and the mistakes she'd made ten years ago and these people who she suspected were still playing games with each other—just as Megan had taught them.

Hurrying upstairs, she changed her mind about looking for more of the heirlooms tonight. After a bubble bath, she wrapped herself in her robe and pulled out the list to see how much she had left to find. Too much. She set the list aside as she stepped to the window. The group had gathered around the campfire. She noticed that Jason and Patience had joined them. The scene appeared to have taken on a party-like atmosphere again sans Claude and Devlin.

Casey watched for a moment from her partially opened window. She could smell the smoke, hear the crackle of the fire when it wasn't being drowned out by laughter and chatter. She could tell that everyone seemed more relaxed. Because Claude was gone? Devlin as well?

She caught the scent of rain on the breeze and looked to the west, where thunderclouds had formed over the mountains. She'd just closed the window when her cell phone rang, making her jump. Her phone was lying on her bed. She stepped to it. "Hello?"

"Hey, Casey." It was Finn on the phone. She felt a wave of warmth move through her before she remembered where they'd left their earlier conversation. He'd had to leave right after dinner tonight because of an important call. "I ran down to the store before it closed. I got this craving for cookie-dough ice cream."

"Seriously?"

"Don't laugh. Can I pick up anything for you? I'll share my ice cream if you're interested. I don't know about you, but I had to have a treat."

She could hear the noise of traffic and voices in the background. "Cookie-dough ice cream sounds great. Let me know when you get back."

There was a smile in his voice when he spoke. "You got it."

She disconnected, smiling to herself. Why did the man have to be so darned sweet? That was when she heard the footfalls outside her door.

Not again, she told herself as she looked around for her shoulder bag—and the gun inside it. But this time the footfalls continued on past her door without stopping.

She stood listening, holding her breath. It could have been anyone, she told herself even as she checked to see who was at the fire. The same people as before except for Claude and Devlin.

She felt a shudder at the thought of being alone in the hotel with either of them. Because one of them knew the truth? Her gaze flew to her bathroom mirror. The words were gone and yet she still saw them clearly in her mind. *I know what you did*

Down the hall, a door slammed. Her drapes blew in on a gust of wind, bringing the scent of rain as the sky darkened. She moved to close the window.

She'd just changed into jeans and a T-shirt when her cell phone made her jump again. She snatched it up. "Hello?"

"I'm down in the kitchen," Finn said without preamble. "One or two scoops?"

"Two. I'm on my way." She disconnected and looked around the room. Her mouth felt dry, her limbs weak. Finn was right. Someone was manipulating them both. He had no idea why. But Casey thought she did as she headed for the kitchen and Finn.

IT HAD BEEN IMPULSIVE, calling Casey from the store. He'd wanted to get her alone after their talk earlier had been interrupted. But that wasn't the only reason he'd called her. He'd had a bad feeling after he and Jason hadn't found Devlin.

He'd assumed everyone would be down at the campfire, leaving her alone in that monstrous place. If Devlin and Claude had really left. If one or both of them hadn't pulled the note and perfume stunts. If there wasn't more going on here than it appeared. He didn't trust any of them.

Everyone was a little too quick to blame Claude. It made Finn nervous to think that if Claude hadn't really left, he could come back and do whatever damage he wanted without any of them being the wiser.

Finn had been concerned that Casey might be a target from the moment he'd realized she hadn't sent the reunion invitations—and that some of the staff seemed to have some animosity toward her. He'd never met her grandmother, but he knew she would have wanted him to keep Casey safe.

At the same time, he found himself getting in deeper and deeper with her. That almost kiss had only made him realize just how deep. Hell, he'd half fallen in love with her from what her grandmother had written about her over those years when they'd been together in this hotel.

Once he'd met her… He thought of her standing at the open shower holding that gun on him. He chuckled to himself. It was simple. The woman had enchanted him because of the stories he'd heard about her. Once he'd met her, he'd been smitten. He'd never once thought she could have murdered Megan. Even now, knowing that she was holding back something, he still didn't.

He'd been hiding out for months, using Megan as an excuse not to take that next challenge after he'd sold his business. He'd lost both parents, lost his drive. He'd dropped out of life. Then Casey Crenshaw had walked into his shower.

Finn had felt the chemistry and suspected she had, too, even as she was threatening to have him arrested for trespassing. She'd made him want to join the human race again. Making an offer on the hotel had forced him to come out of hiding. He knew it wouldn't be long before the media found out. He wasn't looking forward to the headlines again, but he could handle it.

But now he could feel the clock ticking. The reunion would be over after tomorrow. Casey might be planning to leave as soon as she'd packed up her grandmother's things. That was one of the reasons he'd called her from the store. He felt alive when he was with her. He wanted to spend as much time as he could with her.

He'd also really been craving cookie-dough ice cream.

He was just glad it had gotten her out of her room. Now, if she would just tell him what it was she was hiding.

At a sound, he turned, a smile instantly coming to his face at just the sight of her in the doorway. "Two scoops," he said as he finished filling their bowls.

"I know who left the note that got us to Megan's old room," she said as she watched him. He turned to look back at her. "Jason. I recognized his handwriting from a grocery list he made." Finn swore. "Who knows why? He was probably just trying to stir things up. He seems to be enjoying this reunion a little too much."

"He's jealous."

She stared at him. "What?"

"You haven't seen the way he looks at you?"

She shook her head. "You are so wrong."

Finn looked as if he wanted to argue the point but let it drop as he handed her a bowl of ice cream. "Want to sit in here or out in the main hall?"

"Here is good," she said, glancing around the large industrial kitchen before moving to one of the chairs at the staff table.

"This is where I ate all my meals," she said as he took a seat at the corner of the table near her.

"You didn't eat in the dining room with your grandmother?"

She shook her head. "Not a chance. It was hard enough with the rest of the staff when I ate with them. They were always careful about what they said around me for fear I'd tell Gram on them. They knew right away that I wasn't one of them. And yet I was. I complained once early on to her about one of the staff and found out quickly enough that it wasn't allowed. She used to say getting along with the crew was the best experience I could ask for. She was right. It's helped me with managing a large hotel. I use a lot of her methods to deal with my staff."

"I was in the same situation working with my father in his landscaping business," Finn said between bites. "I quickly learned not to be the son of the boss. It's a good way to get your butt kicked." He laughed. "Also, it keeps you humble to know that, when push comes to shove, you'll be let go before one of your father's valuable employees. Nothing like life's lessons, huh?" he said, lifting his spoon as if in a salute before taking another bite of ice cream.

"You didn't take over your father's business."

"No. It wasn't what I wanted to do. He took it pretty well. I knew he'd built it up for me, and I appreciated that, but I wanted something else." He met her gaze. "You enjoy what you do?"

She chuckled. "Most days, I do. After college, getting into hotel management just seemed like the thing to do. It's all I really knew. There is always something that needs my attention. The days just fly by."

"I would imagine it was like that here for your grand-mother."

Casey nodded. "She was definitely busy, but she thrived on it." She looked around the kitchen for a moment before she took another bite of ice cream.

"Are you sad about selling it?"

She nodded without looking up. "I would have loved to keep her legacy alive, but even if I had the resources to keep this old place going, I'm not sure there are enough guests who are looking for this experience in Buckhorn, Montana." After a moment, she met his gaze across the table. "You haven't said what you're going to do with it."

"I still really don't know," he said with a laugh. "But I'm not sorry. And Devlin and his investors are never going to get it."

Casey smiled at that, their gazes locking across the table. Finn felt his heart expand as if filled with helium. Her cheeks seemed to heat before she glanced down at her ice cream again. "This is good. Thank you."

"Glad you were up for it. It wouldn't be half as much fun eating it alone down here." He glanced around the kitchen. "I can't say this place has grown on me, although I do have a greater respect for haunted hotels."

She cocked her head at him, seemingly glad for a change in subject that wasn't quite so personal. "You aren't going to start that again, are you?"

He shook his head. "Guess you'll have to experience the ghosts yourself. Or not. Depends on how long you end up staying."

"Not long enough for the ghosts to know I'm here, I hope," she joked.

He watched her finish her ice cream. A lot of it had melted since she was eating it so slowly. Stalling? Because she liked his company as much as he liked hers?

"Did something happen while I was gone?" he asked, eyeing her. He'd heard something in her tone. "What was it? The noises?" He shook his head. "You are probably used to them since it wasn't that long ago that you stayed here summers. This place was an antique even then. No, I'm guessing it was the footsteps." There was the slightest flicker in her eyes. He nodded, chuckling as he got up to rinse out his bowl.

"It wasn't a ghost," she said to his back. She finished her ice cream and brought her bowl over. He took it from her, washed it, and as he dried his hands, he leaned against the counter, facing her.

"I just know there were nights when I wanted to be anywhere but in this hotel," he said. "The good news is that whoever, whatever, is walking the hallways, it doesn't seem to be dangerous."

"And if you're wrong about that?" He realized that she was more upset than he'd originally thought.

She started to turn away. He grabbed her arm, turning her to face him. The fear he saw on her face made him catch his breath. "I'm sorry I joked about it. So tell me exactly what happened."

She looked defiant for a moment but sighed and told him a story that matched his own experience. "Someone is trying awfully hard to convince me Megan's ghost is in the hotel. Most everyone was down by the fire. So the footsteps I heard outside my door? It had to be Claude or Devlin."

"IT HAD TO be one of them," Casey said again. She could see that Finn didn't believe it, making her more determined. "Who else knew about the perfume except one of the staff?"

"You think Claude and Devlin knew the kind of perfume Megan wore?"

"Maybe not, but Jason did. Also, Megan had the general store here order more of her so-called signature perfume when her bottle got broken. It's really expensive, so someone at the store would have remembered, if either of them had asked."

He looked at her as if he wanted to argue the point, which only irritated her. She needed him to agree. She needed it to be Claude or Devlin. "Isn't it possible Claude only pretended to leave? Or Devlin is still around somewhere, hiding?"

"That has crossed my mind."

At the sound of agitated voices, they both turned toward the kitchen doorway. They could hear everyone come rushing into the hotel and quickly moved to the doorway to see what was going on.

"We just saw Megan's ghost!" Jason announced, sounding winded. The others joined in, all of their voices too high, too animated. She stared at them, seeing both flushed faces and pale ones.

"She ran through the woods, but not before we'd all seen

her," Jen said, hugging herself. She appeared to be shaking. Next to her, all the color had drained from Shirley's face.

"Show me where you saw her," Finn said as he approached the group.

"I'll take you to the exact spot," Jason said and turned to push through everyone toward the door. "Ben and I ran into the woods, but she was gone."

"I'll go with you," Benjamin said. No one else moved.

Casey found herself looking at each of them, trying to tell if this was some joke they'd cooked up. They looked scared. Jen was kind of jumping on the balls of her feet as if not sure what to do with the sudden energy spike. Shirley just looked numb. Even Patience appeared worried, her back against the hallway wall, her arms crossed over her chest. She cut her eyes to Casey as if sensing that she was being watched. "I think we should all get out of here."

The hallway felt alive with fear as Casey stepped past them and headed for the back door. She didn't believe in ghosts. She kept telling herself that as she pushed open the door and spilled out onto the walkway.

There was no one around the campfire as she crossed the large parking lot. Flames rose, and sparks hovered in the air before blinking out. In the dark of the trees, nothing moved. She stood there for a moment before she began to walk toward the woods. The trees behind the hotel and out-buildings were dense. As dark as the night was, it would be black in there. Unless they'd taken a flashlight…

She'd passed the firepit and started into the woods, won-dering how she would ever find the men, when she saw a light bobbing along the ground in the pines. Stopping, she waited as the men came out. Finn was holding the flash-light as they exited the woods. She realized that he'd known where to find one. Sometimes she forgot that he probably knew this hotel better than she did.

"Did you find…anything? Tracks?" she asked, hoping they'd found something to prove that it hadn't been Megan's ghost. Something tangible. Evidence to put an end to this.

"It was impossible to track anything in the dead pine needles," Finn said, dashing her hope.

"Did you see her again?" Jen asked as she, Shirley and Patience joined them.

Jason shook his head and looked at Finn. "You should have seen her," he said, still sounding overly excited. "I heard Shirley cry out, and I turned, and I saw her blond hair, the white dress, the stains on it. I know it was for only a second as she ran through the pines, but her hair and that dress… It was Megan."

Casey scoffed. She had no idea what they'd thought they'd seen, but it wasn't Megan's ghost.

"Why are you questioning this?" Jason demanded. "We aren't the first to see her. Megan's ghost put this hotel on the map for your grandmother."

Casey bristled. "If you're about to say what I think you are…"

"Easy," he said, raising both hands in surrender. "I'm just saying, it was to your grandmother's benefit to have a ghost, for people to see a ghost. You know how people are. Admittedly, it can be a type of fanaticism. But what I just witnessed was her ghost, and I wasn't alone."

She looked to Finn. He had a strange expression on his face as if deep in thought. He really wasn't buying into this, was he?

CHAPTER TWENTY

SHIRLEY HAD COMPLETELY forgotten about Megan—until she saw her ghost. She'd been having fun, drinking more than usual and no longer worried about the motel. It would still be there when this weekend was over.

This was her first vacation in years. She refused to feel guilty about it. So she'd been in vacation mode, enjoying herself, feeling freer than she had in more than a year. Then she'd seen Megan's ghost moving through the woods.

She'd almost peed herself. Her heart was still a sledge-hammer in her chest. She felt dizzy from the booze, from the terror. She'd wanted to run, but her legs were water under her.

When Jason and Benjamin had raced into the woods, she'd stood frozen by the fire, blinking into the darkness, terrified that she would never see them alive again.

"I knew that bitch couldn't be killed," Jen said next to her now. "She's like a damned vampire."

She glanced at her friend. She'd noticed earlier that Jen had been shaking as hard as she'd been. But with Jen, she realized now, it had probably been with excitement rather than fear.

While she suspected the others hadn't wanted to see Megan's ghost any more than she had, she wasn't sure that was the case with Jen. Each night Jen had dressed up to stand by a campfire as if waiting for the dead woman to appear like she had an old grudge to settle.

Shirley glanced at Jen, wondering again why they were friends and why she was still here. She would feel the initial shock and terror slowly crystallizing into something no less scary.

"What if Claude and Devlin are dead?" Shirley asked, her voice breaking. "What if Megan—"

"Megan didn't kill anyone," Finn said. "It wasn't a ghost."

EVERYONE TURNED TO look at him, including Casey.

"But I saw it, too," Benjamin said. "Not that I believe it was her ghost."

"Then what was it?" Jason demanded, sounding almost disappointed.

"I don't know who it was," Finn said, locking his gaze with Casey's. "It could have been Claude or Devlin."

Jason shook his head. "You didn't see her. I did. The ghost had the body of a woman—not either of those men."

Finn wished he had seen her. He told himself that if someone tried this again, he wanted to be there. Next time he would catch them.

"What is that?" Casey asked as she motioned to what he had in his hand, his fingers running over the fibers subconsciously.

He held out his hand so she could see it in the firelight. "This was caught on a branch."

Benjamin gasped as he saw what it was, then began to laugh.

"It's a lock of her hair?" Jason cried.

Finn shook his head. "It was just someone wearing a

wig and a white dress. I found blond synthetic fiber caught on a tree limb."

"What?" Jen cried. "You mean Megan's blond hair wasn't even real?"

It took a moment before anyone laughed.

"It's not real hair," Finn said, showing it to Benjamin. "I suspect it's from a wig."

Benjamin tentatively felt a strand. "He's right. It's synthetic." He sounded more than a little relieved.

Jason swore. "How can you be so sure?"

"Because whoever you saw, it wasn't Megan," Finn said.

"Obviously," Patience said. "She's dead."

"Nor was it her ghost," Finn said. He saw lightning flicker over the mountains and heard thunder. The storm would be moving in soon. "It was just someone who wanted us to believe it was her."

"Why would someone do that?" Shirley asked.

"To scare us," Patience said. "It worked, didn't it?"

"You're drunk," Jason said to her as he slung his arm around her. "We should go inside. I have something in mind. For all of us," he added quickly as Patience shrugged off his arm playfully. Jason grinned. "I found an old Ouija board." There was a groan from the others.

Finn saw Casey looking at Jason with an intensity he recognized. "You're taking this well," she said.

Jason looked up at her in surprise, his gaze locking with hers. "What? The storm?"

"Megan's so-called ghost," she said, clearly angry. "This is the kind of stunt you would pull. Who'd you get to help you? Claude? Devlin? Some barmaid from town?"

He held up both hands, but he was grinning as he said, "You give me too much credit."

Finn witnessed the exchange between the two of them as the first raindrops began to fall. Everyone ran for the hotel, leaving Casey and Finn to bring up the rear.

As they all hurried inside, Finn caught Casey's arm under the shelter of the back door. Rain drummed on the steps below them. "Ready to tell me whatever you were afraid to tell me earlier?" he said. "It's just you and me. And you can trust me. I hope you know that by now."

CASEY HUGGED HERSELF as the storm moved in and the rain began to fall harder.

"I thought it had something to do with Megan and her murder, but now I'm wondering if it's about Jason," he suggested.

"Jason?"

"Casey, clearly there are some unfinished issues between the two of you."

"Not on my end," she said, hugging herself from the memories as well as the cold. A bolt of lightning lit Finn's handsome face. It was followed by thunder booming not far away like the thud of her heart.

Of course he'd picked up on it. Ten years ago, she'd gone into the woods with Jason. He'd said there was something he wanted to show her. Sixteen and unbelievably gullible, she'd gone because she'd had a crush on him. She groaned now at the memory.

She'd actually thought Jason was handsome and funny. What had she been thinking? The kiss had been sloppy and wet, all tongue. Gross. Then he'd grabbed her breast, and she'd shoved him away.

First kisses were supposed to be sweet, something she wanted to remember. But Jason had ruined that. She'd avoided him after that night, embarrassed since he had seemed to be avoiding her as well. Then she'd overheard Megan saying that Jason had told her that Casey was the worst kisser he'd ever had. He'd insinuated that he'd gone even further than he had and that Casey had been all over him.

She'd been horrified and had hated him ever since, especially when he and Megan had become girlfriend and boyfriend—at least, for a while. Every time she saw Megan in the hall, Megan mimed two people kissing and groping each other.

There had been nothing she could say, even if she had tried to defend herself. Casey had put the memory back into a dark corner, hating that Megan and Jason could occupy any of her thoughts. But it was as if someone didn't want her to forget. As if she could.

Why else would they plan this stupid reunion and bring everyone back? Everyone but Megan. She amended that thought quickly. Someone wanted her to believe that Megan's ghost was still here—just as her grandmother had believed it.

Had Anna seen whatever the others had tonight? Her grandmother wouldn't have chased the ghost down and found a strand of blond hair from a wig caught on a tree branch.

"I know what he did," Finn said. "How he lied about what happened between the two of you. Megan told me." That surprised her. "I can also see that he is still attracted to you."

She stared at him again. "Not this again."

He laughed. "The note to try to make you not trust me. Come on. He's like a middle schooler trying to get your attention."

It was her turn to laugh. "You're wrong," she said, shaking her head.

Her laughter died on her lips as he asked, "Is what happened between you and Jason what you were going to tell me about earlier?"

She hesitated. All she had to do was say it was. She looked through the rain toward the forest. This wasn't the place to tell him about the diary. But then again, there was no good place, was there? She shivered as she met his gaze.

"There's a reason you didn't find Megan's diary." She blurted it out. He frowned, not expecting this. "I took it from her room and burned it ten years ago."

He stared at her, surprise in his eyes and something painful to see. He was disappointed. Worse, he was upset with her.

"I didn't read it. None of it. I thought she'd written lies about me. I…" Her voice broke. "I'm so sorry. To think you spent months looking for it—"

Finn pulled her into his arms. "It's all right."

"No, it's not. I lied. I lied to everyone. I didn't think it mattered." She pulled back to look at him. "Can you forgive me?"

He shook his head. "Oh, Casey, is this the secret you've been carrying around for all these years?"

She nodded and buried her face in his chest. "What if Megan had written down who she suspected was stalking her?"

"Don't do this to yourself," he said. "She probably didn't know. Just as we don't know what she really wrote in that diary. It could have been all lies. Honestly, I can't see her even telling the truth to her own diary."

She pulled back to look at him. "You're just saying that to make me feel better."

He shook his head. "No, I'm not. The more I've heard

about her since being here, the more I doubt Megan was capable of being truthful even to herself. She was a young woman who had everything and still wasn't happy. I doubt she would have ever found happiness except in making other people miserable."

Pulling her into his arms again, he said, "I'm glad you told me." He ran his hand down her hair. She closed her eyes, loving the feel of his caress. Being this close to him… Was he really not upset with her?

"You spent months looking for her diary."

"I was looking for a lot more than her diary, trust me." He drew back to meet her gaze. "Fortunately, I found what I was looking for."

She felt the heat of his gaze all the way to her toes as the curtain of rain turned the tiny overhang at the back door way too intimate.

"We should go inside," he said. "You're shivering." He opened the door, and they stepped out of the storm. His cell phone rang. He pulled it out, glancing at the screen before he said reluctantly, "I need to take this."

She nodded and looked down the dim hallway. She could see light. It drew her toward the kitchen, where she could hear the murmur of voices. She knew she wasn't going to be able to sleep. Not yet.

Earlier, out under the overhang at the back door, she'd confessed her darkest secret to Finn. She'd been terrified at how he would take it.

He'd seemed surprised and definitely disappointed. But it was almost as if he'd suspected it all along. Was he also a little relieved that they would never have to read what Megan had thought of either of them?

They'd been so close outside, the shelter from the storm so

intimate. He'd been the first to draw away. Because he hadn't taken the news about the diary as well as he'd pretended?

She knew why she hadn't gone up to her room as she looked around the kitchen. Everyone was gathered around the table where a Ouija board sat next to a large, flickering candle. The faces at the table looked expectantly at it. She hadn't wanted to be alone with her thoughts, her fears, her doubts.

Now she stood in the doorway, knowing she should leave, and yet a part of her wanted to see how this played out. There was no doubt in her mind that Jason planned to use this to his advantage in some way.

"Casey, isn't there something you want to ask Megan?" Jason asked.

She didn't answer, simply watched as he motioned to Patience and Jen, and they hurriedly balanced their fingertips on the edge of the planchette next to his. The candlelight cast an eerie glow over the room as everyone fell silent.

"Let's warm it up a little," Jason said, moving the pointer around the board slowly, his gaze locked on her.

FINN HAD WONDERED why the hotel was so quiet. After his call, he'd planned to head up to his room. Until he saw Casey standing in the hallway outside the kitchen. He recalled Jason mentioning that he'd found a Ouija board. He groaned at the thought as he moved toward Casey.

Earlier outside, all he'd wanted was to carry Casey up to his room. He knew the timing couldn't have been worse. She was going through so much just by being here and dealing with her grief over her grandmother, packing up cherished belongings and letting go of the hotel. Not to mention this murder reunion and the guilt she'd been carrying for so long.

It wasn't the time for either of them to even consider getting romantically involved. He'd been going through his own baggage, and now he would soon own this hotel. He still didn't know what he was going to do with it.

The best thing he could do right now was just be here for Casey. Once this was all over… She hadn't heard him approach but had seemed almost relieved when he'd joined her in the kitchen doorway. With Jason behind this, he didn't like Casey being down here alone.

Jason had grinned when he saw Finn there. "Glad you're both here. This will be fun." Finn highly doubted that. "Let's see if Megan is really still around. Don't pretend you don't want to know." He'd glanced pointedly at Casey.

Now Finn considered those seated around the table. Most of them had spent the day drinking, and from the open beer cans around the table, they weren't stopping now. They looked bored after their ghost scare. If it weren't for the approaching storm, they would still be out by the campfire waiting to see Megan's ghost again. Was it possible Jason had been behind that stunt, just as Casey suspected? He could very well be working with Claude and Devlin.

One thing was clear: Jason had known he had to raise the stakes or he would lose the others to their own devices tonight. But a Ouija board?

"You do realize there is no scientific evidence that a Ouija board is any more than a toy," Benjamin said.

Thunder boomed so loudly that it seemed to shake the hotel walls. They all started at its closeness and then laughed nervously. The lights dimmed as if about to go out. It felt as if the entire room was holding its breath. In the jittery silence, Finn could feel tension replace boredom.

The lights flickered before coming back on. Jason laughed. "Seems Megan is anxious to talk to us." He glanced toward the door where Finn and Casey stood. "Turn out the overhead light. Let's give her what she wants."

Finn reached over and hit the switch, leaving only the candle flickering in the middle of the table and the dim lights from the hallway. Dark shadows filled the edges of the room. He looked at Casey.

He wasn't sure this was a good idea, but then again, she knew her own mind. Like him, she was probably curious to see just how far Jason planned to take this.

"ARE THERE ANY spirits here tonight?" Jason asked the now-silent room.

Casey could hear nothing but her own pulse thrumming in her ears and the sound of the storm raging outside. A bolt of lightning was followed soon behind by a crack of thunder. No one seemed to move, and then the planchette slowly circled the board once more before stopping on *Yes*.

"Are you a good spirit?" Jason asked.

Laughter broke the spell. "Not a chance in hell," Patience said.

Next to Finn, Casey shifted on her feet.

"What's your name?"

For a moment the planchette didn't move. Then, very quickly, it swung to *M*, then *E*, then *G-A-N*. The room had grown deathly quiet, while outside it sounded as if the storm were growing stronger.

"This is ridiculous," Benjamin said, but he didn't get up

and leave. His face looked pale in the candlelight. All of their faces had taken on an eerie glow.

"Where did you die?" Jason asked.

Silence. The pointer didn't move. Casey could hear the tick of the clock, the hum of the refrigerator and the storm as it was attacking the hotel as if wanting in.

The planchette began to move slowly. *B-U-C-K-H-O-R-N.*

"Is there anything you want to tell us?" Again, nothing moved.

Then the pointer hurriedly spelled out four words. There was a collective gasp. *GLAD YOU ARE HERE.*

Benjamin did more than scoff. He started to get up to leave, but Jason waved him back down.

"She'll only appear if we are all here," he said and looked up directly at Casey again.

She could feel Finn watching her. She knew he was worried about where this was headed. He wasn't the only one.

"Megan, we're all here," Jason said. "How do we know *you're* here?"

Silence. It felt heavy against her chest. Maybe this foolishness would—

A cup that had been sitting at the edge of the table suddenly fell. The percussion of it striking the floor and shattering made them all jump. There was a smattering of nervous laughter.

"Megan's here, all right," Jason said. "She isn't going to clean up the mess she made, either." More laughter.

But Casey didn't join in. "Casey, come on. Don't you want to ask her something?" Jason said.

She felt the tension in the room. Her nerves stretched to breaking as she felt Jason waiting for her to say something. And Finn thought Jason had a crush on her? Was he mad?

Walk out. You don't have to do this.

Only she didn't move. A dead Megan didn't scare her. Nor did a live Jason.

"Ask her what she broke of mine," she said, surprised that her voice sounded normal to her ears. Jason looked startled.

He studied her for a moment and then shrugged. "Why not? I believe you just asked her."

The planchette began to move. Casey watched it slowly slide around as if not knowing where to go next. She felt some of her tension release. She was pretty sure that only she and Megan knew the answer. She wanted to laugh since it meant Jason didn't know.

But then the device landed on the *B*. She caught her breath as she watched it move more quickly now, going to the *R*, then *A*, *C*, *E*, *L*, *E* and *T* and stop dead.

She could feel all eyes on her, including Finn's.

"Well?" Jason asked without looking at her.

"It was my bracelet," she said, confirming that Megan *had* told Jason about her favorite bracelet and probably a lot more. Megan had admired the bracelet, then had wanted to take a closer look and then had jerked it, breaking the link. She'd said she was sorry, that it was an accident, but it was just another of her lies.

"I'm sure you can fix it," Megan had said, knowing it wasn't true. "Or maybe not. It looks cheap. I'm sure you can find another one at a thrift store."

Megan had known that the bracelet had been given to her by her grandmother and that it wouldn't have mattered if it had been cheap—which it wasn't.

Casey had never worn it again. The bracelet was still hidden in the bottom of her jewelry box because she couldn't part with it, and also, even if fixed, Megan had ruined it.

"It *was* a bracelet?" Jen asked and then shivered as she removed her fingertips for a moment before putting them back on the pointer.

"Come on," Benjamin said. "If this isn't just a toy, ask Megan what we all really want to know. Who killed her?"

Silence. Casey thought she could hear the beating of everyone's heart in the room. "Who killed you?" Jason asked. The planchette didn't move. Hardly anyone seemed to be breathing.

Nothing happened.

It was Finn who let out a laugh that startled everyone. The pointer jumped across the board. Jen had to wipe her damp hands on her jeans. Patience pulled back her fingers and took a drink of her beer as if she didn't want any part of it anymore.

"Wasn't Megan hit in the back of the head?" Finn asked, clearly aware that was the case. "What if she doesn't know who killed her?"

Benjamin was staring at him. "You don't really believe that she's here, answering our questions, do you?"

He shrugged.

Jason piped up. "She knew about the bracelet. Apparently only she and Casey had known about that."

"Apparently," Casey said, meeting his gaze.

"Finn's right," Jason said. "Maybe she doesn't know who killed her."

"Well, then, that's just sad," Benjamin said. "If you're the killer, wouldn't you have wanted to look her in the eye when you killed her? I would have. I would have wanted her to know it was me."

Jason had his fingertips back on the pointer. The second Jen put hers back on, it moved.

Casey watched it. *F,* then *U,* then *B-E-N.* Everyone laughed except Benjamin.

"There must be something else we can ask her," Jason said.

"Ask her if she's sorry for the way she treated us," Shirley said.

Silence again. They waited. The planchette began to move. *No.*

"At least she's honest," Jen said.

"Does she know what a bitch she is?" Benjamin said. *Yes.*

The group was growing restless. Jason seemed to sense it. "If you had to guess, who wanted you dead the most?"

Silence. Everyone stared at the board. Then, slowly, almost painfully, the planchette began to slide across the board. *B-E-N.*

Ben erupted, shooting to his feet in anger. "I've had enough." He stormed out of the kitchen, shoving past Casey and Finn still in the doorway.

"Any more questions?" Jason asked.

"Tell her to show herself," Patience said, refusing to put her fingers back on the pointer. "No more cup tricks. I want to see her."

"We'll give it a try," Jason said with a shrug. "But since you don't believe in this… Megan, show yourself." Nothing happened.

"I'm with Ben," Finn whispered to Casey. "You ready to go?"

Casey turned on the lights. "I think everyone's had enough," she said to Jason.

The atmosphere in the kitchen changed in an instant as the electricity went out, pitching the room into darkness.

CHAPTER TWENTY-ONE

IT TOOK A MOMENT for the backup generator to come on. Finn found himself holding his breath. No one seemed to move. The lights flashed on and off for a few moments before they remained on.

Jason laughed. "Nice one, Megan."

"Unless you believe that was the storm," Patience said and rose to leave.

"I've had enough, too," Shirley said. "I need a beer and a smoke. It sounds like the storm might be moving on."

"I agree with Shirley," Jen said, getting to her feet. "Megan doesn't have the guts to show herself."

The door behind Casey slammed shut with such a crash that someone let out a startled cry before Jason started laughing. "Tell me that wasn't Megan. You had all better watch your backs."

Finn opened the door. There was no one in the hall. Just a chill wind. Ben had apparently left the back door open on his way out.

Jason put away the Ouija board. "Who's going with me to the bar?" Jen said she would go. Shirley, too.

"Count me in, too," Patience said.

Finn figured they just wanted out of the hotel. It did sound like the thunderstorm was moving on.

"Have fun, but I'm calling it a night," Casey said as she started down the hallway.

Finn might have gone after her, but sensed she needed to be alone. After they had all left, he stood in the kitchen. He'd read in Anna's journal that she'd completely remodeled the space about five years ago. He blinked at the bright overhead lights, all the stainless steel and white cabinets, now that the shadows had all scurried away.

He could see Casey as a girl, propped up on a stool, watching the chefs cook. According to her grandmother, she'd loved the activity, the sound of pots and pans, the smells of the food. The cooks always fed her treats and told her stories about meals that had been served to the rich and famous over the years.

If there were ghosts in this hotel, they were here in this kitchen, he thought as he turned out the lights and headed up for bed.

CASEY TRIED TO shake off what had happened in the kitchen. Her rational mind told her that it had all been a show, orchestrated by Jason. Like Megan, he liked to fool with people. He especially liked to fool with her.

As she got ready for bed, she thought of Finn. It had been so sweet of him to suggest the ice cream. He was so protective and caring. By tomorrow, she would have signed away the hotel and have no reason to stay any longer. Leaving had been all she'd thought about. Until Finn.

It was late when she heard a door open across the hall. Finn must be having trouble sleeping as well. She swung her legs out of bed, moving to her door as if drawn like metal to magnet. She cracked it open, thinking she would thank him again for the ice cream.

"Hey," Finn said and looked glad to see her. He wore a T-shirt and running shorts, his hair wet as if he'd just showered. That certainly brought back some memories. "I like your pajamas."

She realized that she hadn't grabbed her robe. She'd been in a hurry. She hadn't just wanted to thank Finn for the ice cream; she'd wanted to tell him how glad she was that he was here. She couldn't imagine what it would have been like without him even if he hadn't bought the hotel. She also wanted to say that she was glad he wasn't upset with her about Megan's diary.

But he smiled at her, and all the things she wanted to say went out of her head.

"Are those moose?" he asked as he stepped closer.

She looked down at her pj's and laughed. "My grandmother bought me these Christmas before last. At least they don't have feet in them."

"I like them." He was close now, so close she could smell the soap from his recent shower. Her memory shot right back to that first day and him naked as a jaybird with water and soapsuds rippling over that incredible body.

"I just wanted to thank you," she said into the tense silence that had fallen between them. "For the ice cream. For…everything." Her skin felt hot, her heart a drum in her chest; she felt as if she didn't dare breathe. He was so close that he would barely need to move to kiss her.

She wasn't that inexperienced girl who'd gone into the woods with Jason. She was a woman who could appreciate a real man's kiss.

"You're most welcome," he said with a slight bow. He hesitated. "We've both had quite the day." He took a step back.

She nodded, hating the stab of disappointment that pierced her chest.

As she started to turn toward her room again, she heard him mutter, "Oh, hell." He caught her hand. She felt her pulse jump as he turned her back to him. Eyes locked with hers, he pulled her closer. Her breath caught again in her throat. She felt as if she'd been headed to this point her whole life.

"I've been wanting to do this from the first time I saw you standing in my bathroom holding a gun on me," Finn said, his voice thick with desire. He encircled her in his arms, drawing her into him as his mouth dropped to hers.

The kiss was tender and sweet, tentative and then fierce in its need. She lost herself in him. Time seemed suspended. She could feel his heart pounding like her own, just as she could feel the heat of him.

As he slowly drew back from the kiss to meet her gaze, his voice was rough with emotion as he said, "I'm not going to let anything happen to you." He cleared his throat. "I just want you to know that I'm here for you." Just across the hall. Just a few steps away.

"You really aren't angry about the diary?" she had to ask.

He looked surprised by the question. "No. I'm just glad you told me. I hope you feel better having done so." She did. Their gazes locked, stealing her breath.

He drew back, letting her go. "Sleep tight," he said with a slight bow. "Watch those bedbugs."

She grimaced. "Not funny."

"Better than ghosts," he said, then mugged a face.

"Yes," she said, smiling, the kiss still warm on her lips, branded in her memory as the best kiss ever. "Anything is better than ghosts." Even as she said it, she knew that wasn't true. A killer would be worse. A killer pretending to be a ghost.

WORKING LATE AT night alone in the underbelly of the hotel was taking too long. The explosives were set, but laying the electrical detonator fuse, which was just a long length of electrical wire, took precision if the explosives were to go off as planned.

Guessing at how much fuse to put between the various bombs was the tricky part. The idea was to cause them to go off one after another in a chain reaction.

Just being down here with all this dynamite was so dangerous that a person often had to wipe the sweat away. A hand trembled at even the thought of what could happen with just a wrong move as the fuses were connected to each bomb.

But the alternative would be much worse. The fallout too much to bear.

The coil of wire was hefted, and the fuse was strung from one support spot to the next. So close now, working only at night, when no one would think of coming down to investigate the noise. It was almost done.

Once all the wire was laid, all that was needed was a battery. When it was time, the electrical current would be sent through the wire, causing it to heat up and ignite the flammable substance on the detonator end, which in turn set off the primer charge, which would trigger the main explosives.

Kaboom! Kaboom! Kaboom!

The bigger they are, the harder they fall. Oh, how the Crenshaw would fall! But before it did, if anyone got to snooping around and came down into the underground maze of tunnels below the hotel… Well, that couldn't happen. It wasn't quite ready yet. There was one thing that had to be done first.

CHAPTER TWENTY-TWO

Sunday

JASON HAD NEVER had trouble sleeping. Usually he'd had enough to drink after work—he used the term *work* loosely since he sat behind a desk in his beautiful corner office to do the ridiculously easy jobs his father thought he couldn't screw up.

Everyone in the company was aware that he couldn't be trusted to follow through. In his boredom, he often missed deadlines, did a sloppy job or totally blew off the menial assignments. He was a joke. A bad joke.

He pushed that thought away as he stood at the window looking out at the darkness. He'd only taken the job here at the Crenshaw that summer because he'd put off applying anywhere else. When his father lost it, threatening to find him a job if he didn't, he'd been desperate and had taken the first thing that came up on his computer.

There had been one opening left. It was the perfect job—cleaning hotel rooms and serving guests for tips. It was exactly the kind of summer job that would piss off his father. And it had.

He'd actually enjoyed the work, though, because he was good with the guests. He knew rich people. He'd grown up around them his whole life and knew what made them happy. He'd been great at it.

Megan had struggled, since she'd always been on the other end that made the demands—not satisfying them. She'd hated the job from day one.

He laughed to himself now as he remembered how she'd struggled even to make her first bed. "Have you really never made a bed in your entire life?" he'd asked, laughing.

"We have help for that."

"Well, now you're the help," he'd said and showed her. Not that he had any experience, but he'd had a crush on one of his family's younger housekeepers, and he used to love watching her make beds, especially the way she did the tight corners.

That poignant memory of that first day with Megan hurt more than he'd thought it would. For a while, they'd been close. She'd liked him; he was sure of it. Until she didn't.

He stepped away from the window thinking he would try to get some sleep, since Patience had gone back to her room to pack. She was planning to leave. She'd had enough. Unless he could convince her to stay. He just needed to shut down his thoughts for a few hours. Otherwise, he would return to the night Megan died and those shadowy dark woods. If a tree fell in the woods, did it make a sound if you weren't there to hear it? What about a rock to the back of a skull?

CASEY HAD AWAKENED early and, avoiding the kitchen, had finished up her grandmother's tasks. Most of the items were small and would fit in the convertible. A couple of larger items she took down to Vi to have them shipped.

Basically, she was done once she found one more item that hadn't been on the list. It was one of the first books her grandmother had ever read to her here at the hotel. She thought she'd seen it in one of the garden rooms. She headed there now, wishing she'd picked it up earlier. Unfortunately, her mind had been on other things at the time.

She was looking in one of the garden rooms on the ground level when she noticed that someone had been playing Scrabble. The board was laid out on a small table between two chairs. She wondered if it had been one of the last guests. She couldn't imagine that any of the reunion staff had been down here playing.

Without thinking, she began picking up pieces to put the board away when she heard someone enter the room.

"I'm glad I found you," Finn said as he joined her. She stopped what she'd been doing to smile at him. He returned that smile with an amazing one of his own. The man was so beautiful, inside and out, she thought with a rush of emotion.

"Are you winning?" he asked, grinning at her as he motioned to the Scrabble board. She rolled her eyes. "Speaking of words, you do realize that you sometimes make me feel tongue-tied around you? Like right now." He closed the distance between them. The kiss was so natural and yet off the charts as he slowly drew her to him and lowered his mouth to hers. He deepened the kiss, filling her with a sense of promise that had her heart soaring.

"Who needs words," she whispered as the kiss ended.

"They come in handy sometimes." He began to pick up letters from the game board. She watched him, realizing he was writing something. As he finished, he turned the board toward her. He'd written *I have fallen for you.*

She laughed, her gaze locking with his as he kissed her again. The man was an incredible kisser—and not bad at all with words, but that came as no surprise. Was there anything he couldn't do?

"Have lunch with me," he said. His cell phone rang.

He cursed under his breath. "Lunch. Two hours. Meet me here. We'll go out the back door and avoid everyone." She nodded, smiling. He checked the screen. "I have to take this. Later?"

"Later." She watched him walk out of the garden room, his kisses still sending waves of pleasure through her. She was smiling to herself when she looked down again at what he'd spelled out on the Scrabble board.

Impulsively she scooped up the letters and put them in the pocket of her jean jacket. Her whole body seemed to be vibrating. *I have fallen for you.*

AFTER DEALING WITH the fallout from his disappearance and questions about his sanity for purchasing the Crenshaw Hotel in Buckhorn, Montana, Finn found Jason in the kitchen pouring himself a cup of coffee. He looked as if he hadn't been sleeping well. Finn motioned him out into the hallway, wondering where everyone else was, but he didn't ask.

"Has Devlin turned up?"

Jason blinked. "I haven't seen him. When I checked his room yesterday, his stuff was all there."

"What's his room number?"

Jason frowned. "I can't remember, but I can show you."

They headed for the staff wing. Everything was quiet. Maybe too quiet, Finn thought. Jason found the room he believed was Devlin's. Finn knocked. No answer. He knocked again, a little harder. Still no answer. He tried the knob.

The door swung open. Even from the hallway, Finn could see that Devlin had cleared out.

"He probably left," Jason said. "He only came to the reunion because he thought he was going to get a deal on the hotel and land. I doubt his investors are happy with him. I'm sure he's just taken off."

Maybe, Finn thought. It was just that no one had seen him leave. Just like Claude. Both could have just decided they'd had enough and didn't want anyone to give them a hard time for leaving. Finn knew he was probably looking for trouble where there wasn't any. He hadn't forgotten that someone had dressed up like Megan to move through the woods to try to scare them.

They checked. His car was gone. "Let me know if anyone else might have seen Devlin," Finn said, wondering when he'd left. Last night during the Ouija board scene in the kitchen? Or sometime after that when most everyone had gone to the bar?

"Will do." Jason took his coffee and headed for his room. Before the door closed, Finn saw the adult-size lump under the covers of the man's bed. Patience?

He checked his watch and headed upstairs. He had wanted to give Casey as much time as she needed—not just for lunch but before she had to sign over the hotel to him. He hadn't wanted to pressure her. But if Devlin was gone and she still wanted to sell and put this behind her, then he wanted to make that happen today.

Finn didn't like this feeling he couldn't shake. Something was wrong. He was having trouble believing that Claude and Devlin had cooked up the ghost stunt last night any more than they had their disappearing acts. It felt wrong. A clock was ticking down on the reunion. Whoever was behind whatever was going on, it didn't feel over. He felt as if he was waiting for the other shoe to drop.

CASEY HEARD A text come in on her cell phone. She checked it, her heart doing a little bump when she saw it was from

Finn. She was thinking of their kisses earlier when she opened it and felt foolish.

Just wanted to let you know. I have the paperwork. All you have to do is sign on the dotted line and it's a done deal. We can do this at lunch, if you want.

Once she signed, she no longer had an excuse to stay here. She could load up and head back to California. Or stay and what? Her deal with Finn could be closed by lunchtime. The reunion was almost over. Why would she stay? Like Finn said, bad timing when it came to the two of them.

She told herself that she'd been looking forward to the road trip. She'd seen it as a way to unwind before she had to get back to work. She couldn't shake off something that had been bothering her. She felt ready for a change. It was so unlike her. Change had never come easily. But right now, she wanted an adventure. She wanted romance, kisses in the rain. Finn. This was his fault.

But even if she did decide to make a change, she still had to go back to the hotel for a period of time to make the transition easier for them. Was it the job, though, that she wanted to change?

Finn immediately came to mind, making her ache at the thought of leaving here and never seeing him again. As if conjuring him up, her phone rang.

"I'm starving," he said without introduction. "I skipped breakfast, and I suspect you did, too, since I heard you take off early this morning. Ready for lunch?"

"Give me ten minutes." She quickly disconnected and hurried to her room to freshen up. Just the sound of Finn's voice sent a quiver of desire through her. *I have fallen for you.*

But where did they go from here? If anywhere?

Maybe the best thing to do would be to leave after lunch. It wouldn't take her any time to pack her bag and just go. If she stayed...

She knew what she feared. If she stayed, she knew what was going to happen, what she wanted to happen. That meant risking her heart.

Eight minutes later, she was waiting in the garden room when she turned at the sound of footfalls and saw Finn. As always, her pulse did a jitterbug just under her skin.

He was wearing the black T-shirt and jeans like the first day she'd met him. Both fit him like an expensive glove. But it was his smile that was her undoing. She couldn't leave. Not yet. "Hungry?"

"Always," she said with a laugh. It really was so good to see him. They stepped out the side door and took the path toward town. She knew they could be seen from the hotel, but she didn't look back.

It was one of those Montana presummer days that made people flock to the state in carloads. Not a cloud in the vast deep blue sky, the sun bright and warming, the air fresh and cool, it was the kind of day that Casey would always associate with Buckhorn, she thought as they neared town.

"I've been thinking that maybe I should contact the marshal," Finn said. She must have looked as surprised as she felt because he hurried on. "First Claude supposedly leaves. Now Devlin is missing. Yesterday, his belongings were still in his room when Jason checked. But this morning, everything is gone, including his car."

"Maybe he just decided to leave," she suggested. "Or maybe he wants us to believe he did."

Finn frowned. "You have his number? Would you mind trying it?"

She pulled out her phone, found Devlin in her contacts and listened to the call go through. It rang four times before it went to voice mail. "Devlin, when you get this, please call me. It's important." She disconnected. "I left it vague enough that—"

"That message should make him call. He'll think you changed your mind about selling to me," Finn said and smiled. "I'm probably worrying unnecessarily."

"Well, you can quit worrying about me," she said.

He shook his head. "Not happening." He studied her. "You're in danger here. If someone knows about the diary and is worried that you read it…" He rushed on as she tried not to flinch, but he'd seen her reaction. "The killer might think that Megan named them in the diary and that you know."

She realized that she had to tell him. "The first night, someone left a message in my room. *I know what you did.* I didn't know who until I saw the taco-salad grocery list. Jen said Jason had made it out."

"Jason?" Finn swore. "Casey, maybe he's just trying to get your attention. Or maybe Jason is the killer and wants to know if you read Megan's diary. Unless he's just spit-balling and doesn't know who took the diary. Is it possible he wrote that message on some of the other bathroom mirrors?"

She hadn't thought of that. "Maybe he was just goofing around trying to scare me, trying to scare the others." She shook her head. "That would be so like him."

He shook his head. "Still, I don't like this." He raked a hand through his hair in obvious frustration before his gaze settled on her. "As much as I don't want you to leave, I'm glad you're getting out of here."

Casey nodded as they headed down the main drag. The two of them had become close. Maybe too close, given that they were from two different worlds and about to return to them—as if from other planets.

The town was starting to come alive, signaling that summer wasn't far off. There were more cars, campers and motor homes than yesterday. Every year the season began earlier, her grandmother had always told her. It used to start after Memorial Day and end just before Labor Day. The added tourists also signaled that it was time for her to return to California and put the hotel, this town, this life, behind her. Put Finn behind her, too?

They'd almost reached the café when Finn got a call. "Do you mind going on ahead of me?"

"Can I order you something?"

"Cheeseburger and fries and—"

"A chocolate milkshake," she said, finishing for him.

He grinned and gave her a wink. "You've got my number, girl."

Didn't she, though, she thought as he took the call and she entered the café. She'd barely given the waitress their order when he came in looking excited.

"The inquiries I made about Megan's car accident?" he said, keeping his voice down. The café was busy, but no one seemed to pay them much mind. The patrons must all be tourists. "My source found a connection between one of the young women and one of the Crenshaw Hotel staff that summer."

She held her breath. Maybe it *was* possible to solve Megan's murder.

"I thought it would be the family of the woman who was killed," Finn hurried on before she could ask. "But it was one of the women who survived, the one who is now in a wheelchair because of her back injuries. Her older brother had met Claude when he toured the medical school."

"Claude?" Casey felt surprise quickly turn into fear. "You think he took the job here that summer to kill Megan?"

"He could have just wanted to get a little justice, but then things went too far," Finn said. "Or he could have told someone else about what Megan did and that person did what Claude couldn't. I don't know. Didn't you say that you thought he and Megan had hooked up? Maybe she'd beguiled him, and he realized he couldn't hurt her."

"Claude swore she did a number on him. You saw how he was Friday night at the campfire. But that could have been an act for us so we weren't surprised when he left." Casey thought back to that summer. "Megan and Claude were hot and heavy until Megan broke up with him. He didn't take it well."

"Maybe Megan found out why he'd really come to the Crenshaw."

She tried to imagine Claude as a killer and realized it wasn't such a stretch. There was something cold and clinical about him. "You really think he was the one who murdered her?"

"I don't know, but he knew who she was and what she'd done when he came here ten years ago. I doubt she knew that he had a connection to one of her friends she'd almost killed and had injured badly enough that she was in a wheelchair."

"What if we're right and Claude never really left because Megan isn't the only score he wants to settle?"

"So where does Devlin fit in, if he does?" Finn said.

Their burgers came and they spent the rest of lunch talking about anything but the Crenshaw, the staff and Megan. Finn opened up to her, telling her more about himself, his life, his dreams. She shared, too. He was easy to talk to because he listened with an intensity that she appreciated. He admitted that most women he'd dated had only been interested in his money and what it could buy, even before he'd sold his business for a small fortune.

"I love what I do," Casey said. "But, truthfully, I'm ready for a new adventure. I might take some time off when I get back and do some traveling."

"Where do you want to go?" he asked, leaning toward her, anxious to hear.

"Italy, Spain, Greece." She laughed, and he joined her. It was a warm, happy sound that filled her with joy.

"I'd love to take you to all of those places and more."

She told herself it was just an offhand comment a man made to a woman. She wasn't going to take it seriously. "I haven't really been anywhere, but I've been happiest on the beach in California."

He smiled across the table at her. She felt it to her core. "Sounds like it's high time you did whatever you want. You'll definitely be able to afford to with the profits from the hotel and land."

As the waitress cleared away their dishes, Finn drew out an envelope. She didn't have to ask what was in it. "You want to do this here?"

"As good a place as any," she said, her voice cracking a little.

If he noticed, he didn't say anything. The waitress produced a pen as she wiped down their table.

"Did you have your lawyer look them over?"

"I trust you. But I also emailed the preliminary forms you gave me earlier to the family lawyer. He didn't have a problem." She turned to the pages she needed to address and hesitated only for an instant before she began to sign. When she reached the last page, she signed with a flourish and slid the papers back across the table to him.

"I'll text my bank and have the money transferred to your account right now." He pulled out his phone. A moment later her own phone dinged to let her know the money was now there.

It was done. Casey waited to see how she felt. Relieved? Sad? Instead, it felt anticlimactic. She was now basically rich. Her plan had been to invest the money wisely. And she would—at least, most of it. But she would quit her job. She would travel. She would go on that adventure. So why did she feel like crying?

They wandered back to the hotel. She could feel time slipping away.

He stopped just outside the hotel garden-room door and turned to her. "Just the thought of you leaving… I was thinking that maybe tonight—" His cell phone rang. He swore under his breath as he looked at the screen. "This is another reason I dropped out of sight. I have to take this. Unfortunately, I am no longer missing, and this one is important."

"It's fine," she said. "I need to pack, anyway."

"Tonight, then." His phone rang again. Swearing under his breath once more, he moved away to take the call.

CASEY FELT HER eyes burn with tears as she said to his retreating back, "Tonight." She'd seen the promise in his deep blue gaze and felt her own promising one. Tonight. This was one promise she planned to keep no matter what.

Back upstairs, she began to pack, but her heart wasn't in it. So much had changed since she'd come back here. She looked around the room, suddenly filled with an overwhelming sadness. When she'd arrived, she'd thought saying goodbye would be hard, but not this hard. This hotel was the last of her grandmother. Once it was gone…

She reminded herself that it *was* gone and wiped her tears. It was time for a change—just as she'd told Finn. She needed to do something else after all these years of being involved in hotel management. She could blame her grandmother's death for this. Or selling the hotel. But in reality, it was all Finn. Meeting him had made her yearn for more than she'd let herself accept over the past ten years.

She knew she needed time to sort it all out. Nothing had gone as she'd expected when returning to Buckhorn, but in some ways it had turned out so much better. She had sold the hotel, gotten more money than she'd expected and felt good about whom she'd sold it to—even though she had no idea what he would do with the hotel and the land.

It didn't matter. Not anymore. Telling Finn about the diary had been a weight off her shoulders—just like selling the hotel. If Finn thought it would help, she'd tell the marshal. The diary was gone, either way. They would never know what Megan had written.

She told herself she'd done what she'd come here to do. By tomorrow morning, everyone who was still here would be leaving. Except Finn?

He hadn't really said what his plans were. But she couldn't imagine him giving up—until forced to. He had really expected something to happen over this weekend that would force Megan's killer out into the open. That was why he'd been so worried about her. Now he knew why the killer might be coming for her. Believing that Megan had told too much in her diary? Convinced that Casey hadn't just read it, that she'd lied about sending out the reunion invitations because she was no longer going to keep the killer's secret?

Well, if true, wouldn't Casey have said or done something by now? Maybe Finn was right, and they'd all been looking for closure. Or facing the ghosts of their past. Devlin and Claude must have felt the same way since apparently they'd left early. Or maybe they hadn't left at all. Maybe the worst was still yet to come.

It was up to Finn now to decide what to do with the information he'd gathered. The car wreck, Megan lying about driving, Claude being a friend of a friend who might or might not have come here that summer to seek revenge on Megan. Would the marshal take it seriously after all this time?

She finished packing, leaving out only the clothing she would wear tonight and in the morning when she hit the road. "I know this isn't the ending you'd hoped for, but I can't see any other way." She said it aloud to her grandmother, hoping Anna would understand. She hadn't come here to solve a murder. She didn't even think Finn was going to pursue it any further.

Casey checked her phone and noticed she'd gotten another call from the family attorney in California. He'd told her there was more to her grandmother's will than just the Crenshaw. But she'd been anxious to get the sale completed, promising to meet with him when she got back.

"When will you be returning?" Hamilton Freeman had asked her the last time they'd talked on the phone. "There are some personal matters to discuss. It was important to your grandmother. You know how she was."

Yes, she knew. "I won't be gone more than a week."

"Fine," he said. "Call me when you get back." She'd said she would.

His texts were about the sale of the Crenshaw and merely clarifying that she would be returning to California this coming week. He hoped they could meet and wanted to know what day would work best.

Casey pocketed her phone, since she didn't know when she was leaving, tonight or in the morning, or when she'd make it back to San Francisco. As she did, she thought she heard thunder rumbling in the distance. Moving to the window, she spotted dark clouds on the western horizon. Another thunderstorm was on its way. From the tower, she used to love watching storms roll in.

CHAPTER TWENTY-THREE

FINN FOUND CASEY in the tower. He stopped at the entrance momentarily, awed by the sight of her. The dramatic light from an approaching storm shone in her fiery red hair. He'd seen the storm coming when he'd gone looking for her. He loved storms and had a pretty good idea that she did, too. So he'd known where to find her, the one place to watch the clouds roll in.

She stood looking out as if in wonder, as if in anticipation. She appeared like an angel, the storm light making her radiant and even more beautiful, as if that were possible. He held his breath and didn't move, wanting to savor this moment.

She must have sensed him, though, because she turned, her gaze falling on him and softening. He smiled and felt his heart skip.

"Were you looking for me?" she asked, tilting her head, her ginger ponytail falling over one sunburned shoulder.

He hesitated. Leaving was the safest thing for her to do, especially now that he knew the truth. Still, he didn't want to let her go. He couldn't shake the feeling that if he did, he might never see her again.

"I figured you'd be up here." He closed the distance between them, his desire for her a driving force. She tilted her head to meet his gaze, and he knew he was going to kiss her. She knew it, too. He saw it in her eyes, in the way her lips parted ever so slightly. He couldn't remember ever wanting a woman like he did this one.

His touch was gentle on her sunburn, but she came willingly enough into his arms. He drew her close and slowly dropped his mouth to hers. She tasted like strawberries and sunshine. Her lips parted, and he deepened the kiss, losing himself in the taste and smell and feel of her.

"Casey." He said her name like a mantra, like a prayer. She leaned into him as he wrapped her in his arms. How could he ever let her go—even temporarily?

LIGHTNING SPLINTERED THE sky and illuminated the tower, throwing everything into sharp contrast. For that instant, she memorized Finn's face in that amazing light. Then dark clouds blew over the landscape, taking the light with it. Thunder boomed, rattled the old windows, causing Casey to draw back.

As the storm moved in, so did the wind. It roared, pelting the glass with rain. She'd been in some amazing storms over the years, but this spring squall darkened the sky as if a curtain had been dropped over the sun. The storm matched her mood.

This felt like the end to something she never wanted to end.

Casey locked eyes with him, the moment suspended in time. She thought of when she'd turned to find him standing in the tower doorway. Her heart had floated skyward, glowing in the rays of sunlight piercing the storm clouds. She hadn't been able to move, let alone breathe, as he'd stepped to her. Even as her mind tried to argue that she didn't know this man, that she couldn't trust her heart, she'd known better. A man like Finn? You didn't need weeks, even months, to know what was in his heart.

He moved to the door and locked it. As he turned back to look at her, she felt her pulse take off at a gallop. She ran to him, throwing herself into his arms as he pulled her close for another searing kiss. This was where she belonged. She'd yearned for his touch, for his kisses, for him without knowing it was going to be him. As if it had been written in the stars, her grandmother would have said.

As his mouth took possession of hers, she believed that with all her heart and soul.

When the kiss ended, they locked gazes. They needed no words. They both wanted this more than their next breaths.

Finn took her hand, weaving his fingers with hers as he drew her to him again. Her heart thundered like the storm. She could see desire burning hot in his eyes, hear his ragged breath now so like her own. Neither of them could wait the time it would take to get to a proper bed in this hotel full of them. His mouth was on hers, kissing her hungrily, his hands buried deep in her hair.

He pressed her against the door, melding his body to hers as she frantically pulled off the T-shirt he wore and pressed her palms against the hard contours of his chest, his skin hot with desire. He lifted her higher to bury his face in the hollow between her breasts. He held her there with his body as his fingers adeptly unbuttoned the top of her sundress to get to her already-hard nipples. She arched against his mouth as he laved each with his tongue, making her cry out with a burning need like hot lava at her center.

She worked at the buttons on his jeans as he lifted her sundress hem and drew down her panties. His fingers found her hot center. She arched against him. Her desire for him had reached a painful peak. She wanted him, wanted this.

Released from his jeans, he entered her, pressing her against the solid wooden door, and she nearly wept as she clung to him, rocking with his movements as he took her higher and higher until she felt the incredible release.

He drove into her, groaning in pleasure as he came. For a while, he held her there, eyes locked. Carrying her over to the Persian rug in the middle of the floor, he lay down with her. "Casey." He said it all in that one word. She fell into his arms, her chest rising and falling as she tried to catch her breath. Never in her life. Never had she felt like this.

Finn pulled her closer, holding her as if he never wanted to let her go.

CHAPTER TWENTY-FOUR

"I'M GLAD I SOLD the hotel to you," Casey said later when their breathing had finally slowed and the heat of their bodies had cooled. The thunderstorm had moved on, leaving the air crisp with the scent of fresh rain. They lay on their backs on the rug staring up at the rain-dimpled glass overhead. Finn had never felt so at peace. The afternoon had faded away into evening with their lovemaking. But for a while, it was as if they had stopped time.

Finn drew back to look at her. He realized that there was nothing keeping her here now. Tomorrow morning, she'd leave along with the others. "Your grandmother's list—"

"I have everything on it. Vi will be shipping the bigger things. The rest I'm taking back to California."

He realized he was holding his breath. "Then there is nothing stopping you from leaving in the morning?"

She leaned back to look at him. "What?"

"I don't want you to go." The words were out before he could call them back. "I can't bear the thought that now that I've found you… I don't want to be away from you, even for a few days, let alone weeks, while I sort this all out."

Casey smiled. "I don't want to go. But I have a job."

"A job you said you want to change."

"I have to go back at least for a few weeks so they can find another hotelier."

"I know." He cupped her cheek and looked into her beautiful summer-blue eyes. He was still afraid for her. He had too many suspicions. Claude and Devlin were still missing. Until he heard that they'd returned home... He groaned. "I know you have to leave for so many reasons. But it won't be the last you see of me."

Her smile broadened, her eyes twinkling. "I'm glad to hear that. What will *you* do?"

He shook his head. "I'll probably start making arrangements to salvage much of the furnishings before I see about having the hotel demolished, the debris hauled off and the land made ready to sell. I'm sure there are other developers out there who would be interested. Devlin's contacts aren't the only ones."

He saw her reaction and drew her to him. "I thought it's what you wanted."

"I thought it was, too. It still is. I'm just feeling... sentimental."

Finn held her closer, kissing the top of her head. "If you want the hotel—"

"No." She drew back and met his gaze. "I don't. It's time to move on. Even my grandmother understood that. She just hoped..." She didn't have to finish.

He knew. "She hoped that Megan's murder would be solved first. I still think it will happen. I plan to talk to the marshal with the new evidence I've collected. I'm hoping he will be able to track down Devlin and Claude to make sure they aren't...in some kind of trouble."

CASEY FROWNED AS she saw the concern in his expression.

"It's just a feeling," he said quickly. "I'm more worried about what will happen before this reunion is officially over."

"More ghost tricks?" she joked and saw that his concern ran deeper and darker than that. She shivered. He rubbed his hands along her arms. "What aren't you telling me? From the day I arrived here, I've had the feeling you really believe the Crenshaw is haunted."

He sighed. "There's something I need to show you."

Once dressed, they went down to his room, closing the door firmly behind them. Casey had picked up on his tension. She stood in the middle of the room as Finn went to his duffel.

"I found this when I was searching the hotel for Megan's diary."

She couldn't imagine what he'd found. But just the mention of the diary made her stomach roil. If he'd found something, why hadn't he mentioned it before now?

He pulled out a small notebook in a plastic bag. He turned toward her, and she had a moment of panic. What if there had been two diaries? What if she'd taken the wrong diary? Megan and her head games. It would have been so like her to keep two.

He unzipped the bag and took out the notebook. "It's pretty dusty. I have no idea how long it's been hidden under the stairs." He opened it, found the page he was looking for and handed it to her.

She stared down at what was written there, instantly relieved to see that the handwriting definitely wasn't Megan's. Megan had always been doodling on any and everything she could find when she was supposed to be working. Whoever had written this, it hadn't been her.

With each word she read, her heart began to pound harder. The text sent chills through her. "Who wrote this?" He shook his head. "This can't be real." But she knew better. There was an authenticity to it. She could almost feel the writer's pain as well as the darkness that surrounded the killer in him.

She quickly handed back the notebook, feeling as if just holding it connected her with the writer in some awful way.

"It just confirms what's been bothering me since I began digging into the hotel's history." He put the book back into the plastic bag as if he thought it might be some sort of evidence. Then he returned it to the duffel bag and came back with a sheet of paper. He motioned for her to join him on the edge of the bed.

Sitting down beside him, she hugged herself against what else he'd discovered.

"I made a list of young women who went missing over the years after either working at the hotel or staying here," he said.

Did she remember people going missing?

"Even before I found the notebook, I'd seen entries in your grandmother's journal about female staff going missing. Often it would appear they had left, but they never returned home. The law assumed they had run away, I would imagine because the cases were never solved."

Casey couldn't believe this. "I never knew any of this." She realized that she would have been back in California before it became evident that one of the female staff hadn't returned home. Her grandmother had never mentioned any of this.

"I got to thinking," Finn was saying, "Anna had a lot of return guests each summer. What if one of them was a serial killer?"

She shot to her feet. This wasn't possible. She didn't want to believe it, and she could see it was one reason he hadn't mentioned it before now. "It sounds like you had too much time on your hands."

"I tried to match up the years that young women went missing with return guests."

She stared at him. "And?"

He shook his head. "I really thought I was on to something, but I didn't have any luck. But these women's disappearances were never solved. Because they were from somewhere else, they kind of fell through the gaps in the system." He tossed the paper aside.

"How many?" The words came out high and tight. She didn't want to believe this. Her grandmother had known; that was how Finn had found out. No wonder she'd wanted Casey to put an end to it by finding Megan's killer.

"Eight, not including Megan since her body was found. That's why I thought she must have been killed by one of the staff. But now...now I'm wondering if I was wrong about that. She could have been number nine, but the killer didn't have time to move her body."

Feeling stunned, Casey couldn't speak. Nine young women. She'd thought it had just been Megan. But what if there *had* been others? She thought of the ghost sightings over the years. They'd all been young women. She swallowed, still refusing to believe in ghosts.

"I plan to turn over what I've discovered to the marshal," Finn was saying. "It might not go any further than that. But I have to try. Megan said she'd discovered something dark and sinister in this hotel. I thought she was just being overly dramatic. But if true, then her killer might not have been one of the staff at all. Maybe there was someone else in those woods that night."

Casey hugged herself tightly.

He moved to her quickly and drew her close. "I didn't mean to upset you." She shook her head against his strong, solid chest. "I think we could both use a glass of wine to celebrate the sale. Let's hope your grandmother left a bottle or two in the wine cellar."

She didn't feel much like celebrating, but she could use a glass of wine. What she wasn't sure she wanted to do, though, was venture down into the basement of the hotel. It had always given her the creeps.

"Are you really telling me that, in the months you've been here, you haven't already looked in the wine cellar?" she asked, giving him a side-eye and a grin as she tried to hide her discomfort.

CHAPTER TWENTY-FIVE

FINN PRETENDED TO be offended, then laughed. "I couldn't find the key, remember? But I'm betting you have one. But before we go down to the dungeon, I want to go outside. There's supposed to be a full moon tonight."

They stepped out onto the patio off the kitchen. The air was crisp and damp and wonderful in the aftermath of the storm. Standing there with him, Casey felt even more light-headed. What was it about this man that he'd broken down her barriers? He'd gotten to her and in such a short time. It terrified her even as goose bumps of excitement ran across her skin.

She stared up at Montana's big sky filled with stars. It was so beautiful that it stole her breath away—just as being here with Finn on such a night made her heart beat faster.

"I'm hard-pressed to pick a favorite spot at this hotel, but this one is definitely up there, and I don't have to climb all the way up to the tower, which is also one of my favorite places," he said and grinned. "Especially now."

She felt her cheeks heat with the memory of their love-making in the tower. Like him, she'd never think of that room without thinking of the two of them in the throes of lovemaking.

"The sky is incredible," he said quietly.

She looked up at the black velvet studded with tiny jewels of light and wondered how many nights Finn had stared up at the stars alone. This man and this amazing night were like magic. She felt herself opening all the way to him, surrendering to him, to this night, to whatever the future held, while at the same time saying goodbye. "It is so hard to let this place go."

He turned to her, sympathy in his gaze. "I can imagine. Hard to let go of anything you've loved and lost." She could see that he knew the feeling. She felt raw with emotion. He made her ache for him, wanting more.

"You do realize that Jason was also behind all that in there with the Ouija board," she said as she tried to rein in her emotions. "I don't think he's dangerous, just—"

"Just annoying?" Finn said and laughed. He had a wonderfully musical laugh. She thought she would never tire of it. "I wouldn't be surprised to find out he sent the invitations."

"Guess it doesn't matter now," she said and looked off into the distance. They were quiet for a long while, both staring up at the night sky.

"Did you see that?" he said, excitement in his voice.

She had. She'd made a wish on it—just as she had as a girl. "I haven't seen a falling star in so long because of living in the city. I'd forgotten what the sky was like here. I've missed it."

He stepped to her. "I hope you made a wish." She didn't move, didn't breathe as he closed the distance between them, between their lips. He kissed her gently, only their mouths touching for a few moments before he cupped the back of her head with his hand, his fingers burrowing deep in her long hair as he drew her even closer and deepened the kiss.

She breathed him in, relishing the feel of his mouth,

the taste of him on her tongue, the strong, male feel of his body molding to her own soft curves. She sighed contentedly as he slowly drew back to look at her as if he'd never seen her before.

"THE MOON," CASEY SAID on a gasp, making him turn to look over his shoulder. A huge silver moon rose up over the black silhouette of the mountain. She sounded as if the sight had taken her breath away—just as she had when he'd kissed her.

He wanted to take a mental picture of this moment and keep it always, as he put his arm around her and they watched the moon rise from the dark depths.

"It's beautiful," she whispered, snuggling against him.

"No more beautiful than you." He couldn't bear the thought of letting her walk out of his life—not even temporarily. "Dang, I'm going to miss you," he said, his voice sounding husky.

"Finn—"

"I know," he said quickly. "You'll be safer away from here, and I know it's what you have to do." He didn't want her to go, but he had to let her. He wasn't even sure what his plans were for the future. He now owned a hotel in Buckhorn, Montana. He still had no idea what he would do with it. Maybe give it to the town and let them do with it what they pleased. The idea appealed to him.

But tonight, he would try to make it last as long as he could. "You realize that if we don't go look for that bottle of wine soon…"

Casey nodded as if she knew exactly what would happen. She wouldn't have minded in the least.

"Fortunately, the night is young," he said with a laugh. "To the wine cellar."

They went down to the lobby. Finn watched her go through the keys.

"That's odd. It isn't here," she said.

He'd already looked, so he wasn't surprised as he followed her into the office. She used the key on the ribbon around her neck and opened a desk drawer and pulled it all the way out. A key was taped to the bottom of the drawer.

"My grandmother was always losing her keys. She had an extra made." She shrugged. "We're probably going to find the wine cellar empty since someone has the original key, but maybe we'll get lucky."

He'd already gotten lucky when this ridiculous idea of searching for Megan's killer had led him to Casey. But as they started to venture down into the basement, Casey couldn't get the key to work.

Frowning, she turned to face him. "Someone changed the lock."

"Well, I guess that takes care of that," he said.

"No. Why would someone do that? Can you bust down the door?"

He laughed. "If you're thinking I'm going to rear back and crash into that door with my shoulder... I saw something in the kitchen. Stay here." He returned moments later with a variety of tools, including a flashlight.

It didn't take him long to break the lock. As the door swung open, he looked down into the dim abyss. "You sure about this?"

"I used to hate being sent down to get wine," she said, but he could tell by the look in her eyes that she wasn't going to let that stop her. Clearly she was curious why someone had put a new lock on the door. So nothing was going to stop her.

They dropped down the stairs into a labyrinth of tunnels that carried pipes and conduits, the ceilings low, the smell old and damp with a hint of putrid. He'd known he would eventually have to see what was down here in the underbelly of the hotel. Anna had assured the marshal that Megan's diary wasn't in the locked basement, so he hadn't bothered to break the lock to search. In truth, he'd had no desire to come down here.

CASEY TURNED QUICKLY to the right and headed for the large locked door of the wine cellar. But Finn was shining the flashlight beam the other way into one of the main tunnels that ran under the hotel. A lot of the lights had burned out down here. As her eyes were starting to adjust to the darkness beyond, she saw him studying marks on the dirt floor. "Finn?"

"Something's been digging down here," he said as he squatted down near one spot along the wall. "That's probably the sound we've both heard." He shone the beam over the wall. She could see where the brick appeared to be decayed and disintegrating. "It looks like your grandmother had parts of this basement shored up with new brick and rock over the years."

He rose to his feet, letting the beam of light drop to the floor again as he turned to her. "Probably an animal got in somehow and was trying to dig its way out."

She felt a chill. If she'd had any thoughts of saving the place, she didn't now. Even she could see that keeping the hotel would cost a fortune to maintain it. Seeing where something had dug only made her more anxious to get out of here. She felt as if she couldn't breathe until they got back to the upper floor. She yearned for the fresh air just outside.

Finn stepped to her, gently brushing her shoulder as he did. His gaze settled on her, sending slivers of pleasure rushing to her center. "Let's see about that wine, shall we, and get out of here."

She couldn't agree more as she hurriedly stepped to the wine cellar's large wooden door and went to use the pass-key. When she saw that someone had added a large pad-lock, she let out a frustrated exclamation.

"Problem?" he asked as he stepped closer and saw the padlock. "That's odd, isn't it?"

"Very. Why lock an already-locked door? Why change the lock on the door down here to begin with?" she said.

"What do you want me to do?" He met her gaze and chuckled. "That's right. It is now my wine cellar, so if I want to break it open…" He grinned. "I'm opening it. I'll be right back."

Casey looked around the cold, damp space, wondering who had changed the locks and on what authority. Not that it mattered. She just didn't want to spend any more time down here than was necessary. She was almost regretting the plan to check the wine cellar. She would rather be up-stairs in bed with Finn right now.

She couldn't help but notice that it seemed overly dark down here. It appeared every other bulb had burned out and needed to be replaced. Not that it now had anything to do with her, she reminded herself. She had to let go of this place. Let it be whatever it would be from here on out.

As she waited, she couldn't help remembering another time down here when she'd thought she was alone—and hadn't been. She'd come down to get a bottle of wine for the restaurant at her grandmother's behest.

She hugged herself from the chill that wound round her neck at the memory. She'd just started to open the door when she'd sensed someone behind her. If Megan's ghost was still hanging around this hotel, then she was here right now. Casey swallowed back the bile that rose in her throat as she slowly turned, sensing again something behind her. This time no one was there. Had she really expected to see Megan standing there—just like last time?

The memory was so sharp and painful that she couldn't believe ten years had passed. Megan standing so close that Casey had felt the hair stand up on the back of her neck. She'd turned, catching that cloying scent of perfume, startled to see Megan. Even more startled to see the knife in her hand.

"What—"

That was all she'd gotten out before Megan had pushed her against the wine-cellar door hard enough to take her breath away. She'd expected to feel the bite of the blade, given the wild look in the young woman's eyes.

But instead, Megan pressed a finger to her lips and whispered "Shh" next to her ear. "The monster will hear you."

Casey's heart had been pounding too hard to hear anything but the rush of blood careering through her veins.

She wanted to push the woman away, but Megan was still brandishing the blade in front of her face. She told herself that the young woman was just trying to scare her. It was working.

"You can't—"

Megan silenced her with a hand to her mouth.

They stayed like that for a long moment until Casey had had enough.

She'd pushed Megan away, angry enough to have not cared about the knife. "What kind of stupid game are you—"

"You know about the monster, don't you?"

"What are you talking about?"

Megan eyed her for a long moment, eyes narrowing with anger. "How could I have forgotten? Of course you know. This is *your* hotel."

Was the woman delusional? Or just toying with her?

"They're waiting for this wine," Casey had said, realizing that she didn't care one way or the other about what was wrong with Megan. The woman had been mean to her since day one.

But as she'd reached to unlock the wine cellar, she'd seen that the hand holding the knife was shaking, and there were tears in Megan's eyes.

"Stop pretending that you're the one who's scared."

Megan let out a snort. "I'm not scared of you, pip-squeak. I hope the monster gets you." She wiped at her eyes and stormed off.

"Put that knife back in the kitchen where you found it," Casey had yelled after her.

"This should get it open." The sound of Finn's voice made her jump. "Sorry. You all right?"

She nodded and swallowed the lump in her throat. Megan had been genuinely afraid. Why hadn't Casey seen that? Why hadn't she questioned her further? Because she thought it was one of Megan's stunts.

"Step back," Finn said and went to work on the door to the sound of splintering wood.

Casey watched him cut away wood next to the lock and begin to pry. The lock broke with a crack that was like an explosion in the enclosed space. Casey watched him remove the rest of the large padlock and reach for the handle. He stopped and turned back to her, thinking he would need the key. But as he turned the handle, the door creaked open.

She was almost afraid to look beyond it for fear of what she would see. A stale but familiar scent rushed out. He felt inside for a light switch, and a moment later the wine racks were illuminated—along with the wine bottles.

Finn let out a low whistle. "I did not expect this."

"Me, either." Whoever had put the padlock on the door had kept anyone from raiding the wine. "I knew that when my grandmother fell ill, she closed the hotel, paid to have it boarded up and left everything as it was because she'd thought she would be back. Lars must have done this to keep anyone out." She shook her head, surprised at how much wine was still here as she glanced inside. The wine cellar was large from a time when the many shelves had been full. Now most of the shelves were filled with only dust, and yet there were still a lot of wine bottles.

"Why don't you grab some, and we'll take them upstairs? You can pick," she told him, feeling ill at ease.

He nodded, handed her the flashlight and started into the room but stopped.

"What is it?" Casey moved to look past him. He was staring down at the dust marks on the floor. What she saw sent her pulse into overdrive. Her throat had gone dry. She tried to swallow. "What is that?" she asked, voice breaking as she thought of the animal he'd thought had been digging down there.

"What would make a track like that?" he asked. He

shook his head, but she knew he was thinking the same thing she was. Something had been dragged through the dust.

She stared at the concrete floor and the misplaced dust. The marks went from the doorway deep into the wine cellar. What had been dragged back in there? "Be careful."

"You might want to stay out there for a minute while I check." He didn't have to ask her twice. His tone made goose bumps ripple over her flesh. What did he think might be back there?

She stepped away from the door and crossed her arms as she fought off the chill. The basement was starting to get to her. She desperately wanted out of here and found herself looking over her shoulder every few seconds. Her eyes were still adjusting to the dimness beyond the cellar. She turned on the flashlight and pointed it down the tunnel where Finn said something had been digging.

It was what lay next to it that had caught her eye. She told herself it couldn't be a skull even as the beam told her different. "Finn?" she called, her voice too high, too thin. *"Finn?"*

She jumped at his light touch on her arm. The moment she saw his expression, she knew. All the color had drained from his face. He had his phone in his hand. She watched him hit 9-1-1 before he looked up at her.

"It's bad, Casey," he said. As the emergency-services operator answered, he said, "I need to report a murder. Actually, two murder victims."

CHAPTER TWENTY-SIX

MARSHAL LEROY BAGGINS felt a sense of déjà vu. The last time there'd been a murder at the Crenshaw Hotel he'd been a deputy, green as a gourd and still wet behind the ears. That was when Megan Broadhurst had been murdered.

He remembered then-marshal Hugh Trafton getting the call and looking around the office that evening for someone to take with him to Buckhorn. Everyone else had gone home or was already out on a call. Hugh's gaze had skimmed over him and then slowly come back with a sigh.

"Come on," the marshal had said. "You might as well ride along."

Leroy had been excited to get out of the office. He'd had no idea at the time where they were going or why. They'd gotten into the big patrol car, and Hugh had turned on the lights and siren. Hugh was famous for driving fast.

Leroy remembered that thrilling feeling as they raced through the darkness on the empty two-lane toward Buckhorn. When he'd gotten into law enforcement, he'd thought it would be an adventure.

Not in small-town Montana. The calls for the law were often about checking on some old person in town, barking-dog complaints, a few break-ins and assists on car accidents, which meant directing traffic.

But that night, it had felt like he'd imagined law enforcement would be. There'd been a murder, and Hugh had gotten them to Buckhorn in record time. The town hadn't been a surprise, even though Leroy had never been there before. That was the problem: he'd hardly ever been out of his county before he signed on as a deputy with the marshal's department.

But when he'd seen the Crenshaw Hotel, his eyes had gone saucer-wide. That night it was all lit up, looking so out of place on the edge of that tiny Western town backed up against the pine-covered mountainside.

Seeing how taken he was with the hotel, Hugh told him that presidents and kings had once stayed there years ago. "Now it's just full of ghosts."

Leroy had shot the man a surprised look. "You're just foolin' with me."

"No, I ain't. I wish I was," Hugh had said as he'd parked and killed the engine. "Let's go see what we've got." He had started to open his door but stopped. "You aren't going to faint at the sight of a dead body, are you?"

"No, sir."

"If you feel like you're goin' to upchuck, you get the devil out of my crime scene." With that, Hugh opened his door, and Leroy quickly followed, surprised and a little disappointed when they hadn't gone into the hotel.

Instead, he'd followed the marshal across the parking lot to where some people were standing around a campfire. One of them directed Hugh toward the woods.

He'd never forget walking through those dark woods, chasing after the marshal's flashlight beam and trying to see what was waiting for them. He'd been afraid it was going to be something so gruesome that he might embarrass himself.

That was when Hugh stopped and Leroy saw Megan Broadhurst sprawled facedown on a bed of dried pine needles. Her long blond hair was dark with her blood, and so was her white dress. She'd lost a shoe, so one of her feet was bare.

Hugh had turned to him. "Get your notebook out. Get the witnesses' names back at the campfire. Don't let any of them leave." Then the marshal had stepped to the body, squatted down and checked for a pulse. "Get moving, son," Hugh said. "Don't let them change their clothes, and if they have already, I want what they were wearing."

Then the marshal had gotten on his radio and called for the coroner and more deputies.

Leroy had already called for backup as he turned on the patrol car's lights and siren and raced toward Buckhorn through the darkness. This time they would be going into the hotel—into the bowels of it.

He couldn't help but think about what Marshal Hugh Trafton had said as he'd hit the gas and the Crenshaw Hotel had disappeared behind them that night ten years ago.

"That is one scary-ass place," Hugh said, glancing in his rearview with a shudder.

Leroy had looked at him in surprise. He'd never taken a big, strong, by-the-book man like Hugh to be afraid of ghosts and foolishly said as much.

"Ghosts?" the marshal howled. "Ain't the ghosts that scare me. It's the evil I felt the one time I stepped in that place. Something lurks in the depths. Mark my words. Something dark and dangerous."

At the time, Leroy had kept his opinion of that to himself. He'd silently scoffed as he'd looked in his side mirror, the lights of the hotel barely visible behind them.

Finn held Casey tightly to him as they waited by the back door. The marshal had been abundantly clear. *Don't touch anything else. Stay where you are. Don't tell anyone else. I'm on my way.*

"We're not staying down here. We'll meet you at the back door," Finn had said.

The marshal had sworn. *"We?"*

"Casey Crenshaw and I. She's with me. I'm taking her upstairs."

"I just told you to stay—"

"It's cold down here by the wine cellar, and we both need air," he'd snapped. "We'll meet you at the back door. Everyone else is outside by the campfire. We haven't told anyone, and we won't."

He could almost hear the marshal grinding his teeth. "I'll see you at the back door."

They'd stepped out onto the patio, where they would be able to see when the marshal arrived but no one at the campfire would see them there in the dark. They huddled together, both in shock. He hadn't told Casey any more than he'd told the 9-1-1 operator and the marshal. He'd given his name, his location and said that there'd been a murder.

"It's Claude?" she'd asked, and he'd nodded. "Devlin?" He'd nodded again, and she'd begun to cry. Now they were both silent, comforted by being together with no need for words.

Finn's head was spinning trying to make sense out of everything. Claude and Devlin were dead, locked in the wine cellar of the hotel, killed apparently the same way Megan had been. He didn't think that was a coincidence.

When the first law-enforcement vehicles pulled in, lights

flashing, siren blaring, the marshal had barely gotten out before two more squad cars pulled up.

Marshal Leroy Baggins was much younger than Finn had imagined, but he carried himself like a seasoned veteran. He was tall, lean and all business as he strode up to them. "Finnegan James?"

Finn nodded.

The marshal turned to Casey. "You're the owner of the hotel?"

She shook her head. "I was, but I sold it to Finn earlier today."

The marshal looked from one to the other before turning to his deputies, who were standing beside their vehicles as if waiting for orders. "Cordon off the hotel. Get the names of those people at the campfire, and keep them down there until I tell you different." He turned back to Finn and Casey. "You two, show me where you found the body."

"Actually," Finn said, "it's *bodies*."

LEROY COULD TELL that the last place either of them wanted to go was back down to the wine cellar. He was hit with the smell first, then that feeling of being underground with the weight of the hotel overhead. Nothing about it was pleasant.

Within yards of the wine cellar, he ordered, "Stay here." He saw the drag marks on the floor going into the wine cellar, but none outside it. Stepping closer, he saw what appeared to be narrow tire tracks. That could explain how someone had gotten the bodies in. But how had they gotten them down the steep stairs from the floor above?

"Is there an elevator that comes down here?" he asked over his shoulder.

"No. There's a service elevator near the kitchen, but it was never brought down here because of the cost," Casey said.

Leroy nodded and entered the wine cellar, careful to step around the tracks that were already in the dust. The bodies were at the far back. He crouched down next to the first one. There was no reason to check for a pulse; the man was obviously dead and had been for some time. He did worm out the deceased's wallet, though. Devlin Wright. It appeared the man's head had been bashed in from behind—much like Megan Broadhurst's had.

Letting out a curse, he moved to the second body nearby. The man's ID said he was a doctor. Dr. Claude Drake of San Francisco. He'd also had his skull crushed from behind. Again, just like Megan Broadhurst's. That unsolved case had followed Hugh to his grave, something the old marshal had never gotten over. Now it was coming back to haunt Leroy.

Stepping back outside the wine cellar, he found Casey Crenshaw in Finnegan James's arms. He'd picked up on the energy between the two of them. *Lovers*, he thought. He found that both interesting and suspicious, especially after his initial run of both of their names through his system. Finnegan James had been missing for months and presumed dead. Casey Crenshaw had been a main suspect in Megan Broadhurst's murder.

"Is there a place we can talk upstairs?" he asked.

"There's the main lounge and lobby," Casey said. "If you want more privacy, you can use the office behind the main desk."

He followed the two of them upstairs, sealing the doorway to the basement before they walked down to the main lounge and ordering one of the deputies to seal the entry with crime-scene tape.

Leroy took in the amazing hotel as he did. Ten years ago, he'd promised himself he would come back to the hotel as a guest. He never had. He blamed Hugh for that, even though he'd come to agree that evil did seem to live in certain people—and places.

"Why don't you have a seat out here in the lobby while I talk to Mr. James," he suggested to Casey.

Taking Finn back to the office, he closed the door and said, "Help me understand what's going on here. Imagine my surprise when I ran your name through our system. Everyone thought you were dead, but I'm sure you were aware of that."

"I can explain," Finn said, and Leroy waved him into a chair as he sat down behind the desk and turned on his recorder. Patiently, he listened to the man's explanation.

"You do realize how crazy that sounds. Okay, what's this about a reunion?"

Finn explained. "I have the invitation in my room."

Leroy studied him for a moment before he asked for the names of everyone who'd gotten the invitation.

"I don't know, but I can tell you who showed up," Finn said.

Leroy wrote down the names as Finnegan called them off: Jason Underwood, Dr. Benjamin Travers, Dr. Claude Drake, Jennifer Mullen, Shirley Langer, Devlin Wright and Patience Riley. "And these were the staff members the summer Megan Broadhurst worked at the hotel?"

Finn nodded. "And Casey."

"Yes, Casey. Did you two know each other before this?"

"No."

Leroy did the math in his head. "Who is missing?"

Finn frowned. "Claude and Devlin were the only ones."

The marshal radioed his deputy outside the hotel to do a head count. "It appears that Patience Riley left earlier. You didn't know that?"

Finn shook his head.

As a deputy appeared, Leroy said, "Go with Mr. James here to get the invitation, while I talk to Casey Crenshaw." He looked at Finn. "Send her in on your way out. I hope I don't have to tell you not to leave. I'll want to talk to you again."

CHAPTER TWENTY-SEVEN

THE MARSHAL STUDIED the young woman as she entered the room, remembering Casey Crenshaw from ten years ago. Who could forget that red hair or that face? Her freckles weren't quite as discernible now, but those blue eyes... Those he could never forget.

Just as he hadn't forgotten that she was a suspect in the original murder. In fact, she'd had a huge quarrel with the deceased that had been overheard by witnesses the night before Megan had been killed.

Ten years ago he'd seen fear in those blue eyes. Now he saw shock but also a wariness. "Please have a seat," he said. "Maybe you can tell me what's going on here and how you're involved."

She sat down, took a breath, let it out. "I came to Buckhorn to sell the hotel and property and take a few of my grandmother's things that she wanted me to keep. That's all. I was planning to leave for California tomorrow morning."

He motioned the deputy who'd stuck his head in the doorway to enter and give him the invitation. "Tell Mr. James to wait. I don't want him talking to the others."

The deputy said that the crime-scene crew had arrived and had gone down to the scene, then backed out the door as Leroy read the invitation and looked up at Casey. "Did you—"

"I didn't send those," she said adamantly, as if it weren't

the first time she'd had to deny this. "I'd never seen one before Finn showed me the one he'd gotten in the mail. I have no idea who sent them."

"So everyone who's here was here ten years ago when Megan Broadhurst was murdered."

"Except Finn. He wasn't part of the staff, but he had dated Megan. He assumed that's why he'd gotten an invitation."

"You came here to sell the hotel."

She explained that Devlin had been giving her the runaround, trying to get the price down. "Finn made me a generous offer, and I took it."

"Devlin wasn't happy about this?"

She shook her head. "He was upset because apparently his investors were counting on him to make the deal."

"Who were his investors?"

"I have no idea. He kept that from me, and I didn't really care. My grandmother recently died. I was anxious to get the place sold."

"What was your relationship with Claude Drake?" Leroy asked.

She shook her head again. "I knew who he was because we worked together ten years ago, but I hadn't seen him since or ever really talked to him before he left this weekend. At least, we thought he'd left."

"Why did you question whether he had or not?"

She told him about the ghost stunt. "The lock of hair found on the tree was synthetic. It was someone wearing a wig and a white dress just trying to scare us. Also..." She seemed to hesitate. "I'm sure Finn has probably already told you about the car accident Megan was in earlier that year. It was apparently why her parents had sent her out here to work for the summer. Megan had lied about being behind the wheel. Finn found out that Claude might have taken the job here at the hotel to get some kind of revenge on Megan, since he was friends with the brother of one of the girls who was badly hurt in the wreck."

No, Finnegan hadn't mentioned that. He wondered if it had anything to do with these latest murders or if all of it was tied to Megan Broadhurst and her murder.

"Who had access to the wine cellar?"

"I don't know," Casey said. "I hadn't been down there until tonight. I was surprised to see that someone had re-placed the lock down to the basement and put a padlock on the door."

"You went down to get wine?" She nodded in response. "Who broke the locks?"

"Finn."

He nodded. "I'd prefer you didn't leave town." She didn't seem surprised at his request, and she rose to leave but then hesitated again. "Yes?" He expected her to tell him that she needed to get back to work or some other excuse.

"There's something I need to tell you." He saw her swallow, and he thought, *What now?* "You asked me about Megan's diary ten years ago." He realized he was holding his breath. "I said I didn't know anything about it." She swallowed again. "I wasn't telling the truth. I found the diary before Megan was killed and burned it because she'd been tormenting me and saying she'd written awful things about me in it." Relief seemed to make her body limp. "I didn't read it. I just burned it in the firepit."

He swore silently. She'd interfered in a murder investiga-tion. He doubted she was the only one. "You were sixteen, right?" A nod. "Megan had been tormenting you?" Another nod. "How did everyone feel about Megan?" he asked, suspecting Casey wasn't the only one who'd lied.

She met his gaze. "They hated her. She plagued the entire staff. That's why I can't understand why they would come back here for some stupid reunion."

"Apparently, someone had unfinished business."

FROM OUTSIDE BY the campfire, Jason watched the bodies being brought out of the basement in black body bags. No one had told them anything except that they weren't allowed to leave. He didn't have to guess who was in those bags.

The cold night spring wind whipped the boughs of the nearby pines as the bodies were loaded into the back of the coroner's van. Shirley was crying, Benjamin holding her. Jen stood staring into the fire as if she couldn't bear to watch.

Jason couldn't help but think of Megan. She'd been zipped up for that same ride. Like tonight, he'd stood out in the cold and watched as the body was taken away. Like then, he'd realized he was lucky that it hadn't been him.

The deputy who'd ordered them to stay by the fire had said the marshal would be speaking to each of them before the night was over. Jason had been one of the first to go inside. He'd answered a few questions about why he was at the closed hotel and then the last time he'd seen Claude, then Devlin.

He'd answered the marshal's questions, before being told to not say anything to anyone else. He'd been asked his room number, and a deputy had escorted him to it.

Sprawling on his bed, he couldn't get Megan out of his mind. He was sure Devlin and Claude were dead because of her. He thought of the night he'd gotten his hand caught in the scarf she'd had tied around her neck. She'd actually dressed up to come down to the campfire each and every time as if she wanted everyone to know that she was special.

But that night, alone with her, both of them breathing hard, he'd pulled back from a kiss, and his hand had gotten tangled in that damned scarf.

When he tried to jerk it free, it had tightened around her neck. He remembered the way her eyes had widened in alarm—and something else. It was the something else that had excited him.

He'd twisted the scarf, tightening it around her throat as her eyes widened further. He'd been scared that he might keep tightening it, but even the thought excited him. He'd kept twisting until she writhed on the bed beneath him and clutched at him, digging her fingernails into his shoulders.

That had been the best sex he'd ever had, and Megan had come back for more, each time saying she didn't want it rough.

But the truth was, she did. Until she didn't. Just like Patience.

FINN FOUND CASEY in her room. The moment he walked in, she ran to him. He took her in his arms, kissing the top of her head as she cuddled against him.

"It's just so…awful," she said as she pulled back to look at him. All he could do was nod. There weren't words. He'd feared something had happened to them, just as he feared it wasn't over yet. "Is it true Patience is missing?"

"Jason says she left." He could see that she didn't trust Jason's word on anything. He felt pretty much the same way.

One of the windows was open a crack. He could smell the campfire and see the glow of the fire. But everyone had been brought in and questioned before being sent to their rooms. The deputy had tried to get Finn to go to his room, but Finn wasn't having it. "I'll be in Casey's room. I'm not letting her out of my sight."

"A deputy told me that we're not allowed to leave our rooms tonight. I told him I wanted to stay with you." She hugged him harder. "I don't know when we'll be allowed to leave."

"None of that matters," she said, pulling back to look at him. "Who killed them?"

Finn thought any number of people, including the investors who'd trusted Devlin to make the deal on the hotel, but he only shook his head. Past her, through the window, he could see deputies searching the woods and the outbuildings, their flashlight beams flickering in and out of the trees as they moved.

"I was going to ask you to stay in my room tonight," he said.

She smiled. "I've seen your room. Glad you decided to stay in mine."

"I'm usually neat and organized." She laughed in answer to that but quickly sobered. Tears filled her eyes. He wanted to tell her that everything was going to be all right, that the marshal would find out who had killed Claude and Devlin. But the law had never found out who had killed Megan. Wasn't that why they were all here right now? Except for Casey. She'd come back only to sell the place and move on. But someone had other plans. He still didn't know who that other person was, but he suspected now more than ever that it was the killer and Casey still wasn't safe.

THE MARSHAL HAD just finished questioning Benjamin Travers when one of the deputies stuck his head in the door and motioned that he needed to speak to him outside the room.

Leroy knew bad news when he saw it coming. He excused himself and stepped out into the lobby. He figured it would be another body, Patience Riley's. He'd put a BOLO out on Riley, figuring if she really had left, she'd be picked up soon. He'd been told that she'd left not too long ago, which meant she would still be in Montana.

"We found something." The deputy held up the bag.

For a moment Leroy thought it was some kind of dead animal. "What is it?"

"A wig."

He was about to say *And you think this is important how?* but he stopped himself short of doing that as he remembered what he'd been told about Megan's ghost. Finn had said he'd found a strand of what appeared to be blond hair caught in a tree bough, but the hair had turned out to be from a wig.

"Let's see if the lab techs can get any DNA or hair fibers from it," the marshal said. Finn had said that everyone had just assumed Claude or Devlin was behind the ghost sighting. But if they were already dead...

Just then, Deputy Hepner came up from the basement carrying an evidence bag. Leroy swore under his breath as he braced himself for more bad news. With a start, he saw that the bag contained what appeared to be a human skull. His gaze shot to Hepner.

"There are more," the deputy said. "Those tracks down in the basement that led up to the cellar door? I found what made them. It's a cart that was in an old shed in the trees out back. I think that's how the killer got the bodies into the basement. If I'm right, then there's a tunnel from the outbuildings into the basement."

Leroy saw himself in Hepner. It was one reason he'd been harder on him than the others. "Good work, Hepner."

"Thank you, sir. If it's all right with you, I'll go back to the basement and see if I can find the tunnel."

Leroy gave him a nod and turned back to the office and Benjamin Travers.

WHEN CASEY HAD reached her room, she'd quickly turned on all the lights. She'd felt foolish checking the closet and the bathroom, but she did it anyway.

Moving to the window, she'd hugged herself as she looked out on the familiar landscape. Never in her wildest dreams could she have imagined what was waiting for her at the hotel when she'd arrived just days before—Finn included.

Just thinking of him steadied her as she waited for him to return. He'd gone across the hall to get a few things for the night. She tried to relax. Finn would be here with her tonight, even as she realized that there wasn't much night left. She could see the sky lightening over the mountains to the east. As exhausted as she was, she doubted she'd be able to sleep.

She heard him enter the room and ran to him. He pulled her into his strong, hard body, and she leaned into him. "Something's happening," she said, her voice high and tight as she pulled away from him to motion toward the window. She had spotted the sudden movement in the woods. "You don't think they found Patience, do you?"

"Jason said she left, but…" Jason had said he thought the others had left as well.

The horror of it hit her hard. She realized she'd never believed that any of the staff had killed Megan. Finn had, though. He'd been so sure that there was a killer in the hotel with them. That was why he'd been worried about her.

But she hadn't taken it seriously. Or just hadn't wanted to believe that anyone she knew could kill. Was this what the reunion had been about—just as Finn had feared? Someone had planned to kill them off one at a time?

"You were right," she whispered.

Finn shook his head. "I wish I wasn't." He looked at her as if still worried.

She'd always been so proud of herself for needing almost no one. With Finn, she could let down the protective wall she'd built around herself. She could be not so strong.

As she began to cry, he turned her around, swept her off her feet and carried her over to the bed to lie next to her. She cuddled against him, letting the tears come, not sure if she was crying for the loss of her grandmother or out of fear and regret. It didn't seem to matter.

"This isn't over, you know," he said when she'd stopped crying.

She wiped at her tears and forced a smile. "The place is crawling with deputies."

He nodded, but she could see that it didn't relieve his concern.

Casey felt the lateness of the night in her bones. Her eyes felt sandy, and she found herself blinking as exhaustion began to take over.

"We should try to get some sleep," Finn said.

She didn't believe she would be able to sleep a wink, but still, she closed her eyes as Finn took her hand.

AFTER BEING QUESTIONED, Benjamin couldn't imagine anything worse than spending what was left of this night in this hotel with these people, even with deputies in the hallway. Then again, maybe he could.

"You heard?" he asked the group gathered in the staff-wing hallway. Jason looked worse than even the others, which made him feel a little better.

"We're going to get something to drink from the kitchen," Jason was saying.

"Haven't you had enough to drink tonight?" asked the deputy standing at the end of the hall. They'd been told not to leave the hotel and encouraged to stay in their rooms so they would be safe. "It will be morning soon. You should all try to get some sleep."

"We should do as he says," Jen said, tugging on Jason's sleeve.

"What's wrong with you?" he demanded of her.

"Seriously? You have to ask?" she snapped.

"Other than the obvious," he added.

"We're all scared," Benjamin said. "You going to pretend you're not?" He cursed himself for his need to show these people how much he'd changed. He shouldn't have come here. It made him furious with himself. None of these people cared what he'd done with his life. They didn't even understand what he did for a living or how important it was. It was sick that he'd needed them to acknowledge that he was somebody.

"What is wrong with all of us?" he demanded. "We're all *sick*. We all should have forgotten Megan a long time ago and put that summer behind us. If we had, we wouldn't be here now. We wouldn't be trapped here together."

"The marshal can't keep us here much longer without arresting us," Jason said, shooting a look at the deputy. "They let us all go after Megan was murdered."

"Yeah, well, it's even worse now, wouldn't you say?" Benjamin said. "Which one of you idiots thought this was a good idea?" He glanced at the others, his gaze coming back to Jason.

"It wasn't me," Jason said with a groan. "And we can assume it wasn't Claude or Devlin, so if it wasn't us and Casey swore it wasn't her…" He sighed. "Then it must have been Finn."

"Why would he do this?" Shirley demanded.

Jason raked a hand through his hair. "He was in love with Megan."

Jen nodded. "He did spend months in this hotel by himself looking for her diary or her ghost or whatever. What sane person does that?"

"I don't know," Shirley said. "I think he was looking for something, but it wasn't really Megan. I think he found it in Casey."

Jen groaned. "You're such a romantic."

Benjamin wouldn't let it go. "Whoever wanted us all here must have had a reason."

"Like what?" Jason said. "To kill us all off?"

"Maybe. Or maybe they just wanted Devlin and Claude," Shirley said, almost sounding hopeful.

"Kind of went to a lot of trouble to kill only two of us," Jason said.

"What about Patience?" Benjamin asked, looking directly at Jason.

"She left," he said and looked away. "She had to get home to her husband."

"Maybe whoever is doing this isn't done." They all turned to look at Benjamin where he stood. "Just saying, if one of us is killing off the others…maybe the only way to stay safe tonight is to stay together."

"Or sleep with our eyes open the rest of the night?" Jen demanded. "No, thanks. I have a lock on my room door and a can of bear spray in my pack."

"Don't you mean *our* room?" Shirley said. "Unless you want me to take another one."

"Maybe that's not such a bad idea." Jen said it as if the words pained her.

Shirley let out a huff but looked close to tears. "We've been friends since we were toddlers. You really think I'm a killer?"

"That's just it," Benjamin said. "We don't know, do we?"

"He's right," Jason said and moved a few feet down the hallway. "We should all go to our rooms and lock the doors. Maybe even put a chair under the knob."

"Maybe I'll just go back to the motel." Shirley looked toward the deputy. He shook his head from where he stood down the hallway.

"Stay," Benjamin told her. "The place is crawling with law enforcement. You're safer here. Even with us. At least for the rest of the night."

"Fine. I'll find a room to sleep in and lock the door." Shirley glared at Jen. "Sleep tight, everyone."

FINN LISTENED TO Casey's steady breaths as she fell into an exhausted sleep. He'd held her as she'd cried, then fallen asleep. He'd never known such a strong woman. It made him smile as he looked down at her. The sun was coming up on another day. He hated to think what this one was going to bring.

At the sound of running footfalls outside the door, he carefully pulled away from Casey. She didn't stir as he rose and went to the door to peer out. Two deputies had just run by. He could hear voices down in the lobby. Taking the passkey, he glanced at Casey and then locked the door behind him.

The voices were growing louder down in the main lounge. Something had happened. He thought of the notebook he'd found. In all the confusion, he hadn't mentioned it to the marshal. It might not be anything, but then again, it might.

He hurried across the hall to his room. The notebook in the plastic bag was in the side of the duffel bag where he'd stuffed it after showing it to Casey. He pulled it out and rushed down the dim hallway.

At the top of the stairs, he looked down to see a half-dozen deputies scurrying around. The marshal walked back into Anna's office. For a moment, Finn hesitated. He didn't like leaving Casey alone, worried that she would wake up and be frightened. But he had to know what was going on—and give the marshal what he'd found. He hurried down the stairs and headed for the office behind the desk. The marshal had left the door open.

"What's going on?" For a moment, he thought the marshal wasn't going to answer him.

"Weren't you asked to stay in your room?" the lawman snapped.

"What's happened?" Finn stepped into the room, determined not to leave until he had an answer. "I own this hotel now. If you've found something…"

The marshal nodded with a mumbled curse. "My deputies just found what appear to be old graves in the basement."

"Graves?" He was thinking the hotel had been built on an old cemetery when the marshal clarified.

"Someone has been burying bodies in the basement. Apparently for years."

Finn felt that bump in his bloodstream. "The missing young women."

"I beg your pardon?" the marshal said, looking at him with sudden mistrust.

"I spent months in this hotel, and during that time, I read all of the old journals that Casey's grandmother kept. Every few years, a young woman either who had been staying in the hotel or working here disappeared and was never found. I was going to bring the information to you, along with anything I'd learned about Megan's death." He thrust the bag toward the marshal. "I found this hidden under the stairs to the tower. There's a page in it you might want to read. I think you might be looking for a serial killer."

CHAPTER TWENTY-EIGHT

LEROY HAD TWO fresh murders and counting. Patience Riley was missing. Maybe she'd left. Or maybe she hadn't and they had yet to discover her body. He had more deputies coming from the next town to the west. The crime team had arrived and was processing the scene in the basement. He had deputies making sure no one left the hotel or ventured down to the wine cellar. He'd secured the crime scene as much as he could.

He'd told himself that he had control of the situation, and now Finnegan James had walked in and told him he might be looking for a serial killer?

He could see that the man wasn't going to leave until he looked at the notebook. It almost amused him that it had been put in a plastic bag like evidence. People watched too many crime shows.

It took him a moment. Most of the pages were blank. When he did find it, he was struck by the handwriting. There was something about it that set his teeth on edge even before he began to read. Halfway through, he dropped into the office chair.

By the end, he looked up at Finn. He wanted to argue that anyone could have written this. But he had a basement with God only knew how many bodies in it. The skull he'd seen was smaller than a man's, so he suspected it was that of a young woman.

There was no way he couldn't take this seriously. He started to thank Finnegan for bringing this to him and to order him back to his room when Deputy Hepner appeared in the doorway behind the man. Leroy didn't need any more bad news right now.

But when he saw Hepner's face, he knew that whatever it was, it was much worse than anything else that had been discovered tonight. That was the thing about Hepner: every emotion showed on that face. Right now it was bleached white. He'd seen the man's reaction when they found the graves. Hepner had been stoic, calm, contained. Now the deputy looked terrified.

Leroy felt his heart drop to his feet. "Thank you for this information," he said to Finnegan. "Now, I would appreciate it if you would go back to your room."

The man seemed to hesitate but then stepped past Hepner and out into the lobby. Leroy motioned the deputy in. He could tell that Finnegan was even more curious about what was going on.

Hepner closed the door behind him. "You need to come down to the basement. I found…"

Leroy shot him an impatient look.

The deputy swallowed and whispered in a hoarse voice, "Bombs."

The word was so out of place in the situation that it didn't make any sense for a moment. Not *a bomb* but *bombs*.

Hepner was green but smart. Still, Leroy doubted the kid had ever seen a bomb except in the movies.

"Show me." He rose to his feet, and they left the office. In the lobby, he didn't see Finnegan. Nor was he on the stairs. He didn't have time to worry about him, however, as he followed the deputy down the hall to the doorway to the basement and then into the dark underbelly of the hotel.

At the wine-cellar entrance, Hepner drew him down one of the series of tunnels that handled the utilities. A series of corroded piles and conduits ran along the ceiling. Leroy had to bend down in spots to keep from bumping his head as he followed the younger man deeper and deeper under one of the wings, the smell becoming more dank and stagnant and…grave-like.

"The bombs are all along the outside walls," Hepner said, his voice cracking, as he stopped to shine his flashlight on the first one he'd found.

Leroy stared at the dynamite for only a second before he turned to Hepner. "You say there are more of these?"

The deputy nodded. "All along the outside walls of the hotel, from what I can tell. I saw a half dozen before I came to tell you."

The marshal swore under his breath. Bombs along the outside support walls? This wasn't the first time he'd seen something like this. He had an uncle who specialized in explosive demolition. Uncle Pete had dropped some huge buildings in some of the country's largest cities. He was an expert, dropping them straight down. He did beautiful work, which his nephew had always admired. He'd seen his old newsreels and videos of his jobs and been amazed at how a huge building could just drop to its feet, crumbling into nothing but dust and debris.

"There's a knack to it, kid," Uncle Pete had said when Leroy had asked how it was done. "It has to implode from inside and all at the same time. One little foul-up, and you can take out half the block."

He'd asked if it was scary planting the explosives.

Pete had laughed. "Not if you know what you're doing and it's not your day to die."

"Your uncle's an idiot," his father had said. "He has a death wish. I suppose he didn't tell you about the time they didn't go off and he had to go back in, knowing that at any moment he could be blown to smithereens. Death wish. One of these days, his luck is going to run out."

Apparently that might have been true. Uncle Pete had died in one of his buildings a few years ago. No one knew why he'd gone back inside right before the building blew.

Leroy turned to his deputy, working to keep his tone calm and in control. "When we get upstairs, you're going to use some of those boards outside to board the doors into this place once everyone is out. Then I'm going to pull the fire alarm. I need you and the rest of the deputies to get everyone out of the building. No mention of bombs. Just get them out and yourselves a good distance away from the hotel. Get car keys from the guests and move them as well." He wanted them all to be able to leave when this was over.

Hepner took off down the tunnel back the way they'd come. Leroy followed at a good pace. The hair stood straight up on his neck. He could feel his mortality with each step even as his mind whirled. Who'd done this? And when had these been set to go off? He recalled that the invitations for the reunion had mentioned the hotel was to be destroyed.

Before or after the reunion was over?

As FINN CAME out into the lobby, he caught a glimpse of someone sneaking down the hallway toward the kitchen. Even in the dim light, he recognized Jason. What was the man up to?

He hurried after him. If he knew Jason, he was up to

no good. But when he reached the kitchen, the man was nowhere to be seen. So where had he gone, and what was he doing sneaking around? Probably looking for booze.

Finn hurried down the hallway to the back stairs that led from the kitchen floor to the staff floor. As he pushed open the door to the stairway, he could hear footfalls on the steps. Jason going back to the staff floor?

Letting the door close, Finn turned back to the kitchen. He opened the refrigerator and took out two bottles of water, one for him and one for Casey, then saw a carton of orange juice. Casey would be waking up soon since the sun would be rising. If she felt anything like he did, she'd need something to keep her going.

As he started to leave, he saw the blood on the outside of the refrigerator. It was just a smear. It startled him because it was so fresh. Jason? He saw another smear of fresh blood on the door. Jason hadn't been bleeding badly, because there were no droplets on the floor.

But he had been bleeding.

For just a moment, he thought about following him up the back stairs to the staff wing, but Finn had been gone too long as it was. He didn't want Casey waking up and finding him not there.

He turned with the orange juice and waters and headed for the hallway that would take him back to her when the fire alarm went off.

CASEY CAME AWAKE with a start. The fire alarm was blaring, reminding her of the drills her grandmother used to run with the staff before the hotel opened in the spring. She sat up, disoriented for a moment as if the years hadn't passed.

But as she came fully awake, she remembered where she

was and why. At the same time, she saw that Finn wasn't in the bed next to her. The bathroom door was open. No Finn. She'd fallen asleep in a T-shirt and jeans. All she had to do was step into her sandals. From the window, she saw deputies escorting some of the others outside.

She told herself to hurry. Her heart was pounding. Was the hotel on fire? Hadn't that always been a fear of her grandmother's? Of Casey's? If someone had pulled the alarm by mistake or as a joke, deputies wouldn't be escorting people out of the building, she told herself as she grabbed her purse.

Unlocking the door and stepping out into the hallway, she looked over into Finn's room. The door was open, and the room was empty. Maybe the deputies had already led him out. After locking the door behind her, she hurried down the hallway, headed for the back stairs.

But as she turned the corner, she almost collided with Jason.

"Casey?" He seemed confused and oblivious to the blaring fire alarm.

"We need to get out of here," she yelled over the alarm.

His gaze seemed unfocused. She noticed he had a scrape on his temple. It was bleeding, and he had something in his hands that caught the light. With a start, she recognized the necklace before he quickly pocketed it. The chain appeared to be broken. Her heart flopped in her chest, making her recall Megan breaking her bracelet.

"That's Patience's necklace," she cried and took a step back.

Jason seemed to come out of his daze. He blinked, shaking his head and yelling, "No. No, I didn't." But she could see that the chain was broken, as if it had been torn off Patience's neck. She took another step back, the fire alarm blaring so loudly she couldn't think.

Jason kept coming toward her, trying to tell her something, but she couldn't hear him over the noise. He reached for her as she took another step back, banging into the stairs doorway. Pushing it open, she turned and began to run as quickly as she could down the stairs. She could hear Jason yelling behind her but was unable to make out his words. It sounded as if he were right on her heels.

His fingers dug into the flesh of her shoulder, twisting her around and throwing her against the wall. She hit her head hard. The lights in the stairwell dimmed and then she was falling, arms flailing. She landed, her breath knocked from her body from the jarring fall. She felt pain and then nothing as the lights blinked out.

WITH THE FIRE alarm blaring, Finn dropped what he had in his hands and ran for the stairs. All he could think of was Casey waking up and seeing him gone. His heart was pounding as the fire alarm blared in his ears.

He could hear deputies hollering for everyone to get out of the building. One tried to stop him, grabbing his arm and detaining him for a few lost moments before he broke free. He rushed for the main stairway. Taking the steps three at a time, he reached the landing, breathing hard.

Casey would have been awakened by the alarm. She'd been already dressed. How quickly would she have tried to get out of the building? Maybe she was already outside waiting for him.

He reached her bedroom door. It was locked. He pounded on the door, calling her name over the sound of the alarm as he dug out the passkey from his jeans pocket.

Flinging the door open, he rushed in. She was gone. He felt a wave of relief but still doubled-checked to make sure that she wasn't in the bedroom before he ran for the open doorway.

The deputy who'd tried to stop him was blocking the doorway. The man grabbed his arm with one hand. The other hand was on the butt of his gun.

"Have you seen Casey?" he yelled to the officer, who only shook his head and motioned to Finn that the two of them were now leaving the building.

He broke free and ran back the way he'd come, down the stairs, only to collide with two deputies who escorted him out of the building with just enough force that he didn't fight them.

As he stumbled out into dim daylight, he looked frantically for Casey as he pulled out his phone and tried to call her. It rang and rang before going to voice mail.

Several deputies were moving everyone back from the building. He saw Jen and Shirley and Jason. What he didn't see was Casey. As he turned to go back toward the building, the marshal stepped out, a deputy on each side of him.

CHAPTER TWENTY-NINE

LEROY BARKED OUT orders quickly. He'd done a head count and realized the guests weren't all there. Casey Crenshaw was missing from the small group. That was about when he spotted Finnegan James headed for him. Leroy knew that look. Trouble.

"See if everyone can be put up at the motel," Leroy ordered Hepner. "I still want them all to stay in town temporarily until I can get to the bottom of this. If any of them resist, lock them in the back of your cruiser." Hepner got right on his cell phone to make arrangements as he headed for the parking lot, passing Finnegan on his way.

"Fortunately, a busload of tourists are checking out now," Hepner told him. "They're going to get a few rooms ready."

Another deputy, Henry Wilson, came out of the hotel directly behind Leroy. "There's no one left in the building that we could find."

Leroy considered sending him back in to look for Casey but changed his mind. "Check the other exits. Let me know if you find Casey Crenshaw," he told the deputy as Finnegan reached him.

"Casey's not here. That means she's still in there," Finnegan said. "I don't know what's going on because I don't see or smell smoke, but I'm going back in there to look for her." He started past him for the door.

Leroy put a firm hand in the middle of the man's chest

and shook his head. "No one is going back in there. Don't make me arrest you. She could have come out another door. I have a deputy checking."

But Finnegan was shaking his head. Leroy could see that there would be no keeping him out of the hotel short of cuffing him and throwing him in the back of a squad car.

"You don't want to go back in there," Leroy told him, but Finnegan only shook his head, shoving off the marshal's hand. "You need to go with one of my deputies to the motel."

"I'm not going anywhere as long as Casey's missing. I checked her room. She must have headed out at the sound of the fire alarm, but something must have happened. I have no idea what's going on, but I can tell it's serious." He put his face in Leroy's. "I'm going in. There's only one way you can stop me. Otherwise, we can cover the hotel faster if there are two of us."

Leroy sighed. "You take the north wing. We meet back at the main stairway in ten minutes. No more."

Finnegan gave a short nod. They went back inside and parted company. He could hear the man running and calling Casey's name. Leroy checked the lower floor first, his nerves raw. He'd never been in a building that could disintegrate at any moment.

CASEY CAME TO with a start. She blinked, her gaze unfocused for a few moments. She tried to remember what had happened, why she was lying on the floor, her body aching. As she started to sit up, she remembered. Jason. Falling down the stairs. She blinked again, fighting to clear her head as she started to take in her surroundings. She was still on the back-stairs landing. Her body hurt, but she didn't think anything was broken.

But as she tried to sit up, she realized with a start that she wasn't alone. Jason? Her pulse jumped as her earlier fear returned. She tried to sit up again. As she did, she saw him.

Not Jason.

Emery. He came up the stairs from the darkness. He held a finger to his lips as if he was afraid she was going to scream. Over the fire alarm? Even so, a scream was already racing up her throat. But it didn't reach her mouth before he grabbed her and clamped one massive hand down to forever trap it.

"It's okay now," Emery said. "I have you now." She could feel terror widen her eyes. As she struggled to get Emery's massive, calloused hand from her mouth, he reached behind him. The smell hit her first. It wafted through the air an instant before he pressed the damp cloth over her nose. She couldn't breathe.

With all her strength, she wriggled and fought against him, but it was useless. He was too strong, just like the chemical on the rag he was holding over her nose, his big hand over her mouth. She could feel darkness closing in. If he didn't remove the rag or his hand...

Suddenly both were no longer on her face. She opened her mouth, but nothing came out except for a small, inaudible sigh as she felt some strange drug making her limp as a rag doll.

She tried to get up, terrified, but her large-motor skills didn't react. Her body was no longer taking her commands. Emery lifted her as if she were no more than a child, and instead of heading down the stairs, he carried her up until he came to a landing. She watched in a dreamlike state as he pushed on a spot on the wood-paneled wall and it opened, revealing another set of narrower stairs.

She knew at once where he was taking her.

To the basement.

FINN CHECKED ONE floor after another. The sky outside was lightening with the promise of a new day. He was on his way down the back stairway when he saw something on the landing that he'd missed in his rush earlier. He lurched to a stop and bent down. Blood. It was only a couple of drops. But the droplets hadn't been there long. His heart leaped to his throat.

He told himself that the blood might not even be Casey's. Someone could have been hurt escaping the hotel. But as he took the steps more slowly, looking for more blood, he knew in his soul that the blood was hers. The good news was that so far he'd only seen a few drops, which meant she wasn't bleeding badly.

That was when he saw it. Not blood, thank God. But something just as telling. He recognized the tiny object right away. Just the sight of it sent his pulse hammering at his temples. Stooping down, he picked up a Scrabble piece. *Y.*

I have fallen for you.

He tried to tell himself that the piece could have been there at the back of the step for years. But he knew better. Had Casey picked up the Scrabble pieces? She must have. And put them in a pocket?

Finn knew it was a long shot that one had dropped out when she'd fallen. Or been pushed. He glanced down the stairs that ended at a side entrance. If she'd gone out that way, she would have been seen by one of the deputies.

That meant she was either still in the hotel or...

He tried her phone again. He heard it ringing—in the

stairwell below him. With a chill running through him, he descended the stairs to find her purse where it had fallen.

He canceled the call and went racing back toward the main stairway with only moments to spare. As he came rushing down the stairs, he saw the marshal waiting for him, looking anxious.

"She's not here," the marshal said. "We need to get out now."

Based on the marshal's expression, he knew there was a need to get out of the hotel as quickly as possible. Finn had no idea why, just that the lawman looked scared.

"There's one place we haven't checked," Finn said and headed for the door to the basement, but when he reached it, he saw that it had been barred. And not with just crime-scene tape. Several boards had been nailed over it. "What the hell?" he demanded, turning to the marshal. "I need to go down there."

"No one is going down there." There was steel in the marshal's tone and what looked like terror in his eyes. "Casey isn't down there. It's been sealed since *before* I pulled the fire alarm. Let's check outside and pray that she's shown up."

Finn wanted to tear the boards from the door, but if the alarm hadn't been pulled until after the door had been barred… They rushed out the back. He saw that the deputy had cleared the parking lot of cars and people, so Finn was surprised to see that another deputy was standing at the parking-lot entrance with Jason Underwood. They appeared to be arguing.

When Jason saw Finn and the marshal approaching, he pushed past the deputy and ran toward them. "I saw Casey. In a back hallway. She was acting strange. She took off like someone was chasing her, and then she fell…" Jason's voice broke. "I was hit from behind. That's the last I remember before I found myself out here on the sidewalk, but I had to tell you. Whoever hit me…" He didn't have to finish. Finn already knew that Casey was in trouble.

"How'd you get those scratches on your face?" the marshal asked Jason.

He looked away for a moment. "I stumbled into a wall earlier when I went down to the kitchen for a drink. I was trying to explain to Casey. I guess she thought…"

Finn had a sudden urge to beat the man senseless. "Why were you chasing after Casey?" he demanded, sensing there was a whole lot more to his story.

"She saw me holding Patience's broken necklace, and I guess she thought…"

Finn swore. He could guess what Casey thought.

Jason looked worried. "I tried to stop her and explain, but that damned fire alarm was so loud." Finn saw that the man was close to tears. "I didn't hurt her. I swear."

"When you saw her," Finn asked, "did she have her shoulder bag with her?"

Jason seemed to think for a moment before he nodded. "She did." So she had her phone.

"You say someone hit you from behind?" the marshal asked.

"I couldn't have been out long, but when I came to, I was lying in the stairwell. Casey was gone. I thought she'd already be out here, too."

"You were also the last one to see Patience Riley, who is missing as well," the marshal said. Jason started to put up an argument but was cut off. "Go to the motel and stay there. If you leave town, I'll have you arrested. I'd hold you now in a cell until both Casey and Patience were found, if Buckhorn had a jail."

"I didn't hurt either of them. Patience left, and Casey…" Jason shook his head. "I don't know what happened to her."

The marshal reached for the necklace in the man's hands. "The clasp is broken." His gaze rose to Jason's.

"It was an accident," Jason cried.

"Deputy," the marshal was saying, "take Mr. Underwood to the motel, and make sure he stays there. Take Mr. James there as well."

Finn rolled the Scrabble piece in his fingers as he looked toward the woods. He wasn't going to the motel. He had to find Casey, because all his instincts told him that she wasn't far from here—and if he didn't find her soon…

"Wait," the marshal said as Finn started to walk away. "Where do you think you're going?"

"To look for Casey," Finn said, already striding toward the trees. "Don't worry. I'm not leaving town," he said over his shoulder. "And I won't go back into the hotel." He glanced back at the lawman. Their gazes met for just an instant. He'd heard a deputy say the words *booby trap*, he'd seen the looks on all of the lawmen's faces, and given the way he and the rest had been hustled out of the structure, he had a bad feeling the hotel might blow at any moment.

He had no desire to go back in there, anyway. The marshal said he'd sealed off the basement before he'd pulled the fire alarm. So there was no way someone had taken Casey down there without being seen. Unless there was another way into the basement from inside. Either way, there was no chance that Casey would go back down there on her own. Someone had to have taken her.

As LEROY CUPPED his hands against the rising sun, he watched Finnegan James head into the woods and swore before getting on the radio to Hepner. "Leave Wilson at the motel. Tell him to radio me if there is any change over there or if Casey Crenshaw shows up. You get back over here with the other deputies and secure this place—from a distance."

Disconnecting, he then called the state crime lab and told them what he had.

"The entire building is rigged to blow?" the state's explosive expert from the bomb squad said when he came on the line.

"Are you familiar with the Crenshaw Hotel? It's huge, and it appears that there are bombs set at all the crucial structural supports. Whoever did it appears to be planning to demolish it with an implosion. I had an uncle who was in the business." He answered questions about what type of explosives he'd seen and what size each were.

"How close is it to other structures?"

"It's on the main highway but a few blocks from town. There's a motel down the highway about a block away."

"You have no idea who rigged it?"

"None."

"I'd stay clear of the place."

"You think? What do we do until you get here?"

"Stay a half mile from it and pray. We're on our way, but if you're right, I'm not sure what we can do. I'm not sending my men into a situation like that."

"There's another problem," Leroy said. "We found a bunch of graves in the basement. They might be those of young women who have disappeared over the years. The parents of those women…"

"I hear what you're saying. We'll assess the situation when we get there."

Leroy hung up and looked toward the woods where Finnegan James had disappeared. The man was smart. He might not know how bad things were under the hotel, but he knew enough not to go back inside.

Unless he thought Casey was down there. Then there would be no stopping him, because Leroy couldn't jeopardize his deputies by sending them in there after him.

As Casey slowly surfaced, she felt as if she were walking through a fog and realized she'd been dreaming. Finn had been in the dream. They'd been together, and everything had been wonderful. Until it wasn't. Suddenly they were adrift on a raft of rotten wood. Pieces kept breaking off, and soon it would just be them and the endless sea full of sharks—

Her eyes flew open as the last piece of wood between them and the water broke apart. It took her a moment to realize it had only been a bad dream. Until she took in her surroundings and knew she was in maybe far worse trouble.

The room, if you could call it that, had a low ceiling and stone walls. There was a bare bulb overhead that provided only faint light. The walls had wooden shelves on them that appeared full of all kinds of tools and junk.

The smell alone, wet earth and cold, along with the grave-deep silence, told her she was underground. Her last clear thought had been that she was being taken to the basement of the hotel. But now she wasn't so sure. At each side of the space there was a dark opening, as if they were in the middle of a tunnel. She'd taken that all in within a matter of seconds.

A jolt ran the length of her body as she sensed someone coming from out of the darkness at one end. She tried to move, only then realizing that she was duct-taped to a chair. Her arms were behind her, her wrists taped to what felt like a back slat of the chair. Had she been able to catch her breath, she might have screamed as Emery stepped into the small space. He had to bend over to keep from hitting his head on the boards shoring up the roof.

Her memory came back as her panic soared. Him finding her after her fall. The drug he used to incapacitate her. This room underground where he had her bound to a chair. Terror rocketed through her, sending her pulse hammering in her ears.

"Welcome back," he said in a casual tone that only made her panic grow exponentially. Dragging a small wooden stool over, he sat down facing her. She had the feeling that this wasn't the first time he'd done this very same thing, and that was like a knife to her chest.

"Don't look so frightened," he said, shaking his head as if amused. "You know I would never hurt you or your grandmother. You were both kind to me."

Her mouth was dry as sand. She swallowed. "Where am I?"

"Somewhere safe."

She didn't believe that. "Why have you brought me here?" Her voice broke.

"To protect you."

"Protect me?" She cleared her throat as her gaze fell on a pickax covered with dirt leaning against the opposite wall. She noticed other digging tools. *Burying* tools. Her heart rate galloped out of control. She strained against her restraints, the chair under her creaking.

"Calm down," he said, as if speaking to an unruly child.

"It's your own fault that you're here. If you'd sold the hotel to my sister, none of this would be happening right now. Vi would have kicked everyone out of the hotel, and it would be over by now."

"I don't understand."

Emery sighed and leaned closer. He breathed on her, but she forced herself not to turn away even though his breath was like death warmed over. Absently, he reached toward her. She tried hard not to cringe as he began to stroke her long hair. She felt strands of her hair get caught in his calloused hand. He didn't seem to notice.

"I remember you as a little girl," Emery said and continued to run his hand the length of her hair while her stomach twisted into knots. Her head ached from being drugged. Her mouth was desert-dry. She tried to swallow, tried licking her lips, but she had no saliva.

"Water." The word came out on an arid breath.

He looked surprised but jumped right up. "Sorry, I should have offered." He turned his back on her for a moment. Casey looked around for something she could use to free herself. Behind her were more shelves filled with junk like the ones in front of her. She only had a moment to quickly search for anything that might be within reach. The room was so small, her chair had been pushed back where it was touching the nearest shelf. She leaned back, rocking the chair just enough that she could lock her fingers around a rusted blade about an inch wide from a bow saw.

It would be worthless as a weapon, but she thought she might be able to saw through the tape binding her wrists to the back of the chair when his back was turned.

She'd barely started when Emery turned with a jug of what looked like water but might have been something else entirely. He shuffled over to her, took off the cap and held the large jug up to her lips, tipping it. The liquid came gushing out. She caught a stale, chemical smell and turned her head quickly to the side. The liquid splashed down the front of her, drenching her clothing and sloshing onto the floor.

"What is that?" she managed to say as she tried to spit it back out.

"Water." Emery chuckled. "I forgot your generation doesn't even drink out of the hose anymore. Got to have fancy bottled water." He shook his head as if amused by the changing world.

He held up the jug again.

She shook her head. "It smells funny."

"Now you're just being silly." He grabbed her head with one large hand, cocked it back and poured the liquid over her face.

She tried not to breathe or swallow, but the water was going into her nose, choking her. She gasped and swallowed a huge gulp.

As if satisfied, Emery let go of her and turned to recap the jug and put it away. Casey began to frantically saw at the tape. She felt the blade bite into the flesh of her wrist and winced but didn't stop until he turned back to her again.

"Now, isn't that better?" he asked.

She looked away from his weathered, aged face. She could feel a trickle of blood running down her hand to drip on the ground behind her. She had to get away from him. All her instincts told her that, otherwise, she would die down here. She thought of the graves in the basement, and she knew in her heart that Finn had been right. Those girls who'd disappeared—they'd never left the hotel.

CHAPTER THIRTY

THE SUN SHONE through the pines, painting the forest with gold. Finn hadn't gone far when he saw another piece from the Scrabble board lying in the dried pine needles. As he moved closer, his heart began to pound harder. He stooped down to pick it up, turning the tile to see the letter. *F.*

I have fallen for you.

His gaze lifted to the trees ahead—and the decrepit outbuilding in the distance. She was here. Someone had taken her from the hotel. All he had to do was find her. But he felt as if a clock were ticking toward a deadline, one that had the marshal and his men getting as far away from the hotel as possible.

Rising quickly, he headed toward the outbuilding, watching the ground as he moved, hoping for another tile, another clue, but sure he was on the right track.

The outbuilding, which was probably eight feet square, was set back against the side of the mountain, away from the others. While it looked as if it might fall down at any moment, he saw where someone had shored up the stone foundation.

There were no windows and only the one door. He saw that it had been padlocked. The police had broken the lock when they'd searched it. With the shape the building was in, it being locked was definitely a red flag. Padlocked like the door to the basement, padlocked like the wine-cellar door.

He pushed the door open, not sure what he would find. The officers had already checked the building. The door swung open, and he looked inside. Not that there was much to see. No Casey, that much he'd seen at once. As his eyes adjusted to the dim light inside and the dust settled, he saw shelves along all four walls and piles of junk.

If Casey had been here, she wasn't now. He frowned. Something was wrong. He'd found one of the tiles from the Scrabble board only yards from here. Disappointment made his heart ache. He'd been so sure that whoever had taken her hadn't gotten far. Otherwise the person would have been seen. No vehicles had left since the law had arrived, so she had to be here somewhere.

As he started to turn away, he saw something on the floor. The same tracks he'd seen in the dust in front of the wine cellar. Two narrow tire tracks that ended at the edge of a crack in the floor. His gaze flew to the junk at the other end of the shack where he spotted a cart, the kind used to drag out a deer carcass from the woods.

He moved to the dark crack between the boards and knew he hadn't been wrong after all. A trapdoor.

THE SUN SHONE off the side of the string of motel rooms. "I don't get it," Benjamin said as he sat down on the curb outside Jason's room where the others had gathered.

Jen sighed. "What don't you get?" She'd whined enough that they all knew she wanted to go down to the bar. But the cops had been told to keep them all here until the marshal said otherwise.

"Why are we being kept here?" he said. "Legally, they have to arrest us, don't they?"

"Why don't you tell them that," Jason suggested and mugged a face just in case Benjamin missed his sarcasm.

He studied Jason, wondering if being arrested was exactly why the man was acting so strangely. "Why are you so nervous? You've been acting weird since we were hustled out of the hotel. And what happened to Patience?"

Jason groaned and got to his feet. "If I want to be interrogated, I'll go find the marshal." He stormed into his room.

"Something is definitely wrong with him," Jen whispered. She'd been a lot friendlier after Claude left and before his body was found.

"I just talked to the deputy," Shirley said as she walked up. "He said we can order food from the café. Bessie will bring it over." She looked down at her cell phone. "Well?"

"Can we order from the bar?" Jen asked.

Shirley rolled her eyes. "Come on. I'm locked up here, too."

Her friend laughed. "You *live* here. You're always locked up here."

"Food. Yes? No?"

Benjamin could see that she was losing her patience. "I'll take the grilled-chicken salad with the dressing on the side and an ice tea. No sugar. Make it a large one."

Jen rolled her eyes. "Order me a double cheeseburger loaded with extra fries and a strawberry milkshake. And if she has any of those turnovers left, I'd take a couple of those. Is the marshal paying for this?"

"I rather doubt the county is picking up the bill," Shirley said as she finished taking notes on her phone.

"Then skip the turnovers." Jen sighed and got to her feet. "I'm going in to watch daytime television."

"I'll let you know when the food comes." Shirley glanced around the parking lot. "Where's Jason?"

Benjamin motioned over his shoulder toward the closed motel-room door.

Shirley moved to the door and tapped on it. "Jason?" No answer. "Jason!" She knocked hard.

The door flew open. "What?"

She repeated her spiel. "Well?"

He shook his head. "I'm not hungry."

"Suit yourself, but it might be the only meal you get today," Shirley said. "Have you heard what's going on up at the hotel? I wonder why Casey and Finn aren't here."

"Maybe they were arrested," Jason said.

Shirley groaned.

"They totally could have killed Claude and Devlin. It's possible."

Shirley shook her head. Benjamin could hear her ordering the food as she closed Jason's door and walked away.

"Have you noticed how none of us have mentioned Megan?" he said to no one because Jen had gone into her room. He heard the television come on in Jason's room so loud he recognized the reality show.

Getting up, he headed for his room for some peace and quiet. This couldn't be over soon enough.

CASEY TRIED TO pull her wrists free of the chair and felt the tape give a little. She needed to distract Emery enough that she could finish sawing her way free. "My grandmother—" Her voice broke. "She wouldn't like you...doing this."

"That's not true. I have always tried to protect you and your grandmother from the evil in the world. It's not my fault. It's the Crenshaw, always has been. I felt it the first time I walked in the front door. It has a hidden malevolence that feeds on the dark souls of others."

She stared at him, her heart thumping hard in her chest. He was insane.

"It has to be fed." He looked away, his face going slack with what could have been regret before he turned back to her.

She stared at him as she trembled from fear in her wet clothing. She knew, but she had to hear him say it. "The bodies of those women buried in the basement…"

His rheumy eyes looked vacant for a moment. "I told you. I had to feed the beast. It's not my fault."

"The marshal knows about the bodies. He knows—"

Emery shot to his feet so quickly it silenced anything else she might have said. "That's why it has to end." He shook his head, looking as if whatever he planned to do was her fault. "You shouldn't have invited them all back here."

"I didn't. It wasn't me." She could see that he didn't believe her. "It's true. I swear."

"It doesn't matter now," he said. He reached into a cabinet and brought out a device with buttons. It had several wires hanging from it.

"What are you going to do?" she cried.

"What you wanted. You want the building destroyed? That's what I'm going to do. Blow it to hell."

"You can't!" she cried. "There are still people in there."

"That's your fault. Those people wouldn't be in the hotel if it wasn't for you."

"I didn't send those invi—" Suddenly, it hit her who had. "My grandmother. Oh my gosh." She felt a shudder thinking about that last night with Anna. "My grandmother had them sent."

"Why would she do that?"

"Because she was determined that the killer be found. She knew about my nightmares and thought it was the only way I could move on." It had to be true, she realized. It would have been so easy for her grandmother to set things up with her attorney. Was that what he'd been anxious to tell her about? Anna would be one of the few people who would have known about Finn and his relationship with Megan. "Anna did this to try to help me." She met Emery's gaze and saw how pained he looked. "She said she couldn't rest until Megan's killer was caught."

Emery looked at her, wild-eyed. "It wasn't me. I didn't kill that one."

She frowned in disbelief. "Then who?"

The big man shook his head adamantly. "I didn't touch her."

Casey couldn't help looking skeptical.

"I can prove it," Emery said indignantly as he put down the device with the buttons. He turned around to face the shelves again. She took that opportunity to saw at the tape that bound her wrists. She was so close. Once her wrists were free, she'd be free of the chair as well. She would be able to run, which she knew was her best chance, given Emery's size and strength.

He turned back holding a notebook that she noted resembled the one that Finn had found. He opened it to a page filled with tight scrawl, and she recognized the handwriting and the name *Rosemarie Langley* on the list he'd written.

With a shock, she saw that it had to be a list of names of the young women who had been buried in the basement of the hotel. She tried not to cringe in horror as he pushed it in front of her face. She saw that there were names and information about the women that he must have gotten from their driver's licenses.

"If I had done it, I would have written down her name. See?" he demanded, tapping the notebook with his large, calloused finger. "I never forget. I write down each one. It's just like I told Vi. I don't lie. I write down the names."

All Casey could do was nod as he snapped the notebook shut and turned to put it back on the shelf. Vi knew. That was why she wanted so desperately to buy the hotel. She was trying to help her brother hide his crimes.

She quickly sawed while his back was to her, feeling the last of the tape about to give. Just a little more…

For a moment, he stood there, hunched over, his back to her. She felt the tape give a little more. Once free, she could run. He had his back turned. She could… She tried to pull free of the tape, the chair. The chair creaked, and she saw him freeze.

He turned slowly to look at her, something different in his eyes. "You don't believe me."

"About Megan?" Her voice cracked. She licked her lips and tasted that disgusting water he'd made her drink.

"Vi didn't, either. She told me I had to get the bones out of the basement before someone came to demolish the hotel. I tried." He sounded defeated and scared. "I tried, but then that man moved into the hotel. I could only work late at night. I worried that he would hear me and catch me. I didn't want to hurt him. I tried to scare him away but he wouldn't leave."

Finn. The noises he'd heard. Emery had been banging around in the basement trying to get the remains of the young women out before Casey returned and sold the hotel.

"If you didn't hurt Megan…" Was it possible it was true? Maybe he'd just forgotten.

"It wasn't me," he said, shaking his head.

"I believe you." She realized the moment she said it that she did. He'd been meticulous in writing down the names. He hadn't killed Megan.

With a start, Casey realized that two other names were also missing from Emery's list. "What about Devlin and Claude?"

He frowned. "I don't know anything about them."

"Did you put the padlock on the wine-cellar door?"

"I don't steal. I wouldn't take anything."

"You didn't put the padlock on the door." Her heart pounded as she saw the answer on his face. It wasn't him.

Then who had killed them and hidden them in the wine cellar?

FINN OPENED THE trapdoor and looked down into the semi-darkness. He'd expected a ladder. Instead there were some badly cut steps in the dirt that made the entry more like a chute, the end of which lay in total darkness. In any other situation, there was no way he would have dropped to the edge of the trapdoor, held his breath and shoved off with no idea what was at the bottom.

But he knew in his heart that Casey was down there. He had the two Scrabble board pieces in his pocket. He grabbed the closest thing to a weapon he could see, a steel stake, slid on the hardpacked earth over the few narrow steps and dropped at a rate of speed that should have terrified him. At first he'd tried digging his heels in to keep from falling too quickly, but it hadn't worked. The slope was steep, and it only took a moment to realize that he was out of control. Behind him, he heard the trapdoor slam shut as if he'd triggered the closing.

He barely had time to swear before he hit bottom and came to an abrupt stop. He felt a little dazed as he pushed to his feet in a space that was no more than four feet wide and about six feet high. At six-three, he had to lean over to move.

Glancing back up the chute, all he could see was black. He looked in the only other direction and saw cave-like darkness around him. But in the distance he could make out a light. With the metal stake he'd picked up, he moved toward the light. He hadn't gone far when he heard a male voice.

He slowed as he approached. Then his heart lifted as he heard Casey's voice. But it quickly fell again. Someone had her down here. She was still alive, but for how long?

CASEY THOUGHT OF Finn and everyone else still in the hotel. "Emery, don't do this, please," she said as he replaced the notebook and picked up the device again. He looked like a broken man standing there hunched over in this secret room of his as he pulled out a battery.

She tried to imagine where they were. Under the hotel? And if she did have a chance to run, which way would she go? Maybe if she could warn everyone in time... All she could see was darkness on each side of this slightly larger space.

"Where are we?" she asked him.

"Somewhere safe."

Down here, there was no way of knowing which way to run toward the hotel. "Emery, you need to let me go."

He shook his head. "I can't." He sounded miserable as

he looked down at the device. "Once I connect this to the battery... It's too late." His gaze rose to hers. "I don't have a choice now."

Casey shifted on the chair. She felt the tape give. But what now? Unless she could locate something she could use for a weapon and get her hands on it fast enough... But even if she got away, she still didn't know which way to run. What if she managed to get away, only to run into a dead end?

She heard the sound of a boot heel scuff the hardpacked ground the same time Emery did. Someone was coming. She saw it in Emery's body language; she felt it heart-deep. Finn.

Emery wrapped the loose wires around the battery and pushed the first button.

CHAPTER THIRTY-ONE

LEROY HEARD THE first explosion and turned to look back at the hotel. He'd gotten as far as the middle of the parking lot. Now he stared in awe and horror as small explosions seemed to move along the lower outside of the hotel like dominoes that had been knocked over. He prayed that Casey Crenshaw wasn't inside.

One after another, the explosions began to go off around the building all within a second. Puffs of smoke rose as the building collapsed in on itself as if melting. Smoke and debris rose in the air as the ground shook beneath his feet.

He couldn't move. He watched as the hotel disappeared. Smoke and flying debris rose in the air over it, obliterating the town in the distance.

He realized he'd been holding his breath and now let it out in a gasp.

"Did you see that?" Hepner said, suddenly next to him. There was shock in his voice. "I've never seen anything like it."

Leroy had, from videos his uncle had given him. But he'd never seen it standing only yards away. He had a new respect for his uncle. His father was wrong about his brother. Pete just loved to destroy things in the coolest of ways.

"You don't think she's inside?" Hepner said.

"I hope not." Either way, there was nothing they could do now. He just hoped Finn hadn't gone back in for her and that the two were inside there. He pulled out his phone to call the bomb squad, but as he heard the sound of a helicopter approaching, he pocketed it again.

He could see people in town rushing in their direction. In the silence that followed the last explosion, the cloud began to settle over the smoldering remains of the Crenshaw Hotel. "Let's keep those people back," Leroy ordered, and Hepner jumped to it.

As he stood, still transfixed, he realized that he'd gone from two murders to maybe a dozen. But never in his life had he expected to find dozens of bombs that could have gone off with all of them inside.

Leroy glanced toward the woods and the last place he'd seen Finnegan James. He hoped to see him coming out of the trees with Casey Crenshaw at his side. Unfortunately, there was nothing but the breeze swaying the pine boughs and the smell of destruction in the air.

At least the others were safe.

Then he looked back at the hotel. One corner hadn't come all the way down. He felt a start and knew why. One or more of the bombs hadn't detonated.

FINN FELT THE ground shift beneath his feet. One of the boards holding up the ceiling dropped down, grazing his shoulder painfully. He shoved it aside and pushed through the din, even more frantic to get to Casey. He'd been right. The booby trap had been a bomb. Or a series of bombs, he thought as the ground continued to shake.

He didn't realize that he was calling her name until he heard it echoing around him. "Casey!" He had to get to her. He couldn't lose her. Not after he'd just found her. All these months reading about her and her grandmother. He'd been half in love with her even before she'd appeared like a ghost outside his shower.

It couldn't end like this, and yet he felt as if everything was coming to a point of no return. All these months of looking for a killer, and now he feared the killer had Casey, and if he didn't reach her...

The earth seemed to shudder even harder. He feared the tunnel would cave in on him. On Casey. More dirt fell from overhead. He could barely see a step in front of him, but he kept pushing forward, determined to get to her. "Casey!"

The tunnel seemed to never end. Yet he feared at some point he would reach a wall of dirt where there'd been a cave-in. He told himself he'd dig through it with his bare hands if he had to. His heart pounded as he fought not to breathe in the dust still sifting down from overhead.

But he thought he could see the light growing brighter ahead.

Behind him, he heard the tunnel begin to cave in.

CASEY SCREAMED AND tried to push herself up from the chair. Her legs felt weak, from the drug, from sitting for so long in the same position. But she wasn't able to stand anyway. The ground beneath her feet shook, knocking her back. Dirt fell like dark rain from the cracks between the boards over their heads.

There was a ringing in her ears. Over it, she thought she heard Finn calling her name. Her eyes burned from the dust in the air. Finn?

"Casey!" His voice was faint, but there was no doubt. It was Finn.

As the earth continued to shake, she thought for sure the tunnel would cave in, killing them both—and Finn. Because she'd heard him calling her name. She'd known he'd come, and now it was going to cost him his life.

The air had darkened. She could barely make out Emery's hulking shape. He had fallen, apparently after one of the overhead boards had come down and hit him.

Casey tasted grit in her mouth and tried not to breathe too deeply as she pulled her shirt up to cover her mouth and pushed to her feet.

For a moment, she thought Emery had been knocked out and all she had to do was run—in the direction of Finn's voice calling her name. Just run.

But as she started to take a step, the ground shaking again, Emery groaned and sat up, shielding his head from the debris plummeting down on him.

She realized running wasn't the answer. He knew these tunnels. She didn't. He would catch her—and Finn. She couldn't chance that. Nor could she wait to be saved. She was on her own. Reaching behind her, she groped for something she could use as a weapon.

Her hand closed over a cold, heavy cylinder. It felt greasy, as if it were part of a piece of machinery. It was heavy and fit in her hand, and right now it was all she had, because Emery was struggling to his feet.

Casey took a step forward and winced as she swung the weapon. The heavy metal connected with his skull. Emery grunted and grabbed her wrist. He twisted her wrist so hard she thought he would break it, his grip was so strong. But she stubbornly held on, kicking him as hard as she could as he tried again to get up from the ground to give himself the advantage over her.

Once he got to his feet, she wouldn't stand a chance.

One kick made him howl in pain before he jerked on her

wrist, throwing her off balance. She lost her grip on the weapon as she hit the ground next to him. He was grabbing for her, trying to pin her down, when she heard her name called again—much closer.

Emery heard it, too. He hesitated, and Casey saw her chance. She elbowed him hard in the stomach and rolled away from him. She was on her hands and knees, trying to get her feet under her, when, from behind, she heard Emery lumbering to his feet. He grabbed for her, catching the tail of her T-shirt. She heard it rip, but he didn't let go. She was trying to run but he still had hold of her shirt. He jerked her back. She stumbled and fell, but quickly crab-crawled away from him.

Emery had blood running down his face from where she'd hit him with the makeshift weapon. But it was the look in his eyes that told her he was no longer even pretending to protect her. She was now one of his victims and would be added to his book if she didn't get away.

FINN CAME AROUND a bend in the tunnel and saw the giant looming over Casey. He reacted on instinct, letting out a roar as he charged the big man. As he did, he saw Casey pick up something from the ground. He plowed into the man, catching him off guard and throwing him back against the shelves along the tunnel wall. The man seemed to shake off the blow. Finn could see the older man's strength return as he lumbered to his feet. The giant lunged for him, but before Finn could react, the man suddenly doubled over in a howl of pain. Finn realized that Casey had grabbed up a metal stake from the ground. It was now sticking out from between the man's ribs.

There was a clatter as the shelves gave way and objects

fell around the giant as he went down. Finn stood over him for a moment to make sure he wasn't getting up before he turned to Casey, now curled up against the tunnel wall with a look of horror on her face. She was covered with dirt, her clothes filthy and her T-shirt torn. She'd never looked more beautiful.

"Are you all right?" he asked as he dropped down next to her.

She nodded and seemed to come out of her shock to throw her arms around his neck.

For a moment, he just held her tightly before lifting her to her feet. "We have to get out of here. We can't go the way I came in. This way."

He led her down through the underground tunnel, moving aside boards and debris that threatened to block their way. They both coughed, having breathed in so much of the dust that was only now starting to settle.

She could feel Finn's anxiety and knew that, like her, he feared that they would reach a dead end or a cave-in and not be able to get out. Or, worse, that at any moment they could be buried alive down here.

Then in a dim overhead light she saw what was ahead and felt her heart drop. It was a dead end. Panic rose up in her like a primitive wail. She must have let out a cry, because Finn turned back to her. "Look, there's a ladder up the side of the wall. That means there must be a trapdoor up there."

She hadn't seen the ladder. All she'd seen was the end of the tunnel.

"Stay here for just a minute," Finn said.

She didn't want to stay, but he was already climbing the ladder to try to open the trapdoor. That was when she heard movement behind them. Emery. He was coming. "Hurry," she cried, even as Finn disappeared upward. She could hear him trying to force whatever was covering the exit. Heart in her throat, she could see more debris drifting down. With a final shove, he managed to get the cover to move a few inches, and she caught a glimpse of blue sky, sunshine and pine trees.

Her heart soared until she heard the rumble back down the tunnel. "He's coming," she cried, feeling the panic rising in her again as she looked around for something she could use as a weapon, but she saw nothing. She doubted she could fight Emery off again anyway. Just the thought of stabbing him again made her sick to her stomach. "Emery's coming!"

Finn swore and groaned as he shoved harder, the trapdoor splintering as he threw his body into it. Sunlight poured down through the dust. She gasped in relief as Finn began to climb back down and reached for her hand. She started up the ladder, grasping for his hand, when she felt fingers lock around her ankle. She screamed and kicked with her free leg as she felt her hold on the ladder begin to give way. She heard one of her kicks connect. There was a loud snap like cartilage breaking, followed by an angry cry of pain.

She kicked again and felt the fingers release. Finn grabbed for her and pulled her up, pushing her through the hole left by the splintered trapdoor. She scrambled into the daylight and reached back for him.

Suddenly the ground beneath her began to shake again. She saw a flash of light in the direction of the hotel and heard what sounded like an explosion and then another.

Finn grabbed her hand, and she pulled him up through the opening and onto the dried pine-needle-covered earth beneath her. Then they were on their feet, running away from the tunnel. Behind her, she heard it begin to cave in.

They didn't stop until they were a safe distance away. As they looked back, the tunnel continued to fall in on itself—and Emery.

Casey buried her face in Finn's shirt as he took her in his arms and held her, whispering that she was all right now, that he wouldn't let anything happen to her, that she was safe and that it was over.

Except Casey knew it wasn't.

CHAPTER THIRTY-TWO

LEROY LOOKED UP in surprise as Finnegan and Casey came out of the woods. The sky was filled with smoke and dust, still obscuring the area where the hotel had been. He rushed to them, seeing that they were covered in dust and dirt. "I thought you both were dead."

"We almost were," Finn said. "The tunnel caved in behind us. The man who took Casey didn't make it out."

"Emery Gray," Casey said. "He got me out of the hotel before he blew the hotel up. Did everyone get out?"

Leroy nodded. "Emery?"

"He was the on-site maintenance man for years," she said, her words coming faster. "He didn't kill Megan. Or Claude. Or Devlin."

"He told you that?"

She nodded and coughed, no doubt from all the dust. "He kept a notebook of the women he'd killed. I recognized the handwriting from one that Finn showed me he'd found in a notebook hidden in the hotel. He wrote down the names of every young woman and any information he had about them as if keeping a record for the parents when the day came that he'd have to confess what he'd done. His sister Vi knew. He said she told him not to write anything down, but he said he had to—for the women he'd killed."

Leroy was shaking his head. "That doesn't mean—"

"Marshal, I think you'd better listen to her," Finnegan said.

"The person who killed Megan, Devlin and Claude, it wasn't Emery," she repeated. "He didn't put the padlock on the wine-cellar door. He didn't kill them." Leroy could see that she was stumbling over her words, frantic to get them out, to make him understand before it was too late.

"Get her some water," he said to the deputy standing nearby.

"I don't need water," she cried. "The killer is one of the staff. You have to believe me. I don't think the killer is finished yet. The others…they're in danger."

He studied her for a moment before he pulled out his radio and made the call. "Is everyone still over at the motel?"

"All here."

"You're sure?"

"Two of them are sitting outside. A couple of them went in earlier."

"I think you'd better check on them. I'll wait." He looked at Casey. She held her breath, the deputy seeming to take forever to get back to him.

When the officer came back on the line, Leroy heard the bad news. "Don't touch anything. I'm on my way." He looked at Finnegan and Casey. He couldn't very well leave them here. Motioning to a deputy, he said, "Take them to the motel, and get them a room. I'll get their statements as soon as I can."

Casey grabbed his sleeve, tears in her eyes. "Who's dead?"

Leroy swore under his breath. They would know soon enough. "Jason Underwood."

CHAPTER THIRTY-THREE

LEROY PUSHED PAST the deputy standing guard outside the motel room. As he did, he saw the man hanging from the light fixture in the middle of the room. A chair lay on its side beneath him. The breeze caught a loose strip of bedsheet and lifted it into the air.

"We didn't cut him down after we checked, and there were no vitals," Hepner said. "Might be a suicide. He left a note."

Leroy stared at Jason Underwood's swollen face and protruding tongue and the overturned chair below him before turning back to the deputy. He held out his hand. Hepner put a clear plastic evidence bag into it. Inside he could see the handwritten note.

I've ruined my every chance of happiness I've ever had. Patience, please forgive me. I never meant to hurt you. I never meant to hurt anyone.

"Still no sign of Patience Riley?" Leroy asked Hepner, who shook his head. "Coroner called?"

"On his way. Again," the deputy said.

"Right. Take photos. Then you can cut him down," Leroy said and stepped outside.

In the distance, the smoke and dust had started to settle. The once-famous landmark no longer stood against the western horizon. The Crenshaw Hotel was gone. He rubbed a hand over his face before settling his gaze again on the three standing outside the motel.

He kept thinking about Casey Crenshaw. She was convinced he had more than one killer. As he walked toward the now-even-smaller group huddled outside, he asked, "Any of you know Jason's handwriting?"

Their eyes all widened as they took a look. "Is he...?" Jen asked, and Shirley began to cry.

"It's his handwriting," Benjamin said, and seeing that Leroy obviously needed more than that to convince him, he added, "Here. He wrote me a donation check for some research I'm doing." He opened his wallet and took out the check.

Jason had signed his name and also added in the notation section that it was a donation for research.

Leroy checked it against the alleged suicide note. They matched. He handed back the check and turned as Casey and Finn exited from the patrol car that had just driven up.

CASEY STOOD UNDER the warm spray of the shower and closed her eyes. She'd been through a nightmare, and it wasn't over. A killer had lured them all back to the hotel. She kept thinking about what Emery had said, about an evil that lived in the hotel, an evil that made bad things happen.

She didn't believe in that any more than she believed in ghosts. The evil was in people—not in the walls of a building or even in the basement.

The door of the bathroom opened, startling her for a moment before Finn stepped in. The marshal had gotten them adjoining rooms and let them clean up before they had to give their statements.

Casey knew that Finn had wanted to give her some

space—just not too much, from the look on his face. He'd showered, a towel wrapped around that slim waist.

"I just wanted to be sure you were all right," he said.

She smiled and motioned for him to join her. It took little persuading. He dropped the towel and stepped into the shower, pulling her to him. She leaned into his warm body as the water rippled over them. He smelled good; he felt even better.

Casey looked up into his handsome face. "You saved my life. I haven't thanked you."

He shook his head. "No thanks necessary."

"Finn, I don't know what I would have done if you hadn't been here."

"But I am here." He kissed her gently. "I'll be here as long as you need me, as long as you want me."

"That could be a very long time," she said and kissed him.

It wasn't until they were dressed that she told him her theory about the invitations.

"Your grandmother sent them?" he said in surprise, then nodded. "I suppose there is a way to find out. You said she would have had the family attorney take care of it?"

"Yes, and he's been anxious to talk to me since her death. Anna had already signed the hotel and land over to me, but apparently there was more I was to be told."

LEROY TOOK BOTH Casey Crenshaw's and Finnegan James's statements. He'd just finished with Finn when Hepner called him aside.

"A highway patrolman just pulled over Patience Riley," Hepner said from the doorway.

Leroy couldn't believe that she'd turned up. He'd been

so sure she was dead and they just hadn't located her body yet. "Patch him through to my cell phone."

The moment the patrolman came on the line, Leroy said, "She's wanted for questioning in a triple-murder investigation. Don't let her out of your sight. Can you bring her here?" He'd find a way to keep her under lock and key until he could transport her to the jail. But right now, he wanted to hear what she had to say.

He disconnected and turned to see Hepner waiting.

"That warrant you asked the judge for?" the deputy said. "We got it. Several of the crime techs have gone over to search the Mullen house."

Leroy doubted Vi Mullen would be surprised—if she hadn't already left town, given what Casey Crenshaw had told him.

"She'll want to know about her brother," Hepner said.

Finnegan and Casey had given them the location where they'd last seen Emery, but it could take days to find the body, let alone the room where the man had held Casey, and recover any evidence of the murders.

"He is presumed dead at this point," Leroy said, although he'd learned a long time ago not to presume anything.

It didn't take long for the highway patrolman to bring him Patience. She had resisted arrest so had been cuffed and had her rights read to her by the time Leroy had her back in Buckhorn.

"Why would you resist arrest unless you had something to hide?" Leroy demanded.

"Are you serious? He told me he was taking me back to Buckhorn for questioning. I had no intention of ever coming back here. I just assumed this was Jason's doing. He did everything possible to keep me from leaving. Look,

I'm married. I made a mistake with Jason. I didn't want to see him again." She seemed to notice that Leroy had gone quiet. "What?" She looked from him to his deputy standing by the motel-room door. "What is it you aren't telling me?" The color drained from her face as if she suddenly knew. "Jason. He's…he's dead?"

"Apparently he hung himself."

"That's ridiculous. He might threaten to do something like that, but he would never…" She was shaking her head. "No." She must have realized that he was still watching her closely. "Wait. You can't think I had anything to do with it?"

"He left what appears to be a suicide note."

"I want to see it," she demanded. "I know his handwriting."

Leroy considered it for a moment before he nodded to his deputy, who retrieved the evidence bag with the note in it. He handed it to her.

She stared down at the note through the plastic and frowned. "This is the note he wrote to me before I left. I gave it back to him. This isn't a suicide note."

Leroy had suspected as much. His list of suspects had dropped to three. Benjamin, Shirley and Jen. Benjamin would have been the likely suspect, not that Shirley and Jen didn't seem equally capable.

Hepner appeared, looking like the cat who'd eaten the canary. "The crime team found something they thought you'd want to see. It was found in Dr. Claude Drake's wallet." He held up what appeared to be a note inside an evidence bag. *Meet me in the woods.*

Leroy looked from the note to Hepner.

"Those droplets?" Hepner said. "They appear to be

blood. You can see that the note is old. Dr. Drake had been carrying it around for some time. Probably ten years."

"You think the blood might be Megan Broadhurst's? That he found this—" he met the deputy's gaze "—where she was killed."

"Why else hang on to it all these years? If, for whatever reason, the killer wasn't able to retrieve it at the scene," Hepner said, "Claude could have picked it up. We also found one in the same handwriting with the same wording wadded up and stuffed deep in Devlin Wright's pocket."

Leroy felt his pulse jump. Their first good lead. "I assume you have examined the handwriting of our suspects?" Hepner smiled in affirmation. "Who wrote this note?"

CHAPTER THIRTY-FOUR

JEN GLANCED UP as the marshal walked toward her. She could tell by the look in his eyes that he knew. She smiled to herself, thinking of her mother, who would say "I always knew it would end badly for Jennifer. She just couldn't seem to help herself when it came to trouble."

It was true. When she'd lured Megan into that spot in the woods, she'd told herself she wasn't going to kill her. The rock had just been lying there on the ground as if it was meant to be. Poor little rich girl hadn't seen it coming, but she should have. She'd been asking for it. Before Megan died, Jen had crouched down next to her because, as her mother would tell you, Jen always had to have the last word.

She'd been at the creek when luckily she'd heard the half-drunk Shirley busting through the woods like a herd of elephants. She'd known she couldn't let Shirley see her washing off the blood and getting rid of the rock she'd used to kill Megan, so she'd finished and hurried back to the fire. There'd been no time to get rid of the body. Nor had she known how to, until recently she'd discovered the tunnel from the outbuilding—and that handy hunter's cart.

When she'd sneaked out Friday night to meet with Claude—fortunately, Shirley was a deep sleeper—she'd just happened to see the old man going through the woods. Curious, she'd followed him. She'd seen him go into the shed. Peeking inside through a crack in the wall, she'd watched him lift the trapdoor and disappear through it, the door closing behind him—but not all the way.

She'd been intrigued and had stepped inside the dilapidated outbuilding. As she'd knelt down to lift the trapdoor, she saw why it hadn't closed completely. There was a dusty bone caught in it. Glancing down into the dimly lit space, she could see what appeared to be a sloped dirt drop to the bottom.

Rising, she'd let the trapdoor close.

She'd made only one mistake—the note she'd given Megan to meet in the woods. She'd forgotten to pick it up when she'd left the body to go get cleaned up in the creek. By the time she heard Shirley screaming and returned, the note was gone. One of the staff had picked it up.

She'd known who. She'd seen the smudge of blood on his fingers before he'd wiped it away as he and the others stood over Megan's body. She'd thought then that she would have to kill him. The note was evidence. But then she'd realized that he hadn't taken it to show the marshal. He'd taken it as a memento.

She might have let it go even after the reunion, but he'd opened his wallet that first night to offer to help pay for the beer, and she'd seen it. The fool still had the note. If her handwriting could be compared to that note along with Megan's blood…

Claude had actually come into the woods thinking he was smarter than she was. He misunderstood why she'd gotten him there. He had actually thought she'd gotten him there for sex? That she was that desperate? The boy genius hadn't expected her to be the killer. Like Megan, he never knew what hit him.

Devlin had to go because of that moment at the bar when

he'd seen what everyone else had missed. Jason had been trying to come up with a timeline as to where everyone was when Megan was killed. Jen saw Devlin glance at her and quickly look away. He'd known. Because he'd seen her in the woods that night? She'd seen him. She'd even taken his photo with Megan.

Once she'd started, she couldn't seem to stop. She'd remembered how Jason had felt sorry for her just the other night and taken her into the woods. She would have paid back his kindness, but he hadn't wanted her. He'd wanted to talk about that bitch Megan.

The marshal stepped in front of her. "Jennifer Mullen, you are under arrest for the murders of Megan Broadhurst, Claude Drake and Devlin Wright and wanted for questioning in the death of Jason Underwood. You have the right to remain silent—"

"That's hilarious, Marshal," she interrupted. "I've never been silent in my life."

CHAPTER THIRTY-FIVE

CASEY PUT DOWN the top on the convertible and glanced over at Finn. After several weeks in Buckhorn, they were finally leaving. The marshal said he didn't think they would be called back for Jen's trial. Emery was dead and Vi had thrown herself on the mercy of the court. It was over.

"I didn't want to believe any of them were capable of murder," Casey said as she looked down the main drag and wondered if she would ever see this place again. "But once I realized Emery hadn't killed Megan…"

"You thought it was Jason," Finn said, proving once again how well he knew her, as he buckled up his seat belt.

She nodded sheepishly. "Maybe I just wanted it to be him. Now I feel terrible about that. How did Jen get him to hang himself?"

"I heard drug residue was found in one of the two glasses in the room, along with a bottle of booze."

"So Jen pretended to go to her room, then sneaked in the back door with a bottle and offered him a drink. Still…"

"Jen is a lot stronger than she looks and definitely determined," Finn said.

"Angry and bitter. I saw that in her, but no more than Patience and the others."

"Like Jen's aunt," he said. Vi had broken down and admitted that she'd helped her brother try to scare everyone away from the hotel. Her brother Emery, when she'd informed him that the hotel was going to be sold, had returned to Buckhorn to try to cover up his crimes. He'd confessed to his sister about the women he'd killed and hidden in the underbelly of the hotel.

Vi did everything she could to protect him, including trying to stop the sale and even making an offer herself. When that failed, she'd pretended to be Megan's ghost to try to scare away the people who'd moved into the hotel, starting with Finnegan James, while her brother spent his nights digging up the bodies and trying to remove them. Her brother had shown her the secret passages within the hotel so she could move about without being caught. It had been her in the woods Saturday night.

"I always knew Vi was a force of nature," Casey said. Vi swore that she'd tried to stop Emery. But with time running out, he had taken matters into his own hands. He'd always worked around construction and had some experience with explosives. He decided the only way to end it was to blow the place up, but he couldn't kill Casey. So he'd gotten her out.

"I would imagine the law will go easy on Vi since she was just trying to protect her brother," Casey said.

Finn lifted a brow. "Or merely protecting herself and her reputation in town. The months I lived here, I saw that she was like the mayor of Buckhorn, the way she butted into everyone's business. Imagine if people found out what her brother did. She would have done just about anything so that didn't happen. And she did. She'd dressed up like Megan and run through the woods and sneaked around the hotel." Casey laughed, imagining how embarrassing that would have been for the woman.

She smiled at Finn. She often forgot how well he knew

the residents of Buckhorn. She'd known Vi almost her whole life and agreed with him. "She must be devastated, since she was the first lady of Buckhorn."

"Especially after what was found hidden in her room." Not just the white dress with what had been sprayed on it to look like blood, but also an extra blond wig. Now she was looking at criminal charges, since she'd knowingly helped her brother to try to cover up his crimes. But the marshal said she would probably just get probation.

Her husband, Axel, had filed for divorce and left town. Vi still had the general store, her antiques barn and their house since apparently it had been her family money that had purchased all of it.

"I'm surprised she's staying here, though," Casey said as she looked down the main drag of Buckhorn.

"She has a hundred hours of community service to do, and doesn't her daughter still live here?"

"Tina? Yes. She's pregnant." Baby's father unknown, but she was still living with Lars, and Lars was still having an affair with Shirley at the motel.

The story of the women Emery killed had gone viral. Buckhorn was on the map again, but maybe the ghosts would finally be at peace, as well as those poor young women's families. She felt Finn's blue gaze on her.

"You haven't mentioned the hotel."

She shrugged as she looked down the highway toward the spot where her grandmother's Old Girl had stood. Casey had wanted it gone. Well, it was now. "I came home to sell the Crenshaw. I just hadn't planned to stay around to see it be razed. By the way, I can't take your money now."

"The deal was done before it was destroyed," Finn said

and smiled. "I actually come out better with the loss on my taxes this way."

Casey studied him. "What will you do with the land?"

"I'm donating it to the town. I guess there is talk that it could be a park. Unless there's something you'd like me to do with it."

She shook her head. "I promised my grandmother I would get the things that meant so much to her. I did that. I also promised her I would release Megan's ghost and get closure for myself and her. I never planned to keep that promise, but as it turned out, I got everything and more." Her gaze met his. "Ready?"

FINN LEANED OVER to kiss her softly on the lips. "Ready. It was nice of you to offer me a ride to San Francisco, but you do realize you're not going to get rid of me that easily?"

She grinned. "You have something in mind?" she asked as she started the engine.

His dark gaze held hers. "As a matter of fact, I do. Maybe I'll tell you about it on the drive." He'd come here looking for redemption for not saving Megan. The truth was he'd been hiding out here, looking for something he couldn't name until he'd started reading Anna's journals and had met Casey. He saw her look again in the direction where the hotel had stood.

"Emery believed there was an evil in it that made him do what he did. I wonder if Jen believes that, too?"

He shook his head. "Megan brought her lies and her unhappiness with her. So did the others. I spent months in that old monstrosity. I fell in love with the Crenshaw and its new owner. Maybe we find what we're seeking, even when we don't know what we are really looking for." She turned to smile at him. "Your grandmother believed that we get what we put into life. I think she was right."

Casey shook her head. "My grandmother sent out those reunion invitations. Her attorney told me. She couldn't have been in her right mind."

He laughed. "I don't know about that. She invited *me*. I assume Megan's parents must have told her about me when they asked her to take Megan for the summer. They weren't just getting her away from the fallout from the car wreck. They were getting her away from me. Your grandmother was making sure you and I crossed paths. We both had to put the past behind us, make things right and give her peace of mind. Anna was always worried that one of her guests might have been responsible for those missing girls. She'd never dreamed it was Emery."

"Like he said, Anna was always kind to him," Casey said as she hit the gas and pulled out of the Sleepy Pine Motel parking lot and onto the two-lane blacktop that would eventually take them to San Francisco.

"I'm just thankful that she got us together," Finn said.

"What are you saying? That Anna planned it this way?"

He grinned and tilted his face back to take in Montana's big sky overhead. Sunlight lit his dark hair whipping in the wind and made his eyes shine when he glanced over at her as she gunned the engine. "I like to think she did."

Casey laughed. "I have to admit, it would be just like her." She looked at the road ahead as she sped past where the Crenshaw Hotel had once stood, its scars still visible. But she was no longer dwelling on the past.

She was looking to the future from now on. Not that she had any idea where she and Finn were headed. West, until they hit the Pacific Ocean, was all she knew.

"We can't see the future, and there's no reason to be looking over our shoulders all the time at the past," her grandmother used to say with a wink. "We have to look ahead and have faith that everything will turn out just as it's supposed to."

As Casey sped down the highway, she glanced back in her rearview mirror. Buckhorn, Montana, dissolved into the horizon. Finn turned on the radio, cranking up the music, and she pointed the car toward the ocean, leaving the shadows behind.

EPILOGUE

CASEY ALMOST DIDN'T hear the text ping on her phone over the roar of the ocean waves. She pulled out her cell to see that Bessie Walker had sent her a photograph of the new city park at the edge of Buckhorn.

Smiling, Casey showed Finn. It was as if the Crenshaw had never existed. All that could be seen were grass, mountains and pine trees, sparkling green against Montana's big, open sky. She texted a thank-you and pocketed her phone, thinking her grandmother would be pleased.

The Pacific Ocean lapped at her bare feet as she turned to look out at the sinking sun balanced on the water. Finn came up behind, drawing her back against him as his big hands covered her protruding belly and the baby they'd made growing inside her.

"I wish Anna had lived to see this," Casey said as she placed her hands over Finn's. "Sometimes, I swear I can feel her smiling down on us. She always did love a happy ending—especially if she had something to do with it."

"Funny, but I've been thinking about her lately as well," he said and turned her in his arms to look into her eyes before he kissed her. "I love you, Mrs. James."

She smiled, thankful that they were no longer looking over their shoulders into the past. Their eyes were wide-open with wonder and looking ahead with excitement.

Finn kissed her again and put his arm around her shoulders. They wandered down the beach toward the beach house he'd given her for a wedding present. Today they would finish the baby's room in a pale yellow, since they'd opted to wait and be surprised. But Casey had dreamed that she was having a little girl whom they would name after her grandmother. Probably more of Anna's doing, Casey thought with a smile.

Snuggling against Finn, she couldn't see the future, but she could feel it spreading out before them. As she glanced toward the blue sky overhead, she thought of Montana and her grandmother.

As she did, she wondered if she would ever see Buckhorn again. She could almost hear her grandmother's words. "Have faith. Everything will turn out just as it is supposed to."

* * * * *

Look for the next title in New York Times *bestselling author B.J. Daniels's Buckhorn, Montana series. Read on for a sneak peek where new characters are* At the Crossroads.

BOBBY BRADEN WIPED the blood off his fingers, noticing that he'd smeared some on the steering wheel. He pulled his shirtsleeve down and cleaned the streak of red away, the van swerving as he did.

"Hey, watch it!" In the passenger seat, Gene Drummond checked his side mirror. "All we need is for a cop to pull us over," he said in his deep, gravelly voice. It had reminded Bobby of the sound a chain saw made. "If one of them sees you driving crazy—"

"I got it," Bobby snapped. "Go back to sleep," he said under his breath as he checked the rearview mirror. The black line of highway behind them was as empty as the highway in front of them. There was no one out here in the middle of Montana on a Sunday this early in the morning—especially this time of year with Christmas only weeks away. He really doubted there would be a cop or highway patrol. But he wasn't about to argue. He knew where that would get him.

He stared ahead at the narrow strip of blacktop, wondering why Gene had been so insistent on them coming this way. Shouldn't they try to cross into Canada? If Gene had a plan, he hadn't shared it. Same with the bank job. No one had expected it to go sideways the way it had—especially Gene, from what Bobby could tell.

Concentrating on staying between the lines, he took a breath and let it out slowly. He could smell the blood and the sweat and the sweet scent of a dryer sheet that rose from his shirt, which he'd stolen off a clothesline somewhere in Wyoming. The shirt was too big, but he'd liked the color. Blue like his eyes. It bothered him that he'd gotten blood on the sleeve. The smear kept catching his eye, distracting him.

At a sound behind him, he glanced in the rearview mirror and saw Vic's anxious face. "How's Gus?" Bobby asked, keeping his voice down. He could hear Gene snoring, but not his usual foghorn sound. Which meant he wasn't completely out yet. Or he could be faking it.

"Not good." Vic moved closer, putting one big hand on Bobby's seat as he leaned forward and dropped his voice. "He's not going to make it."

Bobby met his gaze in the rearview mirror for a moment, a silent agreement passing between them. They both knew what would happen if Gene's younger brother died.

"We aren't leaving Gus behind," Gene said without opening his eyes. "He'll pull through. He's strong." He opened his eyes and looked around. "Where the hell are we?"

"According to the last sign I saw, just outside Buckhorn, Montana," Bobby said.

"Good. There's a café in town. Go there," Gene said, making Bobby realize that had been the man's plan all along. "We'll get food and medical supplies for Gus and dump this van for a different ride." He pulled the pistol from beneath his belt and checked to see how many shots he had left before tucking it in again under the jean jacket he'd gotten off the clothesline.

Bobby met Vic's gaze again in the mirror. This could get a lot worse.

He'd recognize that voice anywhere, even though he'd heard it live
and in person just a few times and never so…forceful. He believed
her, but he had no intention of letting her off the hook so easily.

He raised his hands. "I'm LAPD Detective Jake McAllister. Are
you all right?"

A sudden gust of wind carried her sigh down the trail toward
him.

"It…it's Kyra Chase. I'm sorry. I'm putting away my weapon."

Lowering his hands, he said, "Is it okay for me to move now?"

"Of course. I didn't realize… I thought you were…"

"The killer coming back to his dump site?" He flicked on the flashlight in his hand and continued down the trail, his shoes scuffing over dirt and pebbles. "He wouldn't do that—at least not so soon after the kill."

When he got within two feet of her, he skimmed the beam over her body, her dark clothing swallowing up the light until it reached her blond hair. "I didn't mean to scare you, but what are you doing here?"

"Probably the same thing you are." She hung on to the strap of her purse, her hand inches from the gun pocket.

"I'm the lead detective on the case, and I'm doing some follow-up investigation."

"Believe it or not, Detective, I have my own prep work that I like to do before meeting a victim's family. I want to have as much information as possible when talking to them. I'm sure you can understand that."

"Sure, I can. And call me Jake."

Don't miss
The Setup *by Carol Ericson,*
available April 2021 wherever
Harlequin Intrigue books and ebooks are sold.

Harlequin.com